CALL DOWN THE THUNDER

Advance Praise for
Call Down the Thunder

"Populated with dirt-poor Kansans, crooked lawmen, circus freaks, brothel dwellers, klansmen and bank robbers, *Call Down the Thunder* is a proud representative of the Southern Gothic tradition. If Faulkner and Fellini had got together and written a crime novel, this would've been it. Hugely recommended."

— ROBERT HOUGH, celebrated author of
The Final Confession of Mabel Stark and
The Man Who Saved Henry Morgan

"In *Call Down the Thunder* Dietrich Kalteis has done something remarkable: he's rendered the Kansas of the dust bowl 1930s so completely that I felt myself disappearing into this surreal and tragic world. The people, the language and the place itself are fully imagined and alive. Bravo!"

— S.J. ROZAN, bestselling author of *Paper Son*

"*Call Down the Thunder* brilliantly weaves history and fiction to give us a gritty, raw-boned tale of survival and retribution in the 'Dirty Thirties' of depression-era Kansas."

— MARK COGGINS, award-winning author of
The Dead Beat Scroll

"Kalteis is such a skillful writer that you feel you're in dust-bowl Kansas right from page one; you catch yourself talking in the local dialect and thinking twice about parting with a nickel in case one never rolls your way again. The voice, the characters and the setting are brilliantly realized!"

— ANNE EMERY, award-winning author of
Though the Heavens Fall

"Immensely readable, tough but beguiling, *Call Down the Thunder* is a highly original novel: a pacy caper set in ugly times as the dust bowl, the depression and the Klan gang up on a ragbag of dirt farmers, circus folk and one indomitable woman, all hoping to scrape by till the rains come. Laugh-out-loud funny, lump-in-the-throat moving and packed with surprises. I loved it."

— CATRIONA MCPHERSON, multi-award-winning and national bestselling author of *Strangers at the Gate*

"Kalteis does a brilliant job of planting us in this particular time and place . . . Even at its darkest, the story is lifted by a light, engaging touch. A sharp-witted, affecting noir, dust bowl–style." — *Kirkus Reviews*

"Kalteis's love of flawed characters has never been more evident. His razor sharp dialogue is stunning and honest, filled with pathos and humor, no false notes at play here. The line between good and evil blurs in *Call Down The Thunder*. It's a masterful piece of writing."

— JOHN LANSING, best selling author of *The Devil's Necktie*

CALL DOWN THE THUNDER

a crime novel

DIETRICH KALTEIS

Published by ECW Press
665 Gerrard Street East
Toronto, Ontario, Canada M4M 1Y2
416-694-3348 / info@ecwpress.com

Cover design: Michel Vrana
Author photo: © Andrea Kalteis

This is a work of fiction. Names, characters,
places, and incidents either are the product of
the author's imagination or are used fictitiously,
and any resemblance to actual persons, living or
dead, business establishments, events, or locales
is entirely coincidental.

LIBRARY AND ARCHIVES CANADA CATALOGUING
IN PUBLICATION

Title: Call down the thunder : a crime novel /
Dietrich Kalteis.

Names: Kalteis, Dietrich, 1954– author.

Identifiers: Canadiana (print) 20190111607
Canadiana (ebook) 20190111615

ISBN 9781770414792 (softcover)
ISBN 9781773053899 (PDF)
ISBN 9781773053882 (EPUB)

Classification: LCC PS8621.A474 C34 2019
DDC C813/.6—dc23

The publication of *Call Down the Thunder* has been generously supported by the Canada Council
for the Arts which last year invested $153 million to bring the arts to Canadians throughout the
country and is funded in part by the Government of Canada. *Nous remercions le Conseil des arts du
Canada de son soutien. L'an dernier, le Conseil a investi 153 millions de dollars pour mettre de l'art dans
la vie des Canadiennes et des Canadiens de tout le pays. Ce livre est financé en partie par le gouvernement
du Canada.* We acknowledge the support of the Ontario Arts Council (OAC), an agency of the
Government of Ontario, which last year funded 1,737 individual artists and 1,095 organizations in
223 communities across Ontario for a total of $52.1 million. We also acknowledge the contribution of
the Government of Ontario through the Ontario Book Publishing Tax Credit, and through Ontario
Creates for the marketing of this book.

PRINTED AND BOUND IN CANADA   PRINTING: NORECOB   5   4   3   2   1

MIX
Paper from
responsible sources
FSC
www.fsc.org   FSC® C103560

To Andie

. . . ONE

Sonny Myers narrowed his eyes against the gust, felt the rush of cold, the air crackling: static electricity churning and hellfire flashing inside the mass of black looming high over the flat land. The yard a frenzy of whipping sand and debris by the time he got his mule and car in the barn. Felt like the end of times coming. Through the boiling wall of sand, Sonny made out two sets of headlights approaching on the county road. Could be coming for shelter from the duster, but something told him no. Going to the house, reaching inside the door, he took the shotgun and stepped off the porch.

Coming to the door, Clara wanting to have a look.

"Just a blow." He told her to stay inside.

"What you gonna do, shoot it?"

His eyes slits, Sonny stepped into the yard, forcing his steps, having to lean into it, going toward the headlights.

Looked like two pickups stopped down by the mailbox, lights dim against the blasting sand. Doors opened and men got out. Nobody he knew. Best he could tell there were six of them, pulling hoods on. Two going to the bed of the first truck, pulling a long cross from the back. Sonny smelling kerosene and oil from where he stood, halfway to the house. A couple of them fanned to his left, heading for the side of the house, flanking him.

Sonny fired in the air, the only warning they'd get, popping in another shell. Leaving the ones by the trucks, Sonny went after the pair going wide around the house. Couldn't see twenty feet ahead as the duster bore down. Hurrying around the side, his eyes searched for them somewhere ahead of him. One hand against the boards, he made his way around the back, staying low. Expecting an ambush. Ready to shoot if he had to. Getting to the far side before he smelled the smoke. Thinking it was the burning cross. Then he caught figures moving ahead of him.

"Halt," he called, wondering what kind of thing was that to yell. Couldn't shoot, knowing Clara wouldn't stay inside like he told her. No point in shooting his wife. Catching sight of the flames, the cross burning down by the mailbox, the sound of car doors shutting, taillights pulling away.

Then Clara screamed from the porch, stumbling down the steps, hand on the porch rail, she moved along and found him, pointing to the barn. Sonny catching the flicker, another man running from it and crossing the open ground, heading for the trucks. Putting the stock to his shoulder, Sonny fired. Pretty sure he winged the son of a bitch, reaching in his pocket for another shell that wasn't there. The man chased after the trucks and disappeared.

The dry boards caught fast, flames flicked to the roof beams and spread, the straw floor alight and swirling around. Bats flew around the rafters, chickens getting out of there. The mule screaming.

Handing Clara the shotgun, Sonny jumped down along the west side, swatting and kicking at the burning straw with his shoe. The heat like a wall, pushing him back. Slapping at the cuff of his overalls as it caught. No way to get to the back. The heat was too much. Couldn't get to the screaming mule and pull her from the stall. Taking Clara, he turned her for the door.

Driven out, both of them choking from the smoke, blinded by the sand. The flames shooting from the roof, long fingers reaching across to the house. The triangle clanging like mad from the porch post. Wrapping his arms around her, Sonny got her across the yard. A picket struck his back and knocked him down. Clara tugged him to his feet. Getting to the porch. The sand blasting so hard, they could barely see the barn, both getting inside the house. Praying it wouldn't catch fire too.

. . . TWO

A WEEK EARLIER

Lining on the check, Sonny Myers raised the maul. Putting some hip behind the swing, he let the weight bring it down, hitting the log dead center and splitting it. Setting the armload on the porch, more than enough to fill the woodbox. The lower step feeling spongy under his foot. Something else that needed fixing.

Squinting at the sun like he didn't trust it. The orange ball dropping to a hand's width above the horizon. A Kansas day like all Kansas days, the sky bleached and the land perished. Shadows cast off the backhouse, stretching to the barn's west side. Soon the bats would be flitting about the rafters and ridgepole, searching out moths and beetles as the cool of evening set in.

It had been a week since the last duster boiled along the horizon, some calling them black rollers. Tapping a finger at the triangle hanging from the porch post, Sonny guessed it was nearing on suppertime, and no sign of Clara getting back from Hoxie to fix it. He put an eye to the front window, thinking if it wasn't one kind of storm, then he was looking out for another. The two of them not agreeing on much lately.

Wiping the cap across the back of his neck, his skin getting like the leather on his strop, same as the old man's had been. Ears and nose punished from working in the sun. Hands and face tanned brown and the hidden parts white, lending an odd look when his clothes were off. But Sonny didn't care much about it.

Setting the cap back on, he pondered where he went wrong: teaching Clara to drive the old Hudson after the phone company cut their service. Sitting next to her on the bench seat, teaching her to put her foot on the clutch, shift the stick, getting the one-two of putting her right foot down on the gas pedal, easing her left on the clutch. Holding his patience, biting his tongue till she did it without grinding the gears all to hell.

Clara drove to Hoxie every chance she got now, picking up supplies and the mail and catching the latest scuttlebutt at Grainger's store. Emmett and Doris letting her use the phone in back every week, charging a nickel for receiving the calls from Clara's mother over in Topeka. Nine miles of driving from the farm to Hoxie, Clara doing it when the sky promised to hold back the dusters long enough to make the trip without getting caught. This time was different. He got the feeling Clara wasn't coming back this time. Guessing it was on account of the money, or lack of it.

Clara had gone on about the storms blowing away her dreams and any promise of a future, the only thing growing was the heap of unpaid bills on the kitchen table. Anybody who tried living off the land knew that heap just kept piling up, their savings going the other way. Sonny making thirty cents an hour planting the damned government trees, FDR's shelterbelt project. If he wasn't doing that, he was digging holes for the electric company's poles, taking any kind of work he could lean his shoulder into. Barely getting them by. The money Orin left when he passed was nearly tapped and gone. The two of them fighting most of the time, her wanting to go west, him not wanting to hear it, set on staying on the land his family had farmed for three generations.

But he did hear about it, Clara going on how there had hardly been any meat these past six months since Sonny helped neighbor Boyd with his last smoat, hanging it and salting it down, bringing home some side meat and bones for roasting down.

Reaching his tobacco pouch and book of papers, Sonny twisted up a brown smoke and struck a wood match to its end. Wetting a lip, he puffed out the Bull Durham. Didn't need to go check the cupboard for the last of the money either, knowing she took it. Clara getting in his old Hudson truck and heading west. Not coming back.

Goddamn.

A shred of tobacco stuck to his lip, Sonny spit, trying to push that feeling aside, anchoring himself, picturing the land the way it was back before the drought and dusters whipped up and blew most of the topsoil to Oklahoma. How he once stood among the shoulder-high stalks as a boy, miles of wheat going from green to gold, hushing and swaying. Orin teaching him to bale that wheat straw, sweating and tending it. Father teaching son the ways of a Kansas farmer. All Sonny needed was a pair of strong hands, a good mule and the iron of his conviction. Schooling him for Kansas life, saying, "Tie a knot in the end of the rope and just hang on."

What Orin didn't teach him about living on the land, the croppers staying on the low section did. The hired men earning their fifty and found, working the wheat and alfalfa, singing around the supper pots like they had something to be happy about. Sonny learning the dump rake and making windrows. Bundling feed of grain sorghum for the mules, the croppers calling it hi-gear.

Remembered the way his ma fussed about her plum thicket back of the house. Hoeing a patch for her cornstalks, propping her tomatoes on stakes, tending runner beans on poles, cabbages and spinach and coneflowers and bluebells growing along the white pickets. Sunflowers getting leggy and lazy and leaning against the house.

The windmill cranked the water pump, making that scraping sound as it went up and down over the well, the water so cold it made his teeth hurt. Enough good water to keep the tank full and plenty of it for growing. The milking cow lowing, his hand working the teat in the shed, the milk house where they kept the dairy cool. The hog rooting, rolling in mud to cool itself, its snout working everything over. The chicken coop full of hens, their clucking and cackling. Feel under them and you had eggs.

Feeling a fool for not seeing it coming. Clara, the truck and the last of the money, gone without a word. "For better or worse, my eye." And no supper.

Goddamn.

Dragging hard on the cigarette, Sonny saw himself on those Saturday evenings at the horseshoe pit, playing the hands for nickels. Those days when the Selkirks and the Braggs would come around regular in their Model Ts, suppers of venison, that taste of sweet plum tart. His mother had been a good cook, everybody saying so.

The neighboring farms mostly boarded up now, some bulldozed down, the goddamn banks foreclosing and taking the land. Some of the Braggs piling up their truck and shoving on west after the storm the papers dubbed the

Black Blizzard, worst hell Sonny had ever seen. Short time on, old man Selkirk complained about a whistling in his lungs and wasn't long before he passed on, Doc Bletsoe ascribing it to the dust pneumonia. The bankers calling it a shame, but taking his land anyway.

Looking across the vastness, Sonny exhaled, thinking most of the folks he'd known were lying under it or blown on by the winds, going to California. Clara chasing after them.

But he'd stick it out.

"Not running off like all them Okies, no sir. Got a good well and make thirty cents an hour, enough to dig in." Allowing short scraps of the past to temper his conviction. Sitting on that stump till the shadows stretched longer, Sonny stubbed out the smoke, figuring he'd go fry up an egg.

Asking himself, "You got eggs?"

Looking at the sky, his mouth twisted and he shook his head, tossing the butt down and grinding it under his flapping sole. Maybe he could find some hobnails and fix the damned sole. Seemed anything he stuck his feet into lately sprung a hole. His socks in need of mending too.

Goddamn.

. . . THREE

Clara always liked coming here. Grainger's Mercantile reflected the times, its countertop doing duty as charcuterie and post office, tin signs nailed on the wall behind it — Life Savers for a nickel, Red Bud Soda Water, Tower Root Beer, Ace High hair pomade — a blackened pot stove with its coal bucket, unlit due to the unseasonal warm weather. The checkerboard on the nail bucket with its mismatched chairs around it by the window, Emmett Grainger dubbing the spot his exchange bank, the place where the graybeards would end up once they got tired of standing. Their chatter endless and their spending rare.

Top of the counter sat the National register, like the heart of the store. A coffee mill and a line of candy jars of horehound and peppermint. A wrapping paper unit with string on the end. The shelf by the near wall held a scale for weighing and a hotplate where Doris made sandwiches. Any kind you wanted, buttered up and stacked high on her sourdough, came with a pickle and just cost a nickel.

Lightbulbs dangled from the ceiling. Sparse goods and groceries on the wall shelves, bins in the bottom, the top rows mostly empty. Packs of Bull Durham, Lucky Strike

9

and Camel store-boughts behind the counter. A poster tacked on the end of a shelf claimed Chesterfields satisfy. Smuckers jars next to Clabber Girl baking goods and Jiffy mix, Hormel's Spam, shot shells and cartridges. Mary Ann cake pans, sewing notions, Fannie Farmer's books, stacks of khaki, denim and chambray. Past the rounded glass show-case, the smell of garlic and brine coming from the barreled pickles. A stack of pails, a harness somebody had bartered as payment, its padding puffing from a seam. Feed sacks leaned in a row, the ones with the patterns the ladies liked for sewing.

Sealing tape framed the window and putty filled any cracks the tape missed, the Graingers hoping to keep the dusters from blowing sand into the mercantile. Townsfolk stepping on the porch tracked it in, their heels working like little scoops.

The two graybeards were regular as fixtures, standing by the rack of shovels, both in bib overalls with their thumbs hooked in their straps. Albert, the one with gray hair sticking from under a straw hat, was going on about dinosaur bones found at some nearby dig-up. Tyrell took his corncob from the watch pocket, sticking it in the corner of his mouth, the pipe dancing up and down as he spoke back. Turning the talk to Bennie and Stella, Kansas's own bank robbers, speculating they were more notorious than Bonnie and Clyde. Albert pointing out that Sure Shot Stella was the only one of the bunch who hadn't succumbed to the fate of their chosen live-lihood, getting shot. The debate drifted through the place, about as welcome as dust motes.

Peering from the alcove where the wood phone hung, Clara Myers eyed the young mother checking prices marked on food tins in the middle aisle, wearing a scarf as a head wrap, her little ones tugging at her skirt. Her red-haired girl asking about the candy sticks high up on the counter, the boy hopping up and down, unable to see the goodies, the mother telling them to wait and see. Looking up at the bare bulbs, Clara guessed the Graingers had unscrewed half of them, saving money where they could. Heard the radio playing from the back, K-L-X on the air, playing some Artie Shaw.

Talking into the spit cup of what the Graingers called their hotel phone, Clara told her momma how nice it'd be to one day have her own electricity. The receiver in her sun-leathered hand. Feet bare on the store planks, toes wiggling up and down like they were regarding the grain of the pine. She glanced to the counter to see if Doris Grainger was timing the five-minute call, the woman like a hawk, right now appearing to be lost in her ledger. Coming up the aisle, the mother told her kids to stay with her and keep their fingers off things.

"Well, I just can't believe these prices, is all, Momma," Clara said into the phone, the call all the way to Topeka, keeping her voice low. "Dollar sixty-nine a sack of flour, you believe it? Putting patterns on the sacks so ladies can make dresses, and charging whatever they want. Peck of spuds going for thirty cents. Thirty cents! I nearly fell over. And a loaf of bread, a nickel. You believe that, just the one loaf? And a pound of peaches, go on, guess how much?"

"Count your mercies, girl. Hard times dropped on all us. Not like it's just you."

"Hardly worthwhile, me sewing my dolls. Lucky if I get a dime a piece. Them bald-headed Kewpies everywhere you look now. Horrible things, and every kid wanting one instead of mine. Goddamn give up."

"Gonna use up your whole five minutes whining?"

"Well, you asked how it was. And got me going. Just telling you, that's all."

"Look. Fact, you married a dirt farmer, and it's what you get, dirt. Fact."

"Well, here's another fact, Momma, some fresh-air change is coming. Reason I called."

"This again. You gonna tell me you're lighting out, getting your fresh-air change. Let me ask, Sonny know about it?"

"Guess he'll put it together by and by."

"Not gonna ask me to wire more money. Already paying for this call. A woman living off her life savings —"

"Not asking you nothing, Momma. Just saying I'm done stirring broth so thin I'm likely to eat myself hungry. Nothing in it but salt, hardly a wild spud or thistle growing around the place anymore. Telling you I'm going west. That's what."

"A young woman on her own. *Phhft!* You ask me —"

"That's just it. I'm not asking."

"Well, how about all that 'for better or worse'? Said them words, didn't you? In a church. Your lips to God's ear."

"Well, He'll have to get past it too, won't He? Not like He listens anyway. Look around you, Momma." Clara drew her lips tight, pale eyes flashing. Trying not to cry. Bumping her shoulder to the wall, one bare foot on the other. Saying, "Been living with a man more married to the land than he is to me."

Doris Grainger looked up from her ledger, getting Clara's attention, tapping at her wristwatch.

"Yeah, well, guess my time's up, Momma. Call you from someplace on the road . . ."

"Oh, for Pete's sake, you're not really —"

Hanging up, Clara stepped into the aisle. Smiling, not sure why she liked stinging her mother like that, had been doing it most of her twenty-five years, and in spite of the lump in her throat, she was feeling pretty good about it.

The red-haired girl came along the aisle, humming a song, her tiny hand running along the edge of a shelf.

Sweetening the smile, Clara guessed her to be about six years old, blue eyes, cheeks dusted in freckles, a clean sackcloth dress. The pattern from a Sunbonnet Sue flour sack, scuffed and worn ghillies on the girl's feet. Holding the smile, Clara padded to the front, her bunions not hurting so much when she went barefoot. Setting her nickel next to the National register, she thanked Doris Grainger for use of the phone.

"Your amici still on the fritz, hon?" Doris said, knowing the phone company was quick to snip the line on anybody with unpaid bills going past a few months. Just had to flip a page on the register to see the scratchings under the heading of "credit" to know where the Myers stood.

"My what?"

"Amici's the phone, hon. Heard somebody call it that." Doris crinkling her nose.

"Why'd anybody call it that?" Clara looked up at the taller woman.

"Guess . . . I don't know, guess it's supposed to be amusing."

"Huh. Well, duster tore our line down. Think I told you. Anyway, you go talk to them at that Bell company when you got no . . . *amici* to call on."

Doris thinking this wasn't the time to bring up overdue accounts. Doris with a finger on the ledger page. In spite of the counter between them, the closeness of Clara Myers played on her discomposure. Didn't like the way the woman was smiling or the way she said amici. Walking around barefoot. The young mother and two kids lined behind her.

"Oh, while I'm in, how about a pack of chewing gum?" Clara said, pointing to a display box behind Doris.

Taking her finger from the ledger, Doris sighed, saying, "You looking at the Fleer's or the Beech-Nut, hon?"

Tapping her lip, Clara went for the Beech-Nut, saying they had an allotment check due anytime now, same thing she'd said last time. "And Sonny's sure to be getting paid for his planting next week. Square up with you and Emmett soon's any of it comes in."

"Sure." Doris's lips thinned into a smile.

Tearing the edge of the packet, Clara turned and sent an inquiring look to the mother behind her, the young woman pursing her lips and giving a nod. Clara bending and offering a stick of the gum, both the boy and girl looking hopefully to their mother. Her nod sending the little fingers reaching in. The kids thanking her, Clara beaming and telling the woman she was blessed with fine children. She wasn't sure if she'd seen them around town before, guessing they could be croppers just passing through and heading west. She walked out the door, thinking she still had a ways to go before nightfall, hoping to make Oklahoma City.

The mother stepped to the counter. Like Doris Grainger, she watched Clara step barefoot across the porch and to the truck parked out front.

"Don't know how that girl works them pedals like that," Doris said. "Barely reach with her toes."

"Seems nice," the mother said. "She got kids?"

"Don't think she can," Doris said — Doris known about town as having the eyes and ears of one who valued good scuttlebutt and happy to share its nuggets — thinking she ought to charge Clara Myers more than a nickel for the phone calls, always going past her five minutes, but knowing the Myers didn't have the money anyway. Taking the dime from the woman for the two tins of Campbell's, guessing it was the heart of the family's evening meal, a lot of folks mingling in whatever they found growing.

Saying so long, Doris flipped open the ledger and entered the pack of Beech-Nut. The graybeards back to prattling on about roasting up dinosaur bones and having enough to gnaw on for a week. Albert setting up the checkerboard on the nail bucket. Tyrell fetching the spittoon, scraping back a chair, flipping a coin to see who got black. Neither one buying so much as a soda. Doris slapped the ledger closed, got them both looking over. Putting it on the shelf, she sighed, glancing at her own weathered hands.

. . . FOUR

The flavor was gone from it, Clara working the chewing gum long after her jaw got sore.

Sonny would figure it out, sitting on his stump at the day's end, whittling some stick, same way he always did. Waiting on his supper like a man too dumb to fix it himself. She pictured him having to walk the ten miles to town, find out she had been at Grainger's and tanked up at the Conoco. His buddy Handy Phibbs charging the fill-up, watching her drive off in the old Hudson.

Heading south of Garden City, she aimed to hook up with Route 66. Rolling the wheels over the painted lines, she passed a humpback piled high with a family's belongings. Spitting the gum out the window. Feeling free.

Guessed she loved him alright, but she couldn't stick it out. Last thing she heard when she left the house: the announcer, Wilbur Flanders, on the K Radio saying that last duster ripped through from Texas, could tell on account the dust was gray. Red dust meant Colorado, brown from Oklahoma. Dumb announcer joking how Kansas winds were quick to blow it all right back, didn't matter about the color. Wilbur guffawing like a goddamn hick at his own joke.

Clara was done with this dead land and didn't care what the dust looked like. Her hands, as dry as sticks, held the wheel. Taking another stick of gum from the yellow pack, she folded it into her mouth, saying to nobody, "Get away from these Kansas winds, blistering my skin to puckering and peeling." Thinking she'd get herself another Franklin machine, sew up some new dolls, maybe dresses and pretty things to wear, sell them to the Montgomery Wards. Hollywood, the place where they filmed *Goodbye, Mr. Chips* and *Gunga Din*. The likes of Garbo and Harlow and Lombard walking around in clothes she sewed up. Kids of famous and rich folks wanting her little dolls. Paying more than a dime a piece too. Clara chewed, thinking of her dolls wasting away, collecting dust on Grainger's shelf.

Leave Sonny to his goddamn goggles and dust masks, the ones he kept on the milking stool next to the mat and bucket. His seed calendar from last year tacked to the kitchen wall, the kind he and Orin once used for marking the seeding, cultivating and harvesting times. Nothing written on any of them since the drought and the old man dying.

Done with Kansas and done with ladling broth over the potbelly. The two of them sitting across from each other, asking the same dumb questions, "How was your day?" "Fine, how in heck was yours?"

Steering to avoid a rock in the road, she caught the steam coming from under the hood. Didn't like the look of it. Working the pedals the way he taught her, Clara slowed and geared down, drove easy as the steam got worse, then she heard a clanking from under the hood.

It made her mad, nothing going right. She started talking in Sonny's voice, "My day? Why, swell as always, planting my dumb-ass trees? Lost count how many I got in, but made dog wages." Watching the red needle rise on the gauge. What she understood about it wouldn't fill a cotton hat, but she knew it wasn't good. More steam rose, and the clattering got louder. Jamming it in first gear, she pulled to the shoulder and shut off the engine. Middle of no place. Finney County, as best she could tell, the steam hissing and the metal pinging. Goddamn that Henry and Edsel and their Detroit dimwits, building something like this Hudson truck.

She supposed she should wait till it cooled, then hump this heap all the way to the coast if she had to. A few miles at a time. Sleep in it, and when it crapped out for good, she'd ditch it and hitch the rest of the way.

Getting out, she plugged a finger to a nostril and gave a blast, doing the other side, clearing out the Kansas, same way she did every morning. Didn't think to bring the jar of petroleum jelly she kept by the bed. Always smeared a plug up each nostril, the only help against the blowing sand. No point tempting the brown lung.

Then Clara was back to talking in Sonny's voice, "Make your nickel call to Momma, huh? Don't know how come Grainger charges a nickel when it's your momma making the call. A nickel for what, on account of tying up the line?"

Picturing the way Sonny sat over his supper every night, elbows either side of the bowl like he was protecting it, the way he tipped it up, slurping the last of the broth, always reaching for the last biscuit. Never asking if she wanted it. Serve him right to go hungry for a night. Clara back to wiping her tears.

"Never want to hear of my dancing days," Clara thinking it, going to the front of the Hudson, thinking of those times center stage in Topeka. The engine hissed. Clara set her fists on her hips and hissed back.

The sound of the engine faded.

"Care more about your truck . . ." Walking around the side, looking up and down the roadway, she gave the bald tire a kick, forgetting she was barefoot, her big toe getting the worst of it. She eyed the wisps escaping from under the folding hood.

"But, I allow you being a farming truck, you don't hold much for singing and dancing neither. Maybe if you'da come with a radio I could show you some steps, give you a sing-along." Clara wanting to kick the rubber again, thinking she best put on the shoes tucked in the beat-up suitcase with her change of clothes.

Stepping to the center of the road, she was back to talking in Sonny's voice, "Singing in church maybe, but I got a hard time making sense of dancing." Looping her arms, Clara pranced in the lane, the pavement hot underfoot. Sonny seeing dancing an unmanly thing to do. "But it's okay. I got to live where I got to plug petroleum jelly up my nose." She stopped, hearing an engine far off.

It was a farm truck coming north, loaded with scrap. Clara giving a wave, the driver scarcely looking, palming his air horn and whizzing by. Raising up dust.

"Leave a lady in goddamn distress. Jesus. Thought there were only two a's in Kansas." Looking at the disappearing truck, cursing it for rushing off to the next jerkwater place, leaving her out there. Guessing she ought to lift the folding hood and set it on its prop rod the way he showed her. Air it out.

Sitting on the seat, she waited till the red needle dropped, brushing a bug from the seat. More and more bugs all the time, all kinds and sizes. Corn-broomed one yesterday with legs of a centipede, long as her finger. Thinking of the plagues of Egypt, Sonny ignoring all of it, just going on about his rows of trees and the rain coming. Saying the same thing going on nine years now. Meantime they were drowning in sand. The old house sinking in it. Only thing growing was Clara's bad feelings, thinking they'd end with the brown lung like old man Selkirk. "Wake up and the only thing white in the bed's the shape where I been sleeping." Clara got out again, slamming the door, swiping the back of a hand at her eyes.

Going to California if it killed her. Leave Sonny and his goddamn roots, his family all buried here. Remembered him telling her they'd be fine as long as they had a good well. How they put extra deputies on the border, turning folk back at gunpoint. Not knowing what to do with all the ones they already got. Calling them Okies and Arkies. Treating them like bindlestiffs. Folks with no pockets left to turn out and no choice, and the tenants and croppers with even less. Told her he'd seen a handbill tacked up at Grainger's about hundreds of pickers needed. Telling her thousands showed for those jobs, one willing to work for less than the next. Dog eat dog. Jobs going to them willing to work for next to nothing. Folks going thinking it's greener someplace else. "Well, nothing's green round here, Sonny, that's for god-damn sure." She spat, imitating Sonny again, "Nothing but the envy of a better life."

She looked in at the engine, not knowing the first thing about it. "Well, to hell with you and your good well, Sonny Myers. And to hell owing the bank. And that Doris Grainger and her ledger. And that dope at the Conoco. How the hell we ever gonna pay 'em all." She put her arms wide and turned on the empty road, waiting on an answer. Feeling the day starting to cool, she went and got her shoes and jacket from the suitcase. Clara reached under the hood and twisted at the radiator cap. Looking down the filler. Putting the cap back on and sitting back in the truck. Folding another stick of Beech-Nut in her mouth. Her mouth so dry she had to work it to get that sweetness.

"Got but one mule left to pull the sulky, sand claiming the rest. And what the hell you figure we gonna eat? Can't live on mud cats, wild spud and turnip if you're lucky to find them along the creek."

She thumped a balled hand at the steering wheel, honking the horn, thinking if she had to eat one more of those whiskered things . . . "And don't go selling me on no jackrabbit or squirrel neither."

Back to his voice, "Either one goes nice, that pastelie recipe you got's a good one."

"It's posole, you dope." Another thump at the horn, Clara looked out at the empty land. A tear rolled off her nose, catching on her chin. Clara letting it hang there.

So quiet out here, she wished she had her old radio along, keep her from talking to herself. Wanted to hear "Top Hat, White Tie and Tails" or that Gershwin number about calling the whole thing off. Thumping her bunched fingers at the wheel again.

Pretty sure she heard another far-off engine coming.

. . . FIVE

Robbing a bank. Sure, it sounded crazy to Willis Taggart. Handy Phibbs called from Hoxie, talking around it, saying it casual, like it wouldn't land them in prison or get them killed. Willis pushed the idea aside, then found himself thinking about it more and more the past couple of days.

Hitting forty was a milestone, and Willis had let the day slip past, nothing special about it. Running a finger along his mustache, he reckoned he had more gray hair than friends. Mother had passed away and brother Walter hadn't called since their last fight over Happy Mustard's, the traveling show they co-owned and kept touring from Topeka to Cheyenne to Kansas City and back.

There was no party. No candles to blow out. Thinking he might take the bottle of hair dye and brush away some of the years. Go down to Ida Jean's ringer house and pick out a gal. Seeking some pleasure sure beat toasting himself with lonely whiskey.

Again, the thought of robbing a bank came around, Willis grinning at the idea. Never even fired a pistol. The chair-leather creaked under him. Sipping from the glass, he leaned on the pencil and worked some numbers, a thing that used to bring him joy. Fingers that used to put a flourish to the figures, back before the damned numbers went down the shitter. Reaching the Black Hawk from the ashtray, he inhaled over the whiskey taste, blowing a stream of blue smoke across the desk. Watching it curl and thin toward the Grant Wood painting over the mantle. The clacking of Granddad's carriage clock like the heartbeat of the house, coming from down the hall. This sitting room, this house he was born into. This whiskey that had always taken away hard times' edge.

The last parley with Walter went like this: the son of a bitch wanted to cut back the acts till times took a turn. "Ditch the midget," he said, feeling every show around had at least one, nothing new in it and nobody wanting to pay to see them. Walter shook his head at him, saying, "Same goes for the clowns."

His brother's shallow way of thinking got Willis steamed, wanting to sock him on the jaw. Only way for the show to survive was keep up appearances and stand their ground. And by Christ, they were keeping the midget. Cutting acts killed the turnout, such as it was, and that meant going bust and getting swallowed by a bigger fish, like those Barnum and Ringling bastards.

Willis guessed Penelope, Walter's wife, was behind this. Blue-blooded by virtue of her own fallacy, the woman had the man on the short leash of marriage. Never cared for Happy Mustard's once it stopped making money, souring Walter on it and pitting brother against brother. Walter turning his back and letting the day-to-day fall to Willis. No small feat with empty pockets, but Willis kept it afloat, scratching and borrowing where he could. The miles of worthless nothing from one town to the next. Hanging up the chalk-stripes and herringbone every night, sewing new holes in old socks, giving the two-tones a spit-shine, keeping up the image.

No wife to come home to, Willis sidestepped the trapdoor of matrimony, slaked the yearning with the light-skirted gals down at Ida Jean's. Yeah, he was going there tonight, pick a good-time gal to blow the candles on his cake. Lend himself the money from petty cash.

Ida Jean ran an upright joint. The gals under her roof wont to the lab on a stick, leading to some good clean fun. Ida Jean's motto: there's no medicine for regret. And her patrons could get romp and rest easy. Top of that, her house was immune from a police blitz, the chief and half the force likely upstairs in bed. Again the thought came around, robbing a bank. Man, if he got away with it, he could go to Ida Jean's any—

The pounding on the front door had him jumping, slamming his knee on the underside of the desk. Dropping the cigar, he fumbled it into the ashtray and got up, ash spilled down his wide lapels. First thought, Walter remembered his birthday after all, coming for a drink, sneaking out on the warden wife.

The pounding came again. Harder. Willis knowing now it wasn't Walter's knock, tiptoeing and tucking into the front hall's vestibule, waiting a few heartbeats before peeking through the sidelight. Snapping his head back.

A nose pressed flat against the ribbed glass, dark hollows for eyes tried peering in, breath frosting on the pane. He knew the sailor's cap, white with a broad black band. The one called Lips. A goon with a dog face and a slit for a mouth, never said much, that cap tipped low on his head. Mumbling from outside meant he wasn't alone. The other one with the knife slash angling across his right eye, leaving the eye the color of milk. The shadow men had come creeping, collecting for loan shark Whitey Adler. Again the nose pressed the glass, the dark hollows for eyes. Willis wanting to sink beneath the lath. He hadn't paid the vigorish this week. Didn't have it last week either.

Knuckles pounded again and the knob rattled. Then nothing but his heartbeat over the click-clack of grandfather's tall-case clock. The cold wet under his arms sent a shiver. Shifting his weight from one leg to the other. The floor betrayed him with a groan.

He had to get Adler some of what he owed. Maybe he ought to use the money he intended to pay Ida Jean. But he needed that too, worse than ever now. God, if the sky-high rates Whitey Adler demanded didn't kill him, the shadow men just might. You didn't borrow from people like Whitey Adler and not keep up. He'd have to take the last of the payroll and hand it off. First thing tomorrow. Make up some new story for Walter and the performers. But right now, he was going to the ringer house.

Craning his neck, he tried to look out. Nothing showing past the ribbed glass. The fear eased, leaving him with the need to get over to Ida Jean's, get his carnal jones twigged. Just had to splash water on his face, pomade his hair and swish Pepsodent around his mouth. Then stroll over. Get his rocks off.

He was thinking maybe Lips left a note, like a reminder about payment. Sliding the deadbolt back, he kept the chain on and cracked the door, feeling the evening air against his damp skin. One eye peeking past the gap.

A burst like fireworks hit him square, the chain snapped, spitting links, the door knocking him back, his arms whirling, trying to keep himself from falling. And in they came. Willis sputtering blood as his head hit the floor.

Lips loomed over him. A gloved hand reached down and

clapped hold of his collar, pulled Willis to his feet, tillering him backward and slamming him into the alcove wall. The other one, Milky Eye, filled the doorway, jerking the door knob free of the plaster, shutting the door and donning black gloves.

"Hold on, fellas —" the words slapped from Willis's mouth as he was jerked back and forth. The iron taste of blood. Willis was lifted, his feet trailing down the hall, feeling himself rushed backward. "Was just gonna bring it to —"

Plowed into the tall-case clock, the glass door cracking. Lips jerked him back, Willis's feet barely scraping the floor.

Lips set him down, steadied him and stepped aside like a matador.

"Trying to tell you, I'll get it to—"

Milky Eye lunged with his forearm cocked, smashing Willis into the clock again. Glass shards bit into his back. A leather fist flew, his head snapped into the grandfather's moon dial. Milky Eye trying to stuff him inside. Willis clinging with his fingers, trying to keep it from happening, his spine pressed against the weights and pendulum. Finial and pediment snapping as Willis stopped time.

Milky Eye hit him in the groin and let go, Willis flopping to the floor. And Lips pulled the grandfather's tall-case over, letting it topple on him.

Semi-conscious, Willis lay there with the clock pinning him. The blur of big shoes leaving, the door shutting and everything going dark. Some time later, he came around, the sour smell of vomit, feeling it pasted to his cheek and in his ear, the smashed clock pressing down on him, boxing him like a coffin. Hard to breathe. Getting out from underneath.

Pushing a loose tooth with his tongue, he groaned, "Happy fucking birthday." Sliding from under the busted clock, he half-dragged, half-crawled to the den, in no condition for Ida Jean's. Climbing into the chair, taking the cigar from the ashtray, he relit it, careful of it against his broken mouth. Thinking the hell with it, he'd call Handy Phibbs. Robbing that bank was starting to sound like a good idea. A way out of this misery.

. . . SIX

Not getting out of Kansas tonight. The dusk was coming on.

Clara sat on the bumper. The steam had stopped rising from under the hood. Had only been the one truck drive by since she broke down. Likely end up sleeping in the truck.

Then she heard it, coming from a long way off, raising dust behind it. An old Packard with the square cab, the headlights high and on either side of the windshield, the kind of truck they used for delivering the post when she was a kid. This one painted brown, gold lettering down the wood-paneled sides. The driver slowed to a stop and leaned across the seat, calling out the window.

"Got trouble?"

Some kind of scorn would likely have the man driving off. Clara smiled and said, "Darn thing started clunking and blowing steam, then quit. Sure be grateful in case you got some water to spare, mister." Clara sizing the man up, medium height with a hawk nose, bug eyes and bushes for eyebrows and sideburns, looked harmless enough.

"Your lucky day. Water's my game," he said, pointing at the lettering down the side.

Eugene Cobb, Rainmaker.

Getting out, he stuck a bowler on his head, came around the front bumper and said his name, looking over the old Hudson, never seen something on the road with this little paint left on it.

"Rainmaker, huh?" She smiled and said her name.

"Spoken with the note of the skeptic, Clara." Pulling open his passenger door, Eugene took a canteen from behind the seat, giving it a shake and offering it to her.

"You make it?" Taking it, she smiled and had a drink. Couldn't believe how good it felt going down.

"Pumped it fresh this morning."

"Let me ask, how you go about making it rain, Eugene?" She drank some more.

Crooking a finger, he wanted her to follow to the rear of his truck, flapping back the musty canvas. Behind some packs and tubs of supplies stood a kind of mortar on a tripod, strapped to the truck's floor. A simple affair of a tripod base, a long barrel and a bipod mount. The thing painted black with his name painted gold along its barrel.

"That like a cannon?"

"Cannon's more an artillery gun, fires a flat trajectory. Roundshot mostly." He climbed up in back. "What I fire's more of a canister shot, what I call my Cobb-busters."

"Shoot them where?"

"The sky, of course."

"Can I ask why?" She drank some more.

"Causes it to concuss, see? Makes it rain."

Clara looked up at the cloudless evening, the moon and stars starting to show.

"Can see you're a doubting Debbie."

"Never seen a fella do it, blast the sky, is all." She looked at the tubs of sulfur and black powder, bottles of colored liquid, some labeled ether.

"Pack them special, my Cobb-busters." Reaching a hollow tube with welded propellent fins, his name down the side. Cradling it in his arms, he explained about removing the explosive, how he repacked it, then dropped it in the cast-iron tube, how it hit the firing pin and shot into the heavens, the special blast bringing about the rain. Saying, "I calculate the trajectory, windspeed and velocity, you see?" Smiling, Eugene set the missile back down, pushed a pack aside and came up with a jug, sloshing it around, holding it out.

"What's this?"

"Water . . . for your radiator."

"You make it?" She smiled again, handing the canteen back.

Tossing the empty canteen to the corner, he hopped down, took the jug over to her truck, looking under the folded hood. He scraped remnants of seeds and nuts from the radiator, pointing to where some rodent had chewed through the tubes.

Clara leaned in and saw what he was pointing at.

"Little buggers built nests, see there?"

"How far you figure I'll get?"

"Was wondering how you got this far." Shaking his head, he set the hood down. "Need a new hose, at least that."

"Saying I'm damn out of luck."

"Well, I can offer you a lift."

Clara looked up the road, then back the way she'd come, then at him. "Where to?"

"Tucumcari. Got a room booked, place called the Blue Swallow. You got no place else, I can get them to wheel in a cot."

"A cot?"

"Town council's got me booked for two days. Hospitality room. 'Course, you rather, you can stay, sleep under the stars."

"Except you're gonna make it rain."

"There is that." Eugene pointed the way she came. "After I make it rain in Tucumcari, then I'm heading to Hoxie. At the mayor's behest."

She followed the way he was pointing. "Flint?"

"That's it, Mayor Flint. A good man, wired me expenses in advance," Eugene said. "You give him the vote?"

"I'd think twice before giving that man pocky warts."

Smiling, Eugene opened his passenger door, saying, "That's politicians for you. In my game, you get used to fellas talking out of both sides of their mouths."

"So, you've made it happen."

"Rain? How about you see for yourself?"

She looked up and down the 83, saying, "Go see a miracle or stay here and get bit by bugs."

He grinned, saying, "You know, you got me thinking. I could use an assistant, Clara."

"Uh huh."

"Somebody to talk up the crowds, answer questions, sell the postcards. Letting me get focused."

"Postcards?"

He reached in a pack and pulled one out. "Nickel a piece. A big seller."

"Uh huh." She looked at the photo of Eugene smiling next to his truck, holding a Cobb-buster in his hands, the mortar set up on its tripod.

"While I'm setting up, mixing and figuring, putting my attention on my Cobb-busters."

"Blasting the sky."

"That's it."

"So, I get a job and a place to stay?"

"Your lucky day, you ask me." Eugene went and got in the driver's side, smiling out the window at her. Letting her make up her mind.

"One question, Eugene?" She got in.

"Uh huh?"

"Who gets the bed?"

The look in his eyes said it hadn't crossed his mind, but his mouth twisting into a smile said it had.

"How much?"

His smile dropped.

"I mean the job, what you're paying?"

He looked thoughtful, tapping his lip. "How's two bits sound?"

"Half as good as fifty."

"Fifty cents an hour. You're joking, huh?"

She shrugged, looked out the window at the flat land whizzing past.

"How about we call it thirty?" he said finally. "And you can have the bed."

"That come with meals?"

Looking over at her, saying, "I got a choice?"

Clara thinking it would be worth it just to see the look on Mayor Flint's face when nothing happened. "Guess I can stick through Tucumcari, then Hoxie. See how it goes."

"Sounds fair. You figure on taking the 66 west?"

"All the way out."

"California, on your own, huh?"

"Something wrong in that?"

"Just, a woman alone . . ."

"Starting to sound like my old man."

"You're married?"

"That a problem?"

"No, no. Just don't see it much, that's all, a woman traveling on her own."

"Don't see a lot of fellas shooting the sky either."

They were quiet as the next few miles flashed by, then she said, "So you done it before, make it rain?"

"Sounds like you don't think I can."

She shrugged. "I'm from the show-me state."

"Think that's the next one over."

"Born in one place, live in the other." She smiled.

"Boise."

"That where you're from?"

"Where I made it rain. Denver before that." Reaching behind the seat for a copy of the *Denver Post*, he handed it to her, pointing to the photo and article, saying, "Fella wrote it called it a scientific phenomenon. Befuddled the naysayers, tell you that."

She glanced at the article and handed it back, trying to picture the look on Sonny's face when he got wind she was working for a rainmaker. Right there in Hoxie. Wondering if she'd make the front page of the *Sentinel*.

Eugene explained about the outfit she'd wear for the job. "Showy and French, gets their attention."

Clara was fine with it, thinking of the costumes she wore when she danced the Palais, back under the spotlight.

Thinking of her in something skimpy, he reached the flask under his seat, uncapped and sipped. Wiping the rim, he offered it to her, saying, "Takes care of the road dust."

. . . SEVEN

Nothing to eat in the place. Nothing growing in the ground. Getting sore at Clara, Sonny was worried at the same time. Could be the old truck broke down. Nothing to do for it during the night, he spent the hours near sleepless, listening for sounds of her coming back.

Tugging up his trousers at first light, he plodded down the stairs, took Orin's Cooey from over the mantel, reached the box and pocketed some shells. May as well get in some hunting while he made sure she didn't break down on the back road halfway to town. Shoving his feet in the shoes, he remembered he needed to find hobnails and cobble the left one before he fell on his face. And he needed to shove a strip of rubber in the other one, its sole wearing thin. Thinking he could cut a strip from a blown-out tire he rolled home a couple months back, found it out on the 24. Sonny thinking he could use it for patching the roof, but it would work fine for a shoe sole.

Easing out the screen door, he stood on the porch, feeling the chill, the first thin light with its promise of the day ahead. Hitching the strap of the burlap pouch to his shoulder, he took the grain sack from the rocker and went down the steps, skipping the lower one that had gone spongy. Crossing the yard, looking at the drift of sand from the last blow, piled partway up the far side of the barn. Lifting the latch, he pulled the barn door back, both yard birds rushing past him.

"Done your roosting, huh, boys?"

Leaning the gun against the boards, he cast grain into the yard, the birds bobbing and pecking. Pearl giving a nicker from her stall, the mule's way of greeting, wanting Sonny to come rub her nose and the long ears, giving a whinny when he came and talked to her. Sonny working the currycomb across her dappled flank, grateful she'd given up kicking at him a long time back. Still, she found some kind of mule humor in biting him in the pants now and again when he'd bend for the hay. Affection, he supposed.

Taking the bucket out to the pump, he set his foot on the well cap and grabbed the handle. He splashed the water in the trough inside the corral, went for a couple more bucketfuls, then set a pan for the yard birds by the door. Shaking sand from a handful of hay, he fed it to Pearl. Then he led her to the corral and slapped her rump. Pearl going and dunking her white muzzle in the trough, drooling streams from either side of her mouth. Sonny thanking the empty heaven for Orin's hand-dug well that kept on pumping good water. Only thing around here still working.

Closing the gate, he slipped the rope's loop over the post. Taking the Cooey and satchel, he walked down the baked track past the phone pole. Felt the heat of that early sun as it rose up. Sonny keeping an eye out for the scrawny dogs he'd seen, ones the croppers left behind when they moved off, unable to take them with and feed them anymore. Leaving the yard birds on their own, hunting grasshoppers along the fence till the heat of the sun would drive the birds back in the barn, do their searching for crickets in the shade.

Cradling the single-barrel, Sonny walked off the miles as the sun climbed, considering Clara likely drove west as far as the old truck would take her. The ten-mile hike gave him lots of time to think about it. His eyes alert for any movement across the open ground. Recalling the Cooey's recoil that first time he pulled on the trigger. Twelve years old and the gun taught him respect, a sixteen-gauge *whump* that sent him on his ass, left his shoulder smarting for days, a bruise that went from purple to brown to yellow. Didn't ask for Orin's say-so to fire it again till his next birthday. That first volley stayed with him, causing him to flinch and miss next few times he fired it. Orin smiling and saying if he were a jackrabbit, the safest place would be square in Sonny's sights.

Then he was thinking about what Handy Phibbs said, planning to rob the Sheridan Loan and Trust, get Willis Taggart in on it. Clean out the cash drawers and safe. At first, Sonny thought he'd gone mad. Handy telling him he didn't know why he brought it up in the first place, ribbing him about not shooting worth a shit.

The backfire came from behind and made Sonny hop in the road. Took him a beat to realize it wasn't a gunshot. Nobody shooting at him. The old Capitol Coach rumbled up, a family's possessions roped in back and up top. Swinging the barrel to his shoulder, Sonny stepped to the driver's side, smiling at Amos Bragg behind the wheel. A water bottle in a canvas bag and a shovel strapped to the running board. The two gape-mouthed kids up on top. Junior and Wilena looked down and said hey, their freckled faces alight with adventure, youth sparing them the gravity of the times.

"Amos," Sonny said.

"Sonny." Amos squinted at him, then ahead at the road.

"Katey," Sonny looked past him to the wife on the passenger side.

Katey smiled a hello, a solid woman with her hair under a bonnet, well into her second trimester.

"Lighting out?"

Amos gave a nod. "Packing her in, Sonny. You know, nothing to be done for it."

"Were done long time ago, but we tried to stick," Katey said, clapping a hand on her man's thigh. "Bank sent the marshal, serving papers to run us off."

"Can't do that. You fight them."

"Well, they done it, and I got no fight left."

"Sons of bitches." Sonny looked to the lifeless road, waving away a curious dragonfly.

"Won't bury my babies in this dirt," Katey said, her mouth tight with resolve.

All three looking ahead at the dancing heat shimmers.

"Hunting jacks?" Amos said finally.

"Hoping to bag a couple, yeah."

"Clara got Thanksgiving on the mind?" Katey said.

He just nodded, best not to mention about her running off, not wanting to add to their worries. Who knows, maybe they'd pass her up the line someplace and hear it from her.

"Going down by the creek then, uh?" Amos said.

"Yeah, always a good spot."

"Was one time maybe, but ain't hardly been a jack in a long time, Sonny. Think you know it."

"Well, mostly right, yeah, but did catch sight of one up where there's still water, creek goes bit wider." Sonny pointed northwest. "And, well, you never know, huh?"

Amos nodded. "Remember when we was kids, so many of 'em even you could hit one." Grinning at what a bad shot Sonny had been, showing the gap between his crooked teeth. "Bagged four, five that time it rained on one side of the bridge, and snowed on the other."

Sonny remembered.

"Well, all that's gone." Katey put a hand to her stomach. "And anything left living's looking starved, what with no rain."

"It'll come," Sonny said.

"Like them pennies from heaven," she said.

Amos glanced up. "You're not thinking about what Handy said?"

Guessing he meant robbing the bank, Sonny just shook his head. Who hadn't Handy told?

The three of them quiet for a time, Wilena calling from up top, saying it was getting hot as blazes.

"And stinking too," Junior added.

Katey called out her window for them to hush.

Unfolding a worn notice from his shirt pocket, Amos showed it, saying, "See here, pickers wanted."

"California, huh?" Sonny looked at it and nodded. He'd seen the notices posted around town, the promise of work. Five hundred pickers wanted, Sonny betting many times that would show up, but biting his tongue about it.

"Yuh, place called Oxnard. Got orchards big as counties, as far as the eye can see. Pick oranges all day. A place a fella can get himself upright." Amos folded the paper, slipping it back in his pocket. "Drive the days, pitch camp in one of them Hoovertowns if we got to. Get there one town at a jump."

"Would've stopped by and said a proper so long . . ." Katey said.

"Yeah, I know it."

"Tell me you're not thinking of laying in with Handy?" Amos said.

"Have to be crazy."

"Get that way when you're on the last ditch," Amos said. "Well, guess not much point in us choking on this old thing's stink, so I thank you to wish us Godspeed."

"You know I do. Clara too." Sonny tapped his friend's shoulder, rapped his knuckles on the side panel, smiled over at Katey and stepped back. Hoping they got past the armed deputies at the California state line, the ones he heard were turning Okies back by the hundreds.

Amos ground the stick in gear, the truck lurching. "You want a hop-on to the bridge?"

Seeing there was no place to hop, Sonny said he could use the stretch. The beat springs sagging as the old truck rolled on.

"Toodle-loo to Clara," Katey called out the window. "Tell her I'll write."

"Till it rains," Sonny called after them, whispering the few words he remembered from a prayer Orin taught him as a boy. First time in years he felt like he might cry.

The next backfire drowned something Amos called out the window, his arm waving. Dust rose in tufts from the near-bald tires, mixing with the blue exhaust. Junior and Wilena waving from up top. The Capitol Coach bumped over the furrows of drifted sand, shrinking and expanding in the shimmer, till it looked like it was rising in the air, and finally, it was gone.

"Damn jacks was everywhere," Sonny said, thinking about what had been, recalling the rabbit drives Orin took him on when he was a boy, had them all the way down to Texas. Damned jackrabbits eating everything green. Folks rounding them and beating the dumb things with sticks, saving on the shells. Made up crude pens and corralled them over in Boise that time, Sonny watching men and women, their arms going like ratchets, beating, gutting and skinning, leaving the pink carcasses. Turkey vultures circling overhead and waiting a turn. Orin had him gather the skins in sacks and put them in back of the truck, selling the pelts to some mink company. Sonny watching bottle flies landing on the pelts. His arms tired from waving them off while Orin haggled for a fair price.

Calling to mind how he'd woke from the dreams, seeing the look in the men's eyes that time in Boise, swinging their clubs, caught up in the killing, nobody paying heed to the dust roller that blew in. The clubbers dropping their sticks, yelling and running off . . . "Like jackrabbits," he thought, looking at the bleached land. Couldn't eat rabbit again till after he got hitched. Clara proud of her fricassee.

Sand was getting in his flapping shoe, past the hole in his sock, felt it chafing between his toes. Sonny followed in Amos's tire tracks to the old wood bridge that had, just as Amos said, once seen rain on one side and snow on the other. A sign tacked on the bridge post: Eugene Cobb, rainmaker, coming to Hoxie, with Friday's date printed under it. Sonny thinking of the two Kaw out of Oklahoma Mayor Flint hired on, promised to bring the rains. The elected head telling the throng on the courthouse lawn to stand back. Folding their arms, the two Kaw demanded cash up-front. Tucking the bills away, they danced circles, whooped and chanted, dabbed with paint, wearing beads and feathers. One gripping the neck of a rattlesnake, setting it down and dancing behind it, the rainmakers set to follow it in search of the rain god. Till Town Marshal Billy Joe Blake parted the onlookers, pulled his service piece and shot the snake apart, arresting the pair for endangering the public and cheating Shawnee County. Blake and the mayor not seeing eye to eye on much of anything ever since.

A straggle of fiddlenecks dotted the stony bank that ran down to the bridge pilings, once thick with cattails, mallow weeds and marsh ferns, a chalky stripe showing its one-time waterline. Sonny watched the bent flowers, swaying yellow, remembering how floodwater wood used to dam against the timbers when the water rose, muddy and angry with the spring floods.

A patch of grass grew down the middle of the streambed where the mossy algae used to wag in the flow of its waters. The tadpoles him and Emmett used to scoop into buckets, the bull cats that swam in the murky pools. The two of them sitting and jawing while eyeing their cork bobbers.

Stepping over the rocks of the dry streambed, he moved along a fence line mostly buried in drifts of sand. No sign of the buckwheat the jacks used to thrive on. Picking his way past a stand of dogwood, the bark peeled from the trunks. A cicada sang across the empty acres of stubble field, brindled in spots by crabgrass and sedge. Nothing was the way it had been, and nobody worked the fields, harvesting and cultivating for the year ahead.

A mile north of the bridge, the Stanton place looked like a giant fist had come down on its roof beam. Its hay wagon busted up like kindling, one wheel lying next to it. The door of the house knocked out, kids from town coming and busting out the windows the way they did when the families moved off. Everything in the place dusted gray. A manure fork stabbed into the ground in front of the door like an omen.

Sounded hollow when Sonny stepped through the place, curiosity bringing him in, no furniture or belongings, scrapes on the pine boards where the potbelly once stood, droppings from a mouse colony in every corner, shards of glass and rocks lying on the floor. A yellowed newspaper, its headline talking about the worst duster ripping through in April of '34, the *Daily Times* calling it Black Sunday, unleashed from the gates of hell. Nine hundred miles wide and fifteen hundred miles long, blocking out the sun, making day into night and howling across the empty plains. And when it was gone, the sun showed devil-red, and folks were sure it was the end of times.

Sonny set about fixing the damage. Most of the boards had been wrested from one side of the barn, the tar paper stripped from the roof. Sand had lanced through slats of the barn and the coop, taking half the livestock. The windmill was leaning, and the fence line along the west side was gone. No sign that it was ever there.

The *Sentinel* claimed Kansas topsoil was blasted as far as Washington. Houdini in the White House, sitting with his advisors. The bunch of them scratching their heads about drought relief. Farmsteads fell to the banks, and folks gave up and headed west on the 66. Those who stuck it out congregated at church, Catholics, Lutherans and Baptists, all praying for rain and an end to the blasting sand.

Black Sunday left Clara with the shakes, her glands thick and her throat raw, could barely spoon down broth. Wanted to pack up and move someplace the Lord hadn't given up on. Sonny couldn't get a decent crop in, the loam stripped off and blown to Arkansas and Texas, their soil blown back, and no rain to set any of it down. But Sonny wasn't quitting, said he'd hang in till the rain came again.

The money Orin left dwindled down, and the dust-laden grass filled the guts of the remaining mules and milking stock, all but Pearl. By '36, dusters and drought claimed most of everything, leaving a strange silence on the land. Clara feeling bare against the nothingness that lent no peace and no place to hide. Barely a bird singing or cricket chirping. Neighbors packed up and left, the land empty to the horizon.

But the land was in his blood. His people had come in prairie schooners, followed their teams of mules, fought the Cheyenne at Beaver Creek. Did it for what the land promised and for their children not yet born, and the ones that would follow. Planted their crops and drove their cattle, helped build the rails and died here.

For a time after Black Sunday, Sonny kept her from packing up, telling her it would only be worse to leave. Nothing to do but take the bit in her mouth and hang on with the iron of conviction. So she pitched in rebuilding the barn, pounded in the squared nails, hauled up buckets of muck to clear the well. Helped him get the tar felt on the roof, Sonny teaching her how to do a Dutch lap. She tried to revive a garden in ground where no shoots would take hold. Fixing what the local ladies at church called the new Kansas fare: fried dough and corn pone, preserving thistle and tumbleweed in brine, serving dishes of dandelion and creek chub, calling it eat-it-and-like-it. Making broth from just about anything that stuck from the ground. Joking about the names for the recipes they shared after church, dishes that weren't much more than gravy and grits, milk and rice, Spam and noodles. Jackrabbit or gourmet gopher if you got lucky, rag soup if you weren't. Sonny eating it all, saying *mmm mmm* good.

Her spirits held for a time, but the last couple months Clara was back to being careworn. Saying she never loved the land, not the way he did, believing what they shared most was an aversion for Henningan, the president at the bank, after losing the half section to him. The loan had been secured by the half parcel. With the money, they bought the sewing machine, pot stove and churn. Sonny had the Bell company put in a phone line, Clara talking to her momma in Topeka. When the bank's money ran out, they struggled to keep up payments. Sonny taking any work he could find, but it wasn't enough. Henningan stopped by, giving the

43

place an assessing eye, and the half section was gone. Wasn't long after that the Bell company sent a man to disconnect the line.

Going out the door, Sonny pulled out the pitchfork and tossed it aside. On the west side of the house, he swept his flapping shoe at the sand covering the fruit cellar, pulled up its door, the smell of rot greeting him. Letting it slam back down.

Sun getting hot for a November morning, Sonny lifted his cap to swipe at the sweat, then clapped it back on. Out on the barren, he caught a flash of movement along the flintrock — thinking it was the sun playing tricks.

Sitting on a rock, he pushed away the lonely trying to creep in, felt the sun's warmth through the overalls. Taking his canteen, he took a swallow, then rolled a smoke. Stretching and puffing, the sun yellow against his closed lids, he considered his chances of getting a stringer of cat-fish, Clara calling them mudcats. Too far and too hot to trek to that spot on the Saline without the truck. He'd walk the rest of the way to town, get something to eat at Grainger's, then walk back with enough daylight to tend the rotted porch step. Maybe get to the hornet's nest under the soffit at the back of the house, surprised the blowing sands hadn't knocked it to Arkansas. Looking down at the shoe, he lifted his toes, making the leather flap. Making note to get some hobnails from Grainger's while he was in town.

Tomorrow, the government man would come dropping another truckload of saplings. Sonny back to planting the shelterbelts along the property line, earning enough to get by. FDR's latest way of lending a hand, the farming man scraping the earth with harrow and shovel, ripping the dry clods with his plow.

Then he caught movement again. Tipping his cap and shielding his eyes. A jackrabbit as gray as the scrub, raised on

44

its haunches — twenty yards off — its perked ears orange in the sun. It gave a short bound and stopped, raised up again and looked at him. Bringing the barrel up slow, Sonny stood and brought it level, taking a step, then another. Getting his breathing right. When the jack went flat out, Sonny swung the barrel, led it by a length. The stock bucking at his shoulder, the shot ringing in his ears.

. . . EIGHT

The rabbit lending weight to the burlap sack, he walked past the old junker out front of the Lang place, its one headlight busted out, their horse trough on its side. The top of a plow and harrow sticking from a drift. His feet getting sore. It had been a few months since he'd been to Hoxie. Nothing much different. Clara doing the driving since he taught her to handle the old truck, picking up what they needed and making her nickel call at Grainger's.

Recalling the rows of cotton with the bolls flowering, "Kansas snow," Old Charlie Lang had called it. Twelve years old when Sonny came here and learned to chop it, Old Charlie showing him how and paying him fifty cents an acre once Sonny got the hang of it. The windows of the house had been knocked out here too, leaving the place looking soulless.

The corduroy bridge took him across Sand Creek, past a cornfield of dried stalks, mostly blown down, with drifts covering parts of it. The outskirts of town, Mort's Café, tumbled in, part of its frame sticking up with the cellar hole showing. The plague on the land forcing these good folks to pull up stakes and head off. Nothing to be done when the soil just blows everything away.

Hoxie was a speck on any man's map. The county seat with its courthouse, the Bee Hive schoolhouse, the Methodist church at the near end, the Presbyterians at the other. The Sheridan Loan and Trust in the middle. Shops lined the main drag around it, mostly clapboard, paint gone and windows brown from the pelting sand, half the places soaped and boarded. The town's commerce reflecting the state of the Great Plains. One flat-roofed building looking much like the next, save for the faded signs declaring Mozelle's, Hoxie Post & Drug, an arrow to Doc Bletsoe's upstairs, Bertie's Beauty & Dress Shop, the Hoxie Café, Gaston's Grill, Hoxie Medicines & Soda with curb service available, Tanner's Feed, C.A. Tawney's, Phibbs Conoco, Bailey Graham's. Tucker's General & Dry Goods, locked up and boarded since '36, when the Tucker brothers hopped a flat-wheeler and lit out for San Francisco.

Sonny's shoe flapped down the main stretch of Hoxie. Hoisting the sack up on his shoulder, he was thinking, "Got me a jack, wouldn't mind trading for one of Polly's pies." Seeing the shop boarded with its window soaped, Sonny remembering those jammie tarts Polly Rupp dished up back when he was a kid. Nothing like their sweet gooeyness, best when they just come hot from the oven. Orin bringing him in after Sonny endured the lessons from the church lady, Sonny doing his book learning with less fuss and fidget if there was a jammie tart at the end of it.

Gone now, Polly's Pies had been taken by the bank, the place rented to a fellow from Boise calling it Capp's Square Deal 'n Wheel. Hollis Capp buying out folks too strapped to hang on, paying pennies on the dollar for pretty much anything they couldn't rope up on their cars and trucks. Stoves, bedsteads, farm gear and tools, Capp's sign making it known he was mostly interested in scrap metal. Once a month he loaded up a semi-trailer and hauled it away, the town gossips guessing he was selling it for a lot more than he paid. Not well liked about town, Hollis Capp showed no sign of giving a goddamn. The graybeards hanging round Grainger's speculated that Capp's place might catch fire some fine night. Betting there'd be no witnesses. Nobody coming into Grainger's argued.

Going past the courthouse, Sonny caught sight of Mayor Melvin Flint standing nose to nose with Town Marshal Billy Joe Blake. "Another fucking rainmaker, tell me you're joking, Mayor?"

The elected official looking more likely to trade punches than to press the flesh, standing by the Civil War twelve-pounder, one of Price's artillery pieces from the Battle of Mine Creek, local forefathers giving their lives back when the state went by Bleeding Kansas. Flint and Blake at loggerheads since the election back in April, the ballot leaving the marshal and four hundred eligible voters with natural curiosities about irregularities that saw Flint creep into office.

"Not driving your truck today, Sonny?" Flint called.

"It look like I'm driving my truck, Mayor?"

Marshal Blake nodded, liking Sonny's attitude. Saying to the mayor, "There you go again, eluded by the obvious."

Reaching the steps of Grainger's Mercantile, Sonny yanked back the ailing screen door, its hinges creaking like all Kansas hinges creaked. Its rusted handle saying it was time for soda pop refreshment, paint peeling from the Bubble Up emblem.

Stepping into the dim of the place, he crossed the sawdust

floor, said hey to the graybeards sitting over the checker-board, the smell of pipe tobacco filling the place.

"Hey ya, Sonny." Tyrell spoke around the cob pipe, hop-ping a red over two blacks, saying, "Our man of the people out there butting horns with the marshal?"

"Looks like."

"Damn fool's bringing another rainmaker."

"Which one's the fool?"

"Good point."

The graybeards cackling, one mouthful of teeth between them. Tyrell took out his pouch, pinching tobacco in his pipe, tamping it with his thumb. "The one the mayor's got coming goes by Eugene Cobb, out of East Texas. Claims can conjure rain by concussing the heavens, firing what he calls, get this, Cobb-busters, blasting the sky."

"Out of that old twelve-pounder?" Sonny said.

"Got a special mortar back of his truck." Slapping his knee, Albert nearly upset the checkerboard, catching it.

Tyrell saying the mayor dickered down the price. Pointing toward the courthouse lawn. "Sure got townfolk troubled and talking about it."

"Only thing's gonna get a soaking's the county coffers," Albert said.

Saying he was probably right, Sonny went to the counter.

Emmett Grainger peered up over the wire-framed half-specs, one hand going to his ledger.

"Figured you for pulling stakes, Sonny." Setting the ledger aside, the shopkeep reached a case of Sunshine peaches and set them by to the register.

"Know me better 'n that, Emmett."

Taking a screwdriver, Emmett pried at the wooden lid, smacking the heel of his hand at the handle. "Still say the rain's coming?"

"Yeah, but not on account of any rain man."

Turning the case, Emmett smacked at the handle and the lid came loose. Stocking the peach tins next to the Franco-American spaghetti. "What I know's the ground's dryer'n the wife's biscuits."

Sonny recalled biting on those biscuits, time they had supper with the Graingers, asking, "How is Doris?"

"Got the gout, but all things considered, she's fine enough." Facing the labels forward, Emmett wasn't going to let Sonny turn this into old times, saying, "Amos stopped by early, settled up best he could. But guess you know about that."

"Saw him on the road, going someplace called Oxnard."

"A fella's gotta go where there's work. Picking whatever needs picking."

"Migrant work."

"Makes for a day's pay." Emmett aimed one at the spittoon behind him, wiped his chin, saying, "And with mouths to feed, and another on the way."

"Well, sure hope there's plenty of work."

Leaning an elbow down, Emmett let go a sigh, saying, "And your Clara was in too."

"Yeah, a call with her momma?" Sonny not saying she didn't come home.

"Doris didn't have the heart, so, guess it's up to me. That louse of a banker told us plain enough. Can't give out no more credit." Opening the ledger, Emmett pointed to an entry, tapped his finger at it.

"Hell of a thing, a bank." Sonny's hand going to a fist.

"Guess they feel the pinch same as everybody. Henningan come in here using words like tenterhooks and foreclosure and blaming the times."

"You and me, Emmett, we go back to days of short pants.

And you know I'm good for every cent I owe, times being whatever the hell."

"Never doubted it, but these are banks we're talking. Not run by anybody walking upright, but sons of bitches like Henningan, with his soft hands and fancy ties. Skin on his neck like a wattle. Takes orders from bigger sons of bitches, with even softer hands and bigger ties. Not a care for the misery they wreak on folks." Emmett turned and spat again, missing. "Not gonna get run off like old Polly Rupp, so I got to heed what he says. Top of that, at the end of the day, I answer to a higher power." Emmett rolled his eyes ceilingward.

"Wouldn't worry on that. Daniel Henningan sure ain't on no Jesus Road."

"Was talking about my Doris." Emmett aimed a thumb upstairs. "And that banker's got her plenty troubled."

"No offense, Emmett, guess I always figured you for wearing the pants." Sorry as soon as he said it.

"Only trouble with my pants is they got bankers in the pockets. Other than that, they fit just fine." Emmett tucked his shirt in. "You think I lost my stones, you can have a look, decide for yourself."

That got Sonny laughing. "Just came in to see about a tin of beans, go with this rabbit." Lifting the ears from the canvas bag.

"Clara making her fricassee?"

"Didn't come home last night."

Emmett looked at him, finally sucked a breath, letting it out like he was trying to fill the place. Watching a bottle fly land on the ledger, he swatted harder than he needed to, looking at his palm, flicking the mess to the floor. "Alright, Sonny, get your beans. better get a couple. That banker's a son of a bitch. Ought to build a gibbet and lynch him by his goddamn necktie." Emmett considering the box of dolls

Clara had brought in, never sold one of them. "And sure hope you're right about the rains coming. That or we'll all be following Amos. First the farms go, then the stores, and with any luck, the banks too."

"Rain'll come, Emmett." Sonny went down the aisle looking for cans of Van Camp's, taking three and remembering about the hobnails, thinking better of asking about them.

. . . NINE

The red-and-green sign hung from a chain above the doors, pocked by termites: Phibbs Conoco. The lone window was around the east side of the garage, grimed by grease, a couple of its panes boarded. A two-pump place with a stack of oil cans next to the ethyl pump on the right. A sign over the glass globes on the pump tops, declaring a dime a gallon. Small print under that: show cash before gas. Tin signs had been nailed to the boards out front advertising whitewall tires, tubes and Willard batteries.

The twin door on the right hung open. A broadcaster's voice cut through the scratch of a radio set, a news flash of the goings-on in the European theater: "Polish forces caved to the Nazi juggernaut." That country getting sliced up, the hyenas taking the east, the jackals getting the west.

Sonny stuck his head in the door, but Handy Phibbs was already coming out, squinting at the daylight, smiling at him, wiping grease from his hands. The man's shoe was flapping, suffering the same malady as his own. Handy lifting his foot, saying, "Both of us in the slumps, huh, brother?"

"Looks like." Sonny showing his own shoe.

The two of them laughing and shaking hands. Clapping him on the back, Handy pointed to the pump handle, the glass display showing "this sale" set to zero. "See how you forget your truck, guess zero ain't gonna change."

Sonny pointed to the business-closing sign by the door — cash only.

"That banking fucker Henningan insisted I put it up, comes by chewing on me for getting behind in payments, giving out credit, with not much coming back in. Last warning and shit like that. Asked how I was gonna pay him if I got to ask cash only for ethyl? Folks needing credit and learning to fix their own junk. But you think that man listens? Threatened to shut me down just like he did old Polly. Tell you, being part Kickapoo and broke's no way to be." He shrugged. "Reason I say we go ahead and rob him. Not feel bad about it."

"Told you I'd give it a think."

"Sure, sure. Anyway, sorry about Clara taking off."

Sonny gave him a level look. "How you know that?"

"Could say I got a hunch?" Saying it like a question.

Sonny waited.

"Okay. She stopped by for a fill-up, about supper last night. Looked upset and told me to pump enough to get her out of state." Handy pointing to the zero on the display. "Was the last sale I didn't make."

"Didn't charge her?"

Handy shrugged, not mentioning it went on Sonny's tab.

"And you didn't think to call?"

"You got a phone?"

Sonny scraped his shoe along the dirt, felt it going inside the shoe. "Took off with the savings. Woman had time on her hands, go around and find where I stashed it." Shoving a hand in his overall pocket, he pulled out his tobacco makings. "Want to twist one?"

"Would if we wasn't standing in this spot." Handy nodded at the pump, a sticker warning about smoking within ten feet. "'Less you want to get to California ahead of her." Handy smiled, slinging an arm on Sonny's shoulder, stepping past the doors, over to a Moon Roadster parked on the lot, saying, "Over here's fine."

Dark green paint and all washed up, parked next to a traveling show truck with weeds rising through its wheel spokes. A sale sign stuck under the Moon's windshield wiper. Handy slapping his hand flat on the fender, saying, "Sharp deal, n'case you got two-fifty."

"I look like I got that?" Sonny rolled one, putting the makings away, patting pockets for a match.

"Well, you ever want rock solid, Moon Roadster's the way to go. Just tuned this baby up all nice. A man could do worse."

"Know I'm a truck man, right?" Sonny said, striking a match, puffing the smoke to life.

"Yeah, well, Moon's a good one to cut away the back, make a truck of her, you want. And this one's got an easy fifty-thousand life left in her. Just did a valve job on her, replaced the points. Ain't no jalopy."

"Handy, you know I ain't got two-fifty." Sonny knowing what was coming.

"Or you don't mind the color red, got a swell Dodge out back with the flathead six. Let you have that one, hmm, two hundred even. You get an eye for it, I can maybe shave off a little more, you know, for old times, throw in couple gallon cans of oil to boot." Handy pointing to the tower of oil cans. "Valvoline, Opaline, take your pick."

"I'd still have my truck, except you fueled her up, let Clara drive off."

"My fault, huh? Well, guess on the up side, how far you think she'll get in that old tin lizzie?" Leaning against the Moon's patched-up rocker. "Gonna be back before you know it."

Sonny tapped a tire with his shoe, sand spilling out.

"Plus, told you I got a way . . ."

"Yeah, easy money." Sonny looked at him.

"Just walk in and take it." Handy grinned.

Sonny recalled how Orin warned him about staying clear of Handy Phibbs back when they were kids. "Get your gas at the Texaco over by the Presbyterian hall," he warned. "Get Jeff Barnes to pump in half Sky Chief, half Fire Chief. Can't go wrong."

"Or we could make 'shine. Not as likely to get shot," Sonny said.

"Need water to make 'shine. Plus Henningan's got it coming. Now, you ready to hear how we do it?"

"Told you I ain't decided."

"Well, that's fine. While you're doing it, I got something else. Wilbur Flanders at the radio says he wouldn't mind a couple guys hanging around his place, a day or two. Willing to pay."

"Hanging around Wilbur's got anything to do with the bank?"

"Not a thing." Handy shook his head.

"Hang around doing what?"

"Just sitting on the man's porch."

Sonny looked at him, waiting for the rest of it.

"About a week back some fella comes by Wilbur's, says he wants to fix him up with a new sign, the old K-L-X one looking tired, paint peeling, termites chewing it up, the X just hanging by a nail."

"Who's this fella?"

"Just said he was affiliated with the Knights of the Great Plains. You hear of 'em?"

"Shitkickers burning crosses and riding through the night with sacks on their heads."

"Got a hate-on for everybody, Blacks, Catholics and Jews. Hate a guy like me double." Handy showing the cross on the chain around his dark neck. "Wants to trade for some airtime, get word to his members and stir up some new recruits. Wilbur saying he'd have to think on it, figuring what happens when he tells the guy no."

"The reason he wants us on his porch, huh? Get us to do it. Bet he wants us holding shotguns, huh?"

"Hold what you want, long as we scare 'em off."

"And he's willing to pay?"

"Dollar a day just to sit on his porch. Told him we got to start shooting at fellas dressed in bedsheets, riding around with torches, it's gonna be five bucks, plus the ammo."

"Who's gonna pump your gas?"

"Got a kid working part time, don't you worry."

Sonny thinking about getting in his shelterbelt trees, his eyes going to "this sale" on the pump. "Ten cents a gallon, huh? Sweet Jesus." Shaking his head.

"Yeah, and it'll be twelve before the year's out. Just wait and see."

"Water still free?" Sonny reaching in the burlap sack, shaking his empty canteen.

"Be something the day I got charge for it," Handy said. "So, what you want me to tell Wilbur?"

"Got no liking for the hating kind . . ."

"Guess I come upon that naturally myself," Handy said, meaning his skin color. "But I got an idea about that too, how they won't know it's us. Same way we do the bank. Can't miss, you gonna see."

•

Setting the Moon's hood on its prop rod, Handy unscrewed the radiator cap and gave it the one-eye squint, then went to the pump, pumped a few gallons, took an open tin of Valvoline and went round to the driver's side, pulling back the squeaking door. Dipping in his thumb, he dabbed oil along the hinges. Saying, "Stand on the man's porch and make some easy money. A fiver if we got to shoot."

"The two of us playing Pinkertons," Sonny said, leaning his shotgun against the fender, sipping the water Handy poured in the canteen. "And have those sons come after us."

"We do like they do. We put feed sacks on our heads, with holes cut out for eyes. Not gonna know it's us."

Sonny looked at his hands, the blisters from planting the shelterbelt trees. Thinking he'd never made any easy money in his life.

Resting an arm on the Moon's fender, Handy looked toward the Sheridan Loan and Trust. "Same hoods we wear when we walk in that bank. Get that fatso off our backs, pay him what we owe with his own money. How's that gonna feel?"

Sonny smiled, recalled how Orin always pegged Handy Phibbs for watering the ethyl. Smile right at you when he did it. The old man betting as soon as you drove any used crate off this lot, you'd be pushing it the rest of the way home. But Sonny knew a different side to Handy Phibbs.

"So, how about it?" Handy said.

"Farm's bust and the wife's gone. Only thing I got's planting government trees. Maybe not much, but still beats Leavenworth or getting shot."

"We do it right, got nothing to worry about."

"Creepy Karpis, you know about him?"

"Sure, man robbed and killed his way 'cross the Plains."

"Guess he figured the same thing till they caught up with him."

"Okay, forget it. Me and Willis'll get somebody else."

They were quiet a time, both leaning on the Moon, both watching Town Marshal Billy Joe Blake drive past, flipping them a two-finger salute off his temple, parking over by the courthouse, getting out and walking past the Civil War twelve-pounder and going inside.

Sonny nodded, then said, "Okay, well, I'm listening."

Handy laid out the rest, how they'd pull it off, how much he figured to clear, the getaway plan. He waited while Sonny smoked. Finally saying, "Well?"

"Now I'm mulling it."

"That old Cooey single all the gun you got?" Looking at it.

"All the gun I need."

"Remember you shooting it. Couldn't hit the side of a hill." Handy laughed. "You get any better since then?"

"You got no idea." Sonny lifted the flap on the satchel, showing the dead jackrabbit.

. . . TEN

Hanging his arm out the window, Sonny dragged on a smoke, driving the Moon home, the satchel with the rabbit and tins of beans on the seat, gun in the back. Handy let him drive the roadster home, told him they'd work something out. Knowing better, Sonny took the keys anyway. Wasn't going to walk ten miles back with a flapping shoe.

Passing the ghost of a grain elevator, faded letters reading GANO down its sand-pounded side. He rolled a couple miles out of town and pulled into the stone orchard, turning slow enough not to stir the dust. Doing it out of respect. This place where his family rested. A double row of trees his ma had called trees of heaven lined the lane.

Stepping between the plots, he squatted at Orin's, saying some words, pulling up weeds and brushing away sand, the cross with Orin's name and the dates Sonny had carved into the hickory. Pledging to get a proper headstone from the place over in El Dorado soon as he could, match the slate one Orin had made for his mother. He talked to the old man, same way he always did when he came. Telling him wheat was down to thirty cents a bushel, something they used to chew over. Allowing the farm wouldn't clear much this year, but on the upside there was no more beholding to the damn bank, feeling bad lying about it. Looking over and apologizing to his ma for the blasphemy in this place of peace. Telling Orin he was thinking of ordering some hens, breeding up a gang of Bourbon Reds as soon as the rain came. Not mentioning about the Sheridan Loan and Trust, guessing he was crazy to even think about robbing it.

Sonny shifted and tended Imelda Dee Myers's plot, his mother succumbing to the cholera when he was a boy. Lately, he was having a hard time picturing her, the way her eyes looked, the scent of her, the way she wore her hair, afraid she'd fade away some day.

An oriole trilled from one of the trees of heaven, and Sonny stayed a while longer, clearing sand from the grand-folks' plots in the next row.

Climbing back in the Moon, he pushed away those reflections of Orin getting sick, how he tried to hold on as the consumption shriveled him. Fever and night sweats and coughing blood. Nothing anybody could do. Orin passed the year before the drought brought on the first of the dusters. Was a bumper crop that year, in '31. Maybe a blessing Orin hadn't lived to see the wheat turn to an oversupply and its price drop by near half. Then the land went dry and the dusters whipped up and there was no wheat at all. Nothing to sell.

Driving out between the rows of trees of heaven, the long leaves rippling in the breeze, Sonny turned east on the 24. The south fork of the Solomon was near dry as he rolled over the bridge. A sod house stood abandoned, a cropper's place next to it had been tractored. Leveled by a plow blade. Sonny slowed the Moon and humped over a drift of sand across the road.

Heading home, he checked the skyline for dusters. He was late seeing the wrecking pothole. Mashing the brake pedal, he swerved to dodge it. Hopping the opposite shoulder and bucking into the ditch. His ribs banged against the steering wheel, his head thumping the windshield. A spider crack in the glass.

Pushing the door, he got out, touched a hand to his forehead. A little blood, but nothing busted on man or Moon as near as he could tell, just the front axle nosed down in the ditch. Getting in, he twisted the steering and got the wheels straightened. Starting it up again, he tried to back out, the rear wheel spitting sand and gravel at the undercarriage, but it did no good. Taking his canteen, he sat on the rear bumper, had a swallow and waited for somebody to come along.

Waited a half hour before he walked back to the sod house. Calling out, he got no answer. Looked like a big-city outfit came and laid claim, boot prints and tractor tracks through the plowed earth. Folks pushed off like they never mattered. Sonny betting Henningan had a hand in it.

Freeing a couple of fractured boards where the tractor had caught the footing of the porch, he slung the lengths to his shoulder and walked back. Using the shorter board like a shovel, he cleared enough sand from the wheels, then wedged both boards under the rear tires. Easing the damaged Moon back up on the road. Thinking what it would be like, walking into the Sheridan Loan and Trust with the Cooey and yelling, "Stick 'em up!" Wondering if that's how Creepy Karpis did it.

Curling his window down, Sonny drove on, turning onto the county line, swiping his cap across his forehead, tossing it next to the satchel, the air rippling his hair. Recalling the K-L-X newscast coming from the radio inside Phibbs's garage, Wilbur Flanders announcing about the conflict overseas. Sonny half-listening while Handy tried to sell him on this car, giving him the special layaway plan: pay him after the robbery. Sonny imagined bullets ripping over some foreign trench. Fighting alongside fellows in some place that wasn't home, serving his country and doing what was right. Just a matter of time till America sent her troops, that's what Wilbur Flanders said on the news. Sonny thinking if he got called up, he'd have to leave the farm. And with Clara gone . . .

Turning past his mailbox, he stopped in the yard, no light on in the place. Getting out, he grabbed the sack and gun and stepped over the rotting lower step, hooking the screen door with his foot and pulling it back.

Tending Pearl and the yard birds, he got a fire going in the potbelly stove, skinned and roasted up the rabbit, heated a tin of beans on top, then went up to bed. Unbuttoning his flannel shirt, he took off his overalls. Looking at the wedding photo next to the bed as he tried to get to sleep, that look of hope and a fruitful life in their eyes, him and Clara on the church steps. Sonny trying to see her side of things, recalling his boyhood days, back when he and Amos would nab the nun's magnifying glass off her schoolhouse desk, the two of them burning leaves out back after their lessons. Looking at that photo, he felt like burning a hole through it and that promise of a fruitful life.

. . . ELEVEN

"First time that's happened," Eugene Cobb said, looking under the covers. Laying his head back on the pillow, looking like he wanted the earth to swallow him.

"You mean, didn't happen," Clara said, turning her head away, looking at the Red Dog perfume lamp on the nightstand. "What'd you say this is?"

"Supposed to set the mood." Reaching over and past her, he switched it on, saying he paid a dollar for it. Worked okay, soon as the perfume warmed in the lamp, but those glowing glass eyes of the Scotty dog now seemed to be judging him.

"Mood for what?"

"Wait and see." Detangling from the sheet, Eugene sat up in his long johns, swinging his feet to the floor, curling his toes on the cold tiles. The perfume lamp heating up, Eugene turning the dog's eyes away from him, waiting on its smell of sweetness. "Relax a while, then we'll get to work."

"See if your cannon'll fire?" She gave a smile.

"Mortar, not cannon." Not seeing the fun in it, he popped a button on his long johns, poked a finger at his navel, digging some fluff, rolling it between his fingers and flicking it to the floor.

"Got to do that, huh?" she said, watching him.

"Gonna act all Queen of England now?"

Propping on an elbow, she pulled the sheet over her breasts. Running a hand over her tangle of hair, saying, "Sorry you didn't get your dollar's worth, I mean for your lamp, but how about you don't go taking it out on me." She was feeling bad enough, ending up in this man's motel bed. Saying, "What's that smell?"

"The lamp's heating up."

"It supposed to smell like that?"

"Nice scent of pine."

"Whatever gets you over the fence, I guess." Crinkling her nose, she watched his finger go back inside his long johns. "And you think that's what, like grooming?" She fished her foot for her undergarments along the floor. Standing, she wriggled into them.

"Got the room till noon, plus pretty sure I got my second wind coming."

"That your first wind you were passing before?" She smiled, her way of letting him know it was a joke. Getting dressed, she buttoned her shirt, telling herself to shut her mouth; she needed the job, at least till she made enough to get her to the coast. "You fellas all make too much of it. Really. For us girls, it's more about . . . the cuddling, you know."

"You fellas, how many we talking about?"

"Make it sound like you got to pay me like you're some john, like I just let you climb in and out of the bus, huh?"

"Forget it." Too complicated. Eugene reached again and switched off the perfume lamp.

Pulling up her pants, scanning the floor for her shoes. Saying, "How about you drop me back at the highway? Can find my own way."

"How about you walk?"

"Could slap myself on the lip, then start yelling?"

"Okay, I'll give you a ride." Eugene went to the door. "First I'm going to the water closet. That alright with you, Miss Queen of England?"

Watching him go out the door, still in his johnnies. Turning down the breezeway between the room and the one next to it. Waiting till he was gone, this guy in need of romance tips, she went to his jacket slung on the chair, she fished out his smokes, store-bought Parliaments, the kind with the paper filters. Her hand bumped his wallet on the inside pocket. Taking it out, she went to the outside door and leaned against the jamb, opened it and counted, asking herself if she'd lost her mind, coming to a place like this with a man like that. A guy she just met, with money in his wallet.

"Abyssinia, Eugene." She tucked the wallet in a pocket. Firing a match on her thumbnail, she lit up a smoke, seeing the Ford coupe out in front of the next room. A greasy-haired guy coming from the room, glancing over at her along the walkway. Nodded to her. "Hey, doll. Name's Jesse."

"I know you?"

"Just told you, my name's Jesse."

"Nice for you."

"Figure you know bunch of fellas, huh?"

"Well, I don't figure you at all." She shrugged and puffed on her smoke, looking away, wondering how far back to the highway.

"How much?"

She looked back at him, not getting a good feeling from him.

Coming back through the breezeway, Eugene looked over at him, saying to her, "Sure don't take you long."

"You her old man?" Jesse said, grinning.

"Ain't your concern, chum," Eugene said.

"One, I ain't your chum." The man looked at Eugene's truck, the word rainmaker painted down the side. Turning into his room, he called inside, "Hey, Levon, come on out, see what we got here. A hotsie and a fella thinks he's a rain man."

"Not looking for trouble," Eugene said.

"Well, then best get in your rainmaking rig and shove off. Me and Levon'll give the lady a lift." Smiling. "Anyplace she wants."

Levon came to the door half-dressed, taller and broader than Jesse, but bearing a resemblance, his hair looking like it never met a comb. Both of them grinning and taking in Clara.

Eugene shrugged, saying he'd just get his stuff, went past her through the door, left her there smoking. Came back out with his pants on, the Red Dog lamp in one hand, jacket folded over his arm. Holding his palm flat, he looked at her, waiting.

Making a face, Clara slapped the wallet in his hand.

Eugene opened it, seeing the money was there.

Jesse laughed, saying, "She's a hotsie alright."

"The hell's that?" Levon said, looking at Eugene's lamp.

"Red Dog perfume lamp. You light it, and it sets the mood. Here, you want it? Maybe it'll work for you." Eugene set it down, then walked toward his truck, saying to her, "Have a nice day."

Levon stepped over to it, picking up the lamp, watching Eugene getting in his truck, then looking at Clara. "We ain't gonna need this, huh, baby?"

Jesse was rubbing his hands together, saying something about getting licked all over.

Clara shrugged, dropped the cigarette and ground her heel on it. Heard Eugene fire up his truck. Pulling into the street, he backed it up, blocking the driveway. Leaving the engine running, Eugene got out, said he nearly forgot something and went to the rear and pulled back the tarp. Climbing up the bumper, he got in and shoved the mortar to the back, working a crank on the side, he got it aimed at the Ford. Taking his ramrod, he whistled and tamped it in. Then he picked up a Cobb-buster, ready to drop it into the mortar. Looking over, waiting.

"What the hell's he doing?" Jesse said, getting a look at the finned missile.

"Believe he's about to give you a demonstration, gonna call down the thunder," Clara said. "Your car's about to rain all over the road in little bits."

Handing her the perfume lamp, Levon hurried to his room.

"Sulfur, black powder and a few of my secrets," Eugene called, hefting the Cobb-buster.

Levon coming from the room, holding a pistol.

"From this range," Eugene said, "I'd say this baby's gonna peel the paint off the whole car. Enough heat to melt your tires, probably light your tank, and let nature do the rest." Then asking Clara if she wanted that ride.

Looking at Jesse, Clara said, "You starting to feel licked yet, dummy?" Putting some hip into her walk, she went to the truck and got in the driver's side, putting it in gear, and rolling onto the two-lane.

Standing in back, Eugene steadied himself, still holding the Cobb-buster, calling out, "You boys want to follow, just come and try me."

. . . TWELVE

Willis Taggart got the car turned around on the dirt track with grass growing up the center. The spot Lips told him to wait. In sight of the Kansas River. Switching his lights off, then the engine. Sweat beaded his forehead, wet under his arms in spite of the night's chill. Waiting in this place where nobody could hear him yell, in rough shape from the beating.

The windows began to fog, Willis wiped his hand at the glass and cranked down his side window, keeping an eye on the berm, the way they'd be coming. The endless fields and scrub of Tecumseh around him. Just a couple of miles from the city, not a farm around, the landscape stark. The flowing river to his north shimmered, catching light off the moon.

Uneasy about a meet-up in this place, he drew on the Black Hawk and blew smoke out the window, the cigar tip glowing against the dashboard. Whitey Adler picked the spot, wanting to scare hell out of him. Ash dropped down, Willis brushing at it, wondering why he wore his suit. Wasn't the kind of business that needed his only suit.

The two hundred he purloined from the pay packets was all he could get, fifty less than Lips told him to bring,

Willis hoping Whitey Adler would see it as a reasonable amount and keep his dogs off. Spare him another beating. Touching the bundled cash inside his jacket, Willis resisted counting it again. The shortfall in payroll would bring him grief, but dealing with a simpering brother and a bunch of vexed performers was light duty compared to what the shadow men would do if he came without it or didn't show.

After this weekend's shows, he'd get Adler more. The trouble was, the vigorish he'd been paying kept the nut from going down. That and the money he laid down at Ida Jean's ringer house. What Willis needed was a good turnout at the Saturday matinee, that or they'd find his body in some drainage ditch. Whatever Taggart luck he once possessed had dried up like everything else on the plains. The stitch in his ribs made him wince, his fingers touching the bruises and sore ribs under the bundle of bills in his pocket.

He saw the glow of headlights over the berm, and panic rose in his chest. Dragging on the cigar as the lights topped the rise. The Packard rolled up, bathing his Nash's interior.

Show no fear, he told himself. Taking a last drag on the cigar, he opened the door and flicked it away, stepping out, squashing the stub under his shoe. Squinting, he couldn't see past the glare of the Packard's headlights.

Leaving his door hanging open, he jammed his hands in his pockets to hide their Judas shaking. Showing no fear and walking from the safety of the Nash. His hand moving for the bundle of cash, doing it slow.

The driver's window rolled down, and Lips smiled from under the sailor's cap. Pointing a thumb to the back. The rear window rolled down, and Whitey Adler stretched out his hand, his fingers snapping his impatience.

Handing it over, Willis said, "Get some more after the weekend. Have it all to you pretty soon."

Without looking at him, Adler grunted something and both front doors opened, and the shadow men stepped out. Willis backed a step, watching them come. Cut off from the Nash. His bladder wanting to let go like a basket press.

"Look, I know I'm light . . ." Willis held his hands out, then he turned and ran for the berm, the spike of pain not slowing him. Stumbling and falling and running for what he was worth, ripping his suit pants. Willis thinking if he could just make that rise, and maybe the river beyond it.

... THIRTEEN

A tower of crisscrossing planks reached up fifty feet, lilting a few degrees from the lashing of the dusters. A wire-cage transmitting antenna sat at the top. The foursquare house perched on some high ground west of Hoxie. Folks who owned it before had planted cotton here. The whole hillside once covered in the low green and white bolls, yielding three good harvests a year, bales laying out in the fields and waiting to be trucked away. Bottom of the hill, the cropper shacks stood three in a line, made of mud and empty now, from back before the time of the combines and tractors, when men and women worked this land.

Sand piled to the paint-peeled windows on the north side, giving the impression the house was sinking. On the front side, letters carved from a plank lined the porch's fascia, making this the home of K-L-X Radio. The X tilted on its last nail — good chance it would surrender to the next duster. As far as Wilbur Flanders figured, the fellow who stopped by was all wrong, one Braxton Early, with the graying muttonchops, calling himself the grand wizard, asking to have a word with the station's owner or radio personality, at the behest of a local group of reformers. Smiling the whole time he was talking, the kind of smile that said he wasn't going to take no for an answer, the grand wizard offered a replacement to the station's ailing signage, bigger and made of tin with a baked-paint finish, letters so big you could see them from the 24, a half mile off. Glad to do it for a little airtime, a weekly reach-out to stir up new members and apprise existing ones of activities. Claiming it would bring new listeners to K-L-X. The way he put it to Wilbur.

Wilbur guessed the kind of activities, but he didn't want his windows smashed out some night or a cross burning out front, so he told Braxton Early he'd have to think it over. Never cared for these hate-mongers and their night rides and cross burning, running off anybody who didn't match their complexion. Knowing most folks in broadcast range kept their radio sets tuned in, if not for the music and folky wit K-L-X was airing, then at least to catch the wild static warning that overtook the airwaves every time a duster bore down over the plains, giving townsfolk and farmers and haters alike the precious minutes needed to gather their kids and kin and livestock and get everybody indoors to wait it out.

His one-time parlor housed the transmitter panel along the east wall, a power supply running through the wall coming from a pair of generators into the former dining room. Stripped-out and cramped, the kitchen served as Wilbur's announcer's booth. An old card table with chairs on either side.

He busied himself with the microphones and gain controls, his thinning hair combed back, the Brylcreem keeping it looking good, the scent of the bubble lather he shaved with filling the room. He flipped a switch, the red On Air light flashed on above the door, and he stopped the platter from spinning, saying into the mic, "That was 'Diddie Wa Diddie' by old Blind Blake." Wilbur did a quick audio-level check, tapping the microphone, adjusting a dial to rid the on-air squelch. Clearing his throat to the side, he put on his announcer's voice. "And this here's Wilbur Flanders hoping all you folks tuned to K-L-X are doing fine and set for some down-home radio. A thousand watts coming right at-cha from Riley County. And now, folks, it being Friday, and only a day off Thanksgiving, it's time for our local corner . . ." Squelch rose, and he tapped the mic and dialed, then tapped again, smiling across the table. Feeling better having Handy and Sonny sitting out on his front porch.

•

The broadcast sounded through the wall. Rocking in the chair, Sonny liked the morning sun on his arms, the shade retreating across the porch. Handy Phibbs perched on the rail, both of them with a good view of the approach to the house. Downslope to the county road, nothing but an old rusting hull of a Baby Moose, one of those cycle cars nobody ever wanted, Handy thinking of it as the bastard child of a motorcycle and some ugly car. They heard Wilbur inside doing his local corner, pretty light on anything newsworthy, ending it by putting on some Fats Waller, "Stormy Weather."

"Easiest fiver you ever gonna see," Handy said, his scattergun leaning next to Sonny's Cooey against the shakes. A couple of feed sacks with eyeholes cut out draped on the railing.

"Assuming we got to shoot." Sonny rolled a smoke, offered the makings and struck a match.

"Guess we'll see. So, how about the bank?" Handy said it casual, not looking at him as he built a smoke.

Sonny fired another match, holding it out to him, waving it out. "First I thought you took a knock ..."

"Uh huh, and now?"

"Now I'm sure you did."

Handy puffed on the smoke, saying, "Other way to do it is we just snatch up Henningan."

"Like kidnapping?"

"Truss him, blindfold him, and stash him in your barn."

"My barn, huh?"

"Man's family's rich as Rocker-fella. We write a demand letter, just sit and wait to get paid."

"Just like that?"

"If we do it right, could come away with fifty big ones."

"Any slips and it's an easy five to ten."

"Just got to look at the thing positive."

"And what if they say no, his family? God, would *you* pay to get that man back?"

"Karpis and the Barkers got a hundred for that Hamm beer dude, snatched him right from his office. Got double for that banker they took. Read in the paper, nobody liked him either, but family's family."

"Karpis is doing life, am I right? And the Barkers, hell, they all got shot."

"Okay, forget them. We just make it easy. We hit the bank just the one time. Take all we need."

"With everybody in town knowing us. And you being ..."

"What, mixed breed?"

"Was gonna say the grease monkey at the Conoco. Everybody around buying their gas from you. Even Blake could track us down."

"That's why we wear these," Handy said, picking up one of the feedbags with the eyeholes cut out he'd slung over the rail.

75

"Shit, we got company." Sonny nodded downslope at the dust rising, a runabout coming their way on the county road, a truck behind it. They watched a Ford Highboy pull into the driveway, an old Hudson Eight behind it.

"Not a bad old truck, that Hudson, flathead engine with twin cylinder heads, eighty horse," Handy said, handing Sonny one of the sacks, slipping on his, lining up the eyeholes. "And holy shit if that ain't yours."

Sonny dropped the sack and jumped to his feet.

Doors opened and two men got out of the Highboy, the Mulligan brothers, Jesse and Levon, the two from the Griggs rooming house. Three others sat in the Hudson.

"Something we can help you fellas with?" Handy called, holding Sonny by the sleeve, keeping him from storming down.

"Here to see Wilbur Flanders," Jesse, the driver of the Highboy called up, hooking his thumbs in the top of his pants.

"You can leave word. We'll see it gets passed on."

"We're the Knighthawks. Action committee for the White Knights of the Great Plains. And we got to leave word. You ain't gonna like it."

"Sons of bitches." Sonny reached down and slipped on the hood.

Handy hung onto his sleeve, telling him to hold steady.

"And you want to tell me what's with the get-ups?" Jesse Mulligan called back, meaning the hoods, laughing over at his brother.

"Looks dumb, huh?" Handy said.

"On account of the way you're doing it," Levon said. "Now, you clowns want to get Flanders. Tell him the White Knights are set to broadcast the tenets of a true religion, warn folks about the impure and the Christ-killers and Bolsheviks."

"Yeah sure, we'll pass that along," Handy said.

"We go back and all we left's a message," Jesse said, "you're not gonna like what happens next." Flapping back his jacket, showing the butt of a revolver in a shoulder rig.

Levon pulled back his own jacket.

"Well, I tried to reason ..." Handy shrugged, still keeping one hand on Sonny. He reached for the Cooey, handing it to him and let go of the arm. Lifting his own shotgun, he racked the pump, saying, "Here we go."

Popping the breach as he cleared the steps, Sonny reached in a pocket and stuck a shell in his gun, swinging it shut, smelling powder from his morning of hunting. Coming off the steps and moving straight at Jesse, Sonny put storm in his step, not giving the man time to think. "Come and look me in the eyehole, you son of a bitch ... coming to our town and threatening folks."

Turning to see if the others got out of the Hudson, backing him, saying, "Come on, Stonewall, let's show 'em something." Jesse started drawing his pistol, turning back into Sonny's gun butt, getting knocked on his ass.

The Hudson was his own. The worst thoughts whirled around Sonny's head, the truck Clara took off in. These people did something to her. Moving from the Highboy to his truck, he called to the driver, "What the hell you do with my Clara?"

Seeing Jesse get knocked down, the one they called Stonewall pushed open the Hudson's door and got on the running board, pulling the hood over his head — what they did when they spread their terror — then reaching for his pistol, saying, "Clara, that like your cow, buddy?"

Levon came around the front of the Ford, drawing his pistol, looking at Sonny's back.

Handy shot the headlight off the Highboy, getting

everybody's attention, telling the Mulligans, "Your next move better be a righteous one."

Levon tossed down his pistol and threw up his hands.

Holding his head, Jesse got to his feet, letting go of his own pistol.

Didn't bother aiming, Sonny swung the barrel and fired, the windshield of the truck bursting, buckshot pocking holes in the hood, didn't matter it was his own truck.

Flinging open the door, the passenger dove out, the third man jumping from the back, both of them running. Stonewall used the driver's door like a shield, thinking he might get off a shot.

Handy kept his barrels on the two by the Highboy. Telling them to kick their pistols away, then pull off their hoods. Getting a look at Jesse and Levon. "Now, get going, and if you stupid sons come back, you know what you're gonna get."

Getting in the Highboy with the radiator leaking, Jesse got it started and swung a wide arc in the yard, bottoming on the springs, the two of them driving off.

Sonny popped in another shell, saying to Stonewall behind the door, "Gonna ask one more time about my Clara."

Crouching behind the door, Stonewall gripped the pistol, deciding how to play it when Sonny stepped up and kicked the door into him, the man tumbling backward and the pistol falling. Sonny swept it under the truck. Stonewall backpedaled and tried to rise. Sonny putting his foot on the man's chest, pressing him down, watching the Ford Highboy head off, the two others running after it.

"Man's got to be crazy, to shoot his own truck," Handy told Stonewall, walking over, tucking the two pistols in his belt.

"Gonna get even crazier if I got to ask again, how you got my truck?" Sonny said, shoving the barrel against

Stonewall's Adam's apple, his finger on the trigger. Telling him to yank off his hood.

"Don't know shit, mister." Stonewall did like he was told, taking off the hood, saying, "The kleagle just told me to drive. Said they found it abandoned out on the 24."

"And the woman in it?"

"Don't know nothing about that. Honest, I don't."

"Who the fuck's this kleagle?" Sonny said.

"Ain't a name, it's what he is, the kleagle, like a recruiter for the White Knights. Was the grand wizard told him he wants his message on the air. All I know."

"You got a name?"

"Terry — Terrence Bradley, but I go by Stonewall." He looked scared. Not the way the kleagle said this would go, these two with the feedbags on their heads, not intimidated by the holy terror of the White Knights.

"You seen this one before?" Sonny asked Handy.

Handy shook his head. "Only Stonewall I know's one who kicked hell out of those fuckers up on the Potomac. Nothing like you."

"Get up," Sonny told him, taking the barrel from the man's neck. "Where you from, Stonewall?"

"Boise."

Nodding like that didn't surprise him, Sonny cradled the gun in his left arm and shoved with the right, sending Stonewall backward. "I were you, that's where I'd be heading." Pulling off the feed-sack hood, Sonny looked at him and said, "I see your hating ass around Hoxie again, they gonna know where to send the body, and what name to put on your marker. You get me, Stonewall?"

"Yes, sir."

Sonny pointed to the road, Stonewall looking, seeing the dust from the retreating Ford.

"Got about five miles to town," Sonny said, reaching under the truck for the pistol, noting the man's shoes as he bent, saying, "And you're gonna do it barefoot."

Looking at him, knowing not to argue, Stonewall used one foot to shove the shoe off his other foot, did the same on the other side. Reaching to pick them up.

"Uh uhn," Sonny said.

Leaving the shoes, Stonewall started walking.

Waiting till the man was down by the road, Sonny picked one up. He held it against his worn-out shoe, passed the shotgun to Handy and put on his new shoes.

Handy pulled off his own sack, saying it sure got hot under there, the two of them turning back to the house.

Wilbur Flanders stood at the door, an old Colt six-shooter in his hand. "Figure they'll be back?"

Sonny looked at Stonewall hobbling along the gravel road. "Guess we're gonna see."

"Them in the Ford show up at my Conoco and want me replacing the radiator, gonna charge 'em double," Handy said. "Give the money to the Catholics."

The three of them grinning.

Handy looked at Sonny's feet, saying, "How they fit?"

"Not too bad."

•

They sat on Wilbur Flanders's porch the next day, smoking cigarettes and listening to the man inside on the air. Sonny quiet most of the day, with his mind on where Clara had gone. Late in the afternoon, a pickup rolled past, some hay bundles in back, two guys inside not looking toward the house.

"So, how about it?" Handy said, stretching his arms, giving a wide yawn.

"How about what?"

"The Loan and Trust?"

"Not done thinking." Sonny rolled a smoke, patting pockets for a match, finally saying, "How much you reckon we'd get?"

"A couple grand on a good day, easy."

"Bad day and we gonna make the FBI list."

"Just need a good plan, go in like blazes. Put the feed sacks on our heads, make it look like the White Knights done it. Drumming up money for their cause."

"How you mean?"

"We drive up in their stolen truck." Handy pointed at the shot-up Hudson, still on the yard.

"My truck."

"One you're gonna report stolen to the marshal. I patch her up, and we hide her till we're ready."

Hearing Wilbur inside on the air, Sonny looked at the truck, the radiator and grill shot out of it, the windshield gone. Wasn't sure if he was just desperate or losing his mind, worried about Clara, but damn, he sure was thinking about that bank.

FOURTEEN

On Thursday, hitching Pearl to the wagon, Sonny rode to where the forestry men dropped the bags, green ash saplings lined along the telephone pole by the county road. Loading up the wagon, he set them along the trench he'd dug on the east quarter, planned to plant them next to the rows of cottonwood and hackberry he'd put in. The next row would be jackpine, then one of red cedar. The Department of Agriculture sending a man out to the courthouse some months back, telling the gathered farmers how to get it done, making windbreaks along their property lines and between fields to hold back prevailing winds, keep it from blowing away the earth, paying them to do it.

Turning Pearl out in the corral, he loaded the handcart, the one from his days working for the Civilian Conservation Corps. Sonny having double-lied to get into their program, which demanded the men be eighteen and single. He hadn't been either when he signed up, staying at the spike camps, building the fire lookouts, cutting in the truck trails and doing the insect control work that time the grasshoppers came like a plague of Egypt. Left Clara alone to mind the farm while he made wages any way he could.

Laying in the pick, hoe and shovel, filling several jugs of water, he tugged the handcart across the clods and dry ground. He set to work, planting the saplings, filling earth in the trench, tamping them down, pouring water around the roots. Wishing he had one of those tree-planting machines he'd heard about at the courthouse. Uncorking his canteen, he took a swallow, splashing water on his neck. Eating the last tin of beans cold, he watched a prairie dog popping from its hole fifty feet off. Sizing Sonny up, it scurried to the next hole, its network of escape. Sonny saying it was lucky he didn't bring the Cooey.

When the sun started its mid-afternoon slide, Sonny had a third of the saplings in, the rows of trees supposed to grow and hold the soil for future crops. Sitting against the handcart's wheel, he kicked off his new shoes, not in a hurry to go back to the house, the place empty without Clara. Thinking about his forebears coming to this land behind their team of mules held his resolve. Hardworking through the rough times they faced, that's the way he saw them. And he was just like that. Drinking more water, he sang the lines he knew to a Woody Guthrie song about the wheat growin' and the oil flowin' and the farmer owin'.

Reaching the tobacco pouch and papers, he rolled a smoke. Patting his pockets for a match when he heard the clang of the porch triangle. His first thought was Clara had come back. Clanging it like she used to when she called him for supper.

Up on his feet, he felt relief, saying, "Parlor talk's sure to be something." Knowing she'd have a good story to tell. Leaving the cart, he shoved on the shoes and walked downslope and around the house, the triangle clanging again. Sonny thinking what he'd say to her. Anger mixing with the relief. Thinking they'd hash it out, she'd make her

83

point, tell him why she did it, the two of them ending up in bed, middle of the day. Clara saying something like if she knew he'd go at her like that, she'd run off more often. Sonny walked around the side of the house.

And his heart sank.

Daniel Henningan stood on the porch, the fat man in his suit and tie, shiny black shoes and sweat stains under his arms, looking past the screen door. A late-model Flint parked down by the mailbox.

"Well now, banker Henningan."

Startled, the fat man turned, mopping a hankie along his brow. Forcing a smile like winter, collecting himself. "Behind three payments, Sonny Myers. Came to forewarn you. You heard the one about three strikes and you're out?"

"Yeah, times've been tough, and I been planting my trees, and soon's I get paid, you get paid."

"You know it's grounds for forfeiture."

Sonny looked at him, thinking when they robbed this fat bastard, he'd get paid in full. He regretted the day he went to hear the government man named Morgan out front of the courthouse, the man doing a convincing crusade, telling the gathered farmers, all determined to stick it out, about the Emergency Farm Mortgage Act. Explaining it would free up farmer cash by backing it with farmer assets, how the bank would hold their mortgages until better times came around, leaving the farming man in a better stead. Sonny had been fool enough to drive back home with the news, and Clara was quick to see the sense in it. Just as quick to grab her earmarked Sears-and-Roebuck and show Sonny the three-burner kerosene stove, flipping the page to the drawing of the Franklin rotary sewing machine, stabbing her finger at it, her pale eyes excited and wide. Pointing out the Daisy churn, she'd said, "Oh Sonny, never to wear myself down on that vertical plunger. Just imagine it." Smiling at the thought of never collecting another cow pat for the old potbelly stove. Always abhorred cooking meals on it.

The iron of conviction Orin had taught him was no match for those pale eyes and the hex of nature. Sonny wanting her happy. Pressing his hands to her heart, she'd said, "Oh, Sonny, it'd sure make things good around here."

"You understand plain English, sir?" Henningan said, slapping a hand at the papers in his other hand, shaking them like a threat. "Now I need you to sign —"

"Had this fellow come out . . ." Sonny put a foot past the lower step, leaning on the rail. "Name of White, think it was. Parked right where you're parking now. Not wearing a suit, just honest denim, the man's pickup showing the right amount of rust."

"You got a point?"

"Explained about the Frazier-Lemke Farm Bankruptcy Act, signed by FDR himself. This man White putting it plain enough, how it restricts sons of bitches like you from de-possessing honest folks of their property."

"No need for name calling." Henningan frowned at his papers, like they were betraying him. This farmer smarter than he looked.

"Explained how you bankers can't go bloodsucking your interest and putting folks off their land, not no more. Meaning Clara keeps her stove, sewing machine and churn, and we go on owing you. And not a damned thing you can do but wait till we pay up."

"And when, pray tell, might that be?"

"Well, there'll be some from planting my trees. Get the rest soon as it rains." Sonny looked the man in the eye. Depression, drought, dusters and debt been like the farming man's four horsemen. "Bad enough without you people trying to dispossess a man of what's his."

"Got your signature right here." Henningan slapped at the sheaf of pages. Pointing a finger at the ink. "Promising to pay."

"Already holding a quarter parcel, securing the loan." Sonny watched him run the kerchief around his dome, mopping at the sweat again.

"You people get yourself owing, then not paying and acting like you've got no obligations, wiggling out of it on account of some hogwash from Washington. Well, I petitioned the judge, and he agrees I can't take your land, but I can repossess the assets you bought with the money. Long as I prove the purchase." Henningan flipped the pages, showing statements from the merchants. "See right here . . ." Jabbing at the papers. "Default's immediate grounds for repossessing said goods." Looking around the farmstead, Henningan frowned. "Guessing this patch wouldn't fetch enough to cover the cost of bulldozing it to the ground anyhow. But your burner, churn and sewing machine, well, that's another story." Looking at Sonny like he just ate something sweet.

Walking up the steps past him, Sonny went through the screen door and came back out holding the Cooey, smelling of gun oil from being cleaned last night.

"You threatening me?"

"Just showing you something else that's mine." Breaking it open, Sonny dropped in a shell, flipping it closed. "Lock, stock and barrel."

The look in the man's eyes made Henningan uneasy. Turning toward his Flint, he went down the steps, the spongy one at the bottom giving out under his weight, Henningan pitched into the yard, scraping his palms and knees, splitting the trousers up the middle. The fear of God setting the man in full waddle.

Funniest thing he'd seen in a long while, Sonny laughed. The fat man's eyes bugging and his arms whirling as he hurried to his car.

"Going to have the marshal come and run you off, Sonny Myers." Back at his Flint, Henningan mopped with the kerchief, calling across the hood of his car, "Loans work the hardest, and make no mistake, day or night, they never sleep. And when deadbeats like you default —"

Sonny lifted the barrel, set it against his hip and pulled the trigger, watching Henningan jump in and drive out of there, raising the dust along the county road.

·

Town Marshal Blake drove out before suppertime, Hollis Capp from the Deal 'n Wheel driving a truck behind him, another man with him in the cab. Getting out of his car, the marshal adjusted his cap and walked up the drive, followed by the others.

Sonny left the Cooey inside and stepped past the screen, saying, "Hey there, Marshal." Nodded to Capp, sizing him and the other man up.

"Sonny." Adjusting the cap some more, looking around the place, Billy Joe Blake said, "Heard you took a potshot at Henningan."

"That what he said?"

Capp and the other man grinned.

"Claims you shoved him down the stairs. Man's ankle's twisted up, tore up his good suit."

Sonny pointed at the broken step, saying, "Man ought to lose a few pounds, maybe he wouldn't go busting folks' property. Fact, I got a mind to go after damages."

Blake looked at the step, nodding, giving a glance about

87

the place. "Got a mind to ask to see your gun, Sonny, but I guess it's how you put food on the table. Word to the wise, stick to jackrabbits instead of jackasses." He pulled a folded paper from his pocket. "Got an order signed by the judge, afraid we got to repossess your stove, churn and sewing machine."

Nothing he could do but stand there and watch. Hollis Capp and the other man stepping past him, going in his house. Watching while they carried the stuff, grunting, to their truck. Blake told Sonny he was sorry, but there was nothing he could do. He gave the yard another scan, then told Sonny to give his best to Clara. Sonny watching them drive off, getting strong feelings about robbing the Sheridan Loan and Trust, but guessing he'd now be high on Billy Joe Blake's suspect list.

FIFTEEN

The song was about angels, coming through the open doors of Phibbs Conoco. Martha Tilton's voice smooth as silk piping from the crystal set atop the mechanic's bench heaped with wrenches. Tires hung from wall spikes, a porcelain Brunswick sign above them. License plates from Oklahoma, Texas and the show-me state, some rusted and bent, all nailed to the bulkhead above a dismantled carburetor bathing in a pan of petrol on a workbench.

Sitting on the factory stool, Sonny flipped through the grimed copy of *Movie Mirror*, then set it by the radio. Looking to the back, a partition separating Handy Phibbs's quarters: an iron-framed cot, a blackened cooker with a single burner on a crate, clothes heaped on the only chair, Sonny could smell they needed laundering from here. Guessing a couple weeks without Clara, and he'd pick up his own layabout ways.

Next on the air was *Radio Chapel*, part of K-L-X's morning lineup. "Enough inspiration to get you through your day." Announcer Wilbur Flanders put on his Preachin' Jimmy Pratt voice, glory-shouting and talking in tongue, putting it on like he was treading the boards, leading listeners down the Jesus Road.

Handy had promised to keep the radio dialed in, told Wilbur to call a warning over the air if the Knighthawks showed again. Handy would drive out in five minutes flat, be shooting in six.

"Loves when he does Jimmy Pratt," Handy said from under the car. The Zephyr was a '36 and belonged to Mayor Flint, hoisted up in the middle of the garage, Handy's untied boots sticking out from underneath. The ball of one foot showing through a hole in the leather sole an eagle coin could fit through. Setting the oil pan in place, checking the undercarriage. Blood trickling from his skinned knuckles, mixing with the grease and oil. Handy sucked at the blood, hardly giving it any notice. Not a mechanic around who didn't slip with a wrench now and then.

"Yeah, he's something," Sonny said.

"And no sign of any shit since we run them sons off. Likely back in Boise bothering the decent folk there." Draining the old oil, laying on the creeper, half of him sticking out from under the car, Handy scratched down between the buttons, saying the same itch had been dogging him for better than a week. "No visual malady when I haul my britches down, just this itch ..."

"I look like Doc Bletsoe?" Sonny said, not wanting to hear it.

"Wasn't gonna bend and ask you to look in." Letting the pan drip, Handy laughed and took the stub of pencil and calendar page from his pocket, angled so he could write in the tight space, conjuring a list of ailments for the Zephyr, something to show the mayor: crankcase doesn't vent right, suffers poor oil flow, could lead to overheating due to water passages that old Henry Ford should have made bigger. Scratching with the pencil, Handy rehearsed how he'd sell the mayor on the list of repairs.

Sonny watched him roll the creeper out, Handy jotting a couple more ideas: a ring job and intake valves.

"Gonna give the mayor a hosing, huh?"

"Man's got sludge building up on account he motors like a matron, never sends the needle past fifty. A real crime, this baby's dozen virgin cylinders not being used and just begging to rip loose. Hundred and ten horses, can cook right up to ninety. And with transverse springs, let a man rip out on these Kansas roads, blow past any DeSoto or Chevrolet." Handy smoothing a hand along the rocker panel like it was a race horse. "Only thing Ford could've done better'd be on the dead axle in front and the torque tube in back, but I forgive him just for the sheer beauty." Tapping his raw knuckles on the sheet metal.

"Ask me, sounds like you're in love."

"Yeah, that low-raked windshield . . ." Handy smiled. "Got a prow like a speedboat and a grill of chrome. And these sheet-metal curves, yeah, guess I'm in love alright." Handy went about tallying the numbers, thinking the whole shebang would make his rent for the next couple of months. Having some second thoughts, saying, "Maybe leave the rings and intake valves for next bunch of ailments."

"Getting me worried about driving that Moon you gave me," Sonny said.

"There some exchange of cash, a money-down situation I'm forgetting? Handed you the keys, treat you like a brother. Nothing wrong with the Moon. Just some more sweet tin eye-candy."

"So there's nothing wrong with the Zephyr?"

"Not so much, but Flint don't know it. Way I look at it, we vote the man in and he screws us every chance he gets. Just giving him back some."

"Well, on behalf of Sheridan County, I thank you."

Sonny grinned, saying, "And speaking of crime, been thinking it over."

"You know it was dumb, right?" Handy sobering, saying, "You and me talking about robbing the son of a bitch, then you go shoot at him."

"The man fanned my fire."

"Maybe so, but how you gonna keep Blake from looking at you for it? Just put yourself high on the list of whodunits." Handy paddle-stepped the creeper back under the Zephyr.

"Guess it was dumb, but that banking bastard's got a way of bringing it out in me."

"Been thinking how to do it. Thinking I go in the back, you in the front. Have Willis in your old truck out front."

"He get an even split?"

"Without him in the getaway car, won't be splitting anything but the sentence." Finger-tightening the bolts on the pan, Handy gave a quarter turn with the wrench. Sliding back out, he got up, set the paper by the radio, the pencil on top. Wiping his hands on his back-pocket rag, he propped up the hood and got a gallon can of Opaline, unscrewed the filler, set the funnel and poured. Dumping the sludgy engine oil down the commode hole, he chased it with some Red Devil lye. Letting Sonny think about it.

Preacher Jimmy Pratt getting all roused with the Spirit, introducing his listeners to his back-up chorus just come into the studio, calling them his Tabernacs, the group of neighbor ladies clapping their hands and chanting up some uh huhs and amens. Preacher Jimmy calling on the good listeners to plant their own hands on their sets, raise up their voices and be as one, right across the airwaves. The Tabernacs uh huh-ing and amen-ing.

"That Wilbur's sure full of it, I mean the Spirit. Was

thinking of getting him in on it, but the man's too far down that Jesus Road."

Sonny nodded.

The ringing phone got Handy turning the volume down, answering, "Yuh, Phibbs?"

"Handy, it's Willis."

"Speak of the devil." Wiping his cheek with the rag, Handy left a streak of oil. Looking past the DeSoto out front, the Taggart brothers' Studebaker truck waiting on a new fuel line and needing its carb cleaned out. Saying, "Yeah, Willis, still waiting on that part —"

"Never mind that. Got a situation here, more of a swamp of shit. Thought maybe you and Sonny could help me out . . . same way you did Wilbur."

"Shoot."

"Might come to that. But look, not on the phone . . . how about I come see you boys, maybe Saturday, lay things out?"

"Alright."

"You know Dingle's on Route 6, out by Hays?"

"We'll find it."

"How about I buy you boys lunch?" Willis said.

"Next time lead with that." Handy spoke around the phone and relayed it to Sonny.

"Best we don't get seen together." Sonny said they should meet out at his farm.

Handy got off the phone and peeled April from last year's seed company calendar, using it to wipe the grease from his hands. Saying, "Looks like you and me got a new line —"

The rap at the door had him turning. Town Marshal Billy Joe Blake poked his head in, smiling, liked that he caught the two of them off guard, stepping all the way in and glancing around, saying to Sonny, "Keep bumping into you, huh?"

93

"Just stopped by for a tank-up. No crime in that, huh, Marshal?"

"None I know of. You driving the Moon, huh? Surprised, seeing you're busted." Blake looked from Sonny to Handy, trying to read between the lines.

"Owe up to here, same as everybody," Sonny said, looking at Handy. "But between friends, we come to terms."

Handy nodded, asking the marshal if he needed a top-up.

"Just a question I been meaning to ask," Billy Joe Blake said. "You in on Sunday? Thought I saw lights?" Stepping to the Zephyr, Blake looked around and said, "This the mayor's, huh?"

"Yeah, the mayor's. Sunday, hmm . . ." Handy twisted his mouth and rolled his eyes at the tin signs, like he was thinking. "Guess I was maybe in a while, not working though, just counting up oil cans, supplies, you know. No ordinance against it, is there?"

"Bylaw about working Sundays, but taking inventory, guess that's okay." Blake turned to Sonny. "Got a call couple days back. This nice couple on the way to midweek call-to-service, sure they heard shots over by Wilbur's radio."

"That so?" Sonny said. "Hadn't heard, but if you're asking, I was right where you found me yesterday, planting my trees."

"Could be Wilbur's got trouble with pocket gophers again," Handy said.

"Yeah, could be shooting at them," Billy Joe said. "Damn things love that high ground." He nodded to the radio. "That Preacher Jimmy you got on?"

"Getting the folks stirred, all that amen-ing he does, the whole place singing and shaking."

"Fired full of the Spirit, that's for sure," Blake said.

"Like having him on, 'specially on Sundays when I can't make church."

"On account of taking inventory." Blake smiled and adjusted the brim of his cap like it made a difference, then said he'd go ask Wilbur Flanders about it. Looked at each of them and said he'd be seeing them around. The eye contact supposed to mean something. Then he stepped out the doors, walking to his patrol car, looking up and down the main drag. Doing it like he owned the town.

"The hell was that?" Sonny said, watching him drive away, putting his foot on the creeper and scooting it across the garage, stopping against the Wolf's Head Oil sign.

"Man's letting us know he's got an eye on things, place where nobody works on Sundays," Handy said. "Wouldn't worry about it, just likes to come and piss on my post, marking his town."

"Thought it's 'cause you're a halfbreed."

"Maybe that too." Handy grinned, looked up at the Mobil clock, then he became serious. "One thing's sure, three guys knock over the Trust and Loan, that man's gonna come looking hard."

"Just got to be someplace else when it happens."

. . . SIXTEEN

Hearing the triangle, Sonny figured Daniel Henningan was back. Setting the rootball in the trench, Sonny scooped in the dry earth, thumping his fist to tamp it down. Had to be a hundred degrees. Wiping the sweat from his neck, he drank from his canteen. Taking his time, he left the cart and walked down the slope, telling himself to play it easy, no matter how much he wanted to kick that fat man in his plus-sized pants. Coming around the side of the house, getting some words ready, he stopped up short.

Clara stood on the porch, a truck turning at the mailbox and driving off. Eugene Cobb, Rainmaker, painted down the side, Sonny remembering seeing the notice tacked to the bridge when he walked to town.

She looked at him. "Cat got your tongue?"

"So many things to say. Just thinking which to let go first." He went to the steps and put a hand on the rail, looking up at her.

"I don't know, try, 'It's good to see you, baby,' or, 'Where's my damn truck,' or how about, 'You okay, Clara? Thank God, you're alright.'" Clara imitating the way he'd say it.

"Can see you're fine. As far as the truck, it's fine too, at least it was till I shot it." Lifting his foot over the busted step, he went up, grabbed the handle, stopping himself from tearing the screen off its hinges.

"You shot your truck?"

"Long story. Tell you about it later." He walked inside.

"Well, sounds like you know more 'n me."

Sonny heard the rain man's truck disappear down the road, answered, "Except guessing ain't knowing."

She followed him in. "We got anything to eat?" Looking around and saying, "What the hell . . . where's my stove?"

•

The walls of the house held a kind of amity, felt like a ceasefire. The two of them sitting across from each other, a supper of cold leftover jackrabbit with beans. Clara trying to set aside her feeling about her missing three-burner Westinghouse, the Daisy churn and Franklin rotary sewing machine, putting out a loaf of sourdough she picked up at Grainger's. She told about the rainmaker, Eugene Cobb rescuing her up after the Hudson died of thirst. Didn't mention the part about the motel room, but told how she stirred up the crowd in Tucumcari, dressed like a ringmaster in heels, while Eugene Cobb fired his mortar rounds at the sky.

"Why'd a man do that?"

"To make it rain, silly. Tell you, the man's got a knack for doing it too. Read about it in the paper, how he did it in Denver."

"How about Tucumcari. He do it there?"

"It's a nine on ten kind of thing. But he's sure gonna do it here in Hoxie, in case you want to see for yourself."

"With you helping him?"

97

"That's right. Wearing the special outfit. Oh, and it's a paying job too."

"Got to be right here, huh, where everybody knows you?"

"Hardly anybody left that knows me. But how about it, you come and see?"

"Tell you what, if it rains, I'll see it from right here." Sonny tore a chunk of bread and offered it to her.

Taking it, she mopped up the beans, saying, "Could just come and support me."

Looking at her, he started flicking the salt shaker between his fingers. Unscrewing the cap, he poured a little salt in his palm, making a fist around it and letting it trickle out like sands in an hourglass, back into the shaker. Knowing it bothered her when he did it.

Getting up, Clara sighed and took their plates, sinking them in the bucket of hot water, pulling them out dripping, one at a time, wiping them with a cloth bubbling in lard soap, then rinsing them in the other bucket, one with clean water, letting them drip off.

"You done with running off west?"

"For now, I guess." Telling him how she might go on and work with Eugene Cobb while he was setting up in town, maybe the one after that. "See how it goes."

"How you getting to work?"

"Can drive me in your shiny car. One you haven't explained yet. That, or guess Eugene can swing by and pick me up."

"Eugene now, huh?"

"Got a problem with his name?"

"Sounds namby-pamby."

"Want to know how Sonny sounds?"

"Come on, a man goes around and calls himself a rain-maker —"

"That's right, 'cause he makes it rain. Something we sorely could use. Top of that, the job pays thirty cents an hour, something else we can sorely use. What more you got to know?"

"How come it ain't raining in Tucumcari?"

"My job's talking up the folks, explaining how the Cobb-busters work, frees Eugene to figure his trajectory and so on. A question like that, you got to ask him."

"Man shoots off his cannon, tells you it's gonna rain. And you go believing it."

"And you been saying the same thing, better 'n nine years, how the rain's coming, expecting me to believe that. And it's a mortar, not a cannon."

"Think the sky gives a damn what you call it?" Sonny scraped his chair back and stood. "Fine, you want to work for a rain man, go right ahead."

"You think I was asking?"

"Got some ideas myself."

"How to wait for rain?"

"About making money."

"Planting trees and digging holes, wearing yourself skinny."

"You're gonna see." Not ready to tell her about guarding Wilbur Flanders's porch. Or about robbing the Sheridan Trust and Loan. By way of truce, he said, "You want, I can brew up some chicory?"

"Well, guess that'd be nice." She watched him put more wood in the potbelly and go about fixing it, pouring water from the pail to the pot. Something she usually took care of. "Since I'm back and working, making some money, thought it'd be nice to have Momma come for a visit, just a short one." Waiting for a comeback, she added, "You know she ain't been well."

He let go a long breath, saying, "Guess that'd be fine," but thinking that old woman had a way of filling a house. Taking the bucket he kept by the door, he went out to the well. What any man knew about women couldn't fill a hat. Orin's words. The man smiling when he said it. Likely knew more about the gender than most, raised by his widowed mother and an aunt, alongside his older sisters. Married to Sonny's ma for sixteen years.

When the water boiled, Sonny went about fixing the chicory, divvied it between their tins, poured the water over top and let it steep. She set the dishes out on the table to dry, reaching to the bottom of the bucket, getting the cutlery. Taking the offered tin, she said, "How about we sit on the porch? Nice breeze tonight."

Blowing across the top of his tin, he said, "Nothing like good coffee."

"You're right, it's nothin' like that." She smiled at him.

The two of them laughing. He followed her out, holding the screen, swiping sand from the rocker, making a spot for her, perching himself on the rail. Clara setting the lantern down, sitting and gently rocking back and forth.

Sonny asking, "What's she got, your momma?"

"Aching in her joints, mostly. Had it for years, but keeps it to herself."

"Uh huh." Sonny looked up at the night, sipping.

"Get all your trees in?"

"Get another row in tomorrow. Not sure when the truck's coming back, bringing more." Explaining how he'd plant the windbreak on the west side, planting rows five deep, same as the east side.

"Well, you go out in the morning, I'll get the place swept and ready for Momma coming. Get that fine layer of sand that always settles. Set the tub in the kitchen, boil enough water, fill it good and hot so Momma can get a hot soak when she comes, give her some comfort."

"You already asked her?"

"Called when Eugene drove me to town." Not allowing a beat, she went on, "Whole time she's here, guess I'll hear how good things are going for Lizzie and Irenie." She looked up at the night sky, getting those faraway eyes. "Funny, how things run through your mind."

"Like what things?"

"Like the times we went for pie in Penokee, you and me, after the bingo." Her face softened. In the lantern light she looked like she did back then, and it disarmed him. "And the dime movies and soda fountain over in Waldo after the church suppers, you used to take me, remember?"

"Sure I do. You going for the egg cream, me the rocky road. Ordered the same thing every time."

"And that *Broadway Melody*, projected up on the bricks, side of the livery, must've been two stories high."

"Yeah, and us with the best seats in the house." Sonny waved a hand. "And how about that picnic up by Shanty's Mill?"

"Packed up my crispy chicken, them buttermilk biscuits you like. A nice spread on that quilt Katey made us, sitting under that cottonwood."

"Day before we got hitched. Yeah, that was something."

"Sun just so, not too hot, gentle back then and nice on the skin."

"The two of us skinny-dipping, splashing below the mill, middle of the day with nobody around."

"Taught me pinochle that day."

"Taught you more 'n that."

The two of them smiling and sipping chicory.

"Why, Mr. Myers, ain't you a cheek, talking like that."

Something in those million-mile eyes, the lantern flickering, making them shine. Looking at her, he waved a hand at a fat moth, flying too close, hissed and dropped in the cylinder.

"Picked me wildflowers," she said.

"And you stuck them in the lemonade jar."

"And tucked some in my hair."

"Then we waded across, you on my back and the water like ice."

"Flowers spilling from my hair. Nearly dropped me. Had me holding on for dear life."

"Stones were mossy."

"The perfect day."

"Yuh."

"And them tin cans tied on the back. Remember? That jalopy clattering all the way to the courthouse next day, scaring every dog and kid for miles."

Sonny laughed. "Amos wasn't supposed to tie 'em on till after, but who knew, huh?"

Rising from the rocker, she stretched a hand to him, saying, "How about we take a walk?"

"Where we gonna walk?"

"Just come on." Turning out the lantern, she took his hand and tugged him up.

Her hand felt warm. The stirring surprised him, hadn't felt that in a long time. A thought stabbed in: Sonny wondering about her and the rainmaker.

Stepping over the busted stair, she led him across the moonlit yard and around the side of the barn, past the coop and the lean-to. Around the back, she got down on the piled sand, still warm from the sun and soft as a beach. Propped on her elbows, she glanced up at him, guessing he was still bothered about her running off, coming back and stepping out of Eugene Cobb's truck, but betting he was willing to set it aside. Patting the spot beside her, saying, "What's the matter, you forget how?"

... SEVENTEEN

Pumping water the next morning, Sonny went about filling Pearl's trough. Then, setting a pan by the barn door, he got the grain sack for the yard birds. A turkey vulture flying its lazy circles high above like it had all day, its face like a red rubber mask, pinfeathers stretched out like fingers. Sonny calling it a buzzard. Seen his share of grubber birds since the livestock started dying off. Awful things looping in the air, sitting on a fence rail, waiting on something to die, all the patience in the world. Tempted to pull his Cooey off the mantle and give the damned thing a sixteen-gauge blast of how you doing. Picturing Clara jumping from bed. Grinning at the thought.

Thinking again that it sure would be something to get shed of banker Henningan and the Sheridan Loan and Trust. Pay him back with money from his own vault. Get Clara a new stove, churn and sewing machine. Clara calling Henningan a lard bucket since that day they first signed the papers. Sonny wondering what she'd make of robbing the bank, thinking he might tell her.

His mind rolled again to that picnic at Shanty's Mill, twenty miles north of here and all those years ago. Could feel that icy rush of water as he stepped over the mossy rocks. Cuffing his pant legs while she splashed water at him. Catching her from slipping in, he put her up on his back. Felt like she weighed nothing. Taking off their clothes on the opposite bank, stealing glances at each other, skinny-dipping in the chill of the stream's pool, her shrieking from its bite. Watching her running naked through that glade of meadow flowers, the low hills looking purple just past it. Nestled on that cutbank in shade of the cottonwood, its roots cupping the two of them like a hammock. Clara dropping flower petals one at a time into the flow, seeing them float out of sight, nobody knowing where they'd end up. Sonny thinking she was the most beautiful thing he'd ever seen. All of those old feelings rushing back at him after last night. As strong now as it had been that first time. Maybe better.

His mouth was stuck on a smile, and he packed up the handcart, hearing an engine chug along the county road. He got a picture it was Cobb, the rainmaker coming to pick her up. Sonny losing the smile. The Model A came into view, the same one from out front of Wilbur's. The one Handy shot at. Guessing it was the same two men inside, without the masks this time. They slowed, looking his way.

Sonny walked down the drive toward them. The one on the passenger side opened his door and got up on the running board, looking across the roof at him.

"Mask didn't do you much good," Jesse Mulligan said, reaching for his pistol.

Not caring that they knew it was him at the K-L-X, Sonny walked straight to the car.

Dale Telfer cranked down the driver's window, flapped back his jacket to show the butt of the handgun sticking forward, saying, "How about you get in and we go for a ride."

"That a question?" Sonny said, stopping at the window.

Dale turned to Jesse Mulligan on the passenger side, saying, "Ask me, the tables just got —"

The punch was short through the open window, Sonny catching the man on the jaw. Reaching in, he snatched the pistol, pointing it at Jesse, half in and half out of the car. Jesse let go of his pistol and showed his hands.

Sonny heard Clara push past the screen door, turning his head enough to see her with the Cooey between her knees, tying back her hair, then coming down the steps, saying, "Thought you was gonna fix this bottom step, Sonny Myers. Getting tired of all these butt-ins." Walking down the drive, the ponytail bouncing behind her.

"Said I'd get to it."

"Well now, Jesse, right?" Clara smiled, remembering him from the motel. "Don't know what happened to your Kansas hospitality," she said to Sonny. "You gonna invite your friends in for lemonade? This fella can tell you how we met."

"You know them?" Sonny said, looking confused.

"You two hitched, huh?" Jesse said. "Well, small world and all, but we just come for a word with your man here."

"Which word's that?" Clara pressed by Sonny, banging the barrel into the door. "Tell you what, you think on it while I count to three. One . . ."

Telfer put the stick in gear.

"Two . . ." Clara aimed the shotgun after them.

Sonny taking it from her, not wanting Marshal Blake coming back. "Full of surprises, you are, that's for sure." He popped the barrel open. Guessing they'd be back, only next time there would be more than two. Saying to her, "How about next time you load it first?"

"Supposed to say, 'I never loved you more, girl.'"

"Well, you know I do." And he kissed the top of her head. "Think you would've done it? Shot him?" He put his arm around her, walking her back to the house. "Gonna tell me how you know that fella?"

She shrugged. "Maybe when you get that step fixed."

... EIGHTEEN

Gently pressing the ice bag over his eye helped, his punched-up lips not feeling like his own. Leaning back in the armchair, Willis Taggart checked his reflection in the cigar case, the initials W.T. in cursive across the silver plate. His face looked distorted, cheeks puffy, new welts and bruises on top of the ones Whitey Adler's goons pounded on him the first time. Tucking the cigar in the corner of his mouth, careful not to reopen the gash. Setting the case down, a stab in his side followed a throb. Touching the welt there, sure it was from when the tall-case clock got pushed on top of him. Cuts from the busted glass and snapped pulleys on his arms and neck.

His pinstripe hanging on back of the chair looked like he took it off some boxcar drifter, the peak lapel dog-eared and the boutonniere hole ripped. A button missing and the seam torn at the shoulder, lining hanging out like stuffing. Willis hoped the old woman who ran the laundry could work her magic and mend it.

The shadow men had plied their trade, plied it hard and left him whimpering and bleeding out by the muddy Kansas. Whitey Adler had stepped from the back of his Packard, watching, then leaning down, giving Willis one more week to make good, not just the vigorish, this time he wanted all of it. Said his boys had better things to do than bang their knuckles on deadbeats. Next time things wouldn't go so easy. Bad men good at their business. No further notice, no memorandum. All of it coming due in a week, the nut too. His world was closing in.

Dragging on the Black Hawk, Willis looked at the stone-faced couple in the Grant Wood painting, asking, "What say you, I look like a bank robber?" Blood trickling from his lip.

The ringing phone made him jump. Reaching for it, hoping it was Handy, but fearing it was Whitey Adler's man.

"Willis?" His brother's voice.

"Walter, you know what time it is?"

"I want to know what's going on, that's what. Asking you nice before we get a lawyer involved."

"You and the ball and chain, huh? Show me you're serious. The lawyer your idea, or hers?"

Sounded like Walter cupped the mouth piece in his palm, saying something to her. Coming back on the line, saying he had every right to know.

"How about you two buy me out, can run it yourselves. Get your lawyer to draw up the papers. Make it fair and I'll sign it."

More whispering, then, "On something you rendered worthless?"

"As usual, you and the battle-axe got it wrong. Forgetting we're in hard times."

"Call her a name again, and I'm gonna come bust you one, so help me."

"Yeah, well, get in line." Willis hung up and leaned back, thinking of getting a fresh ice bag, press it to his throbbing head. Puffing on the cigar stub. Blue smoke going to the ceiling. God, he was a wreck.

When it rang again, he let it, finally picking it up but not saying anything.

"Think we don't see past your fudging and skimming?" It was Penelope this time. "The way you been going, there won't be a show to put on. Nothing left to sell to the Ringlings."

Willis heard a click, the call disconnected. His temples throbbed, squiggles of light across his vision. Slamming the receiver, he got the cord looped around his sleeve. Jerking his arm to free it, the receiver shot up as if lassoed, cracking him above eyes. The desk and chair rushing up, his head striking the floor.

Lying on the planks, he looked up at the bottom of the chair, feeling the pain settle between the eyes, coming into focus on the dust motes clinging to the fabric underside. Over by the door, glints of rainbow light came off bits of glass from the smashed grandfather clock. Been months since he had to let the maid go. The cloudless sky showed through the wood slats, sun shining through the window. Staying down, Willis thought about Handy Phibbs's plan — used to think he rose a cut above those two, Willis making something of himself since their schooling days, hard times leveling the field — putting his mind on robbing the Sheridan Loan and Trust Company, his eyes on the blind cords, wondering for just a moment if they'd take a man's weight.

. . . NINETEEN

Clara put the radio set near the window, the RCA that Orin brought along with the blue ribbon from the Kansas City fair back in '29. Cost him near ten dollars brand new. Fussing with the angle of the set, Clara twisted the Kolster Loop antenna around to catch a better signal, the broadcast coming in. The battery still good.

Eugene Cobb's voice came over the air, sounding tinny but filling the room, explaining to Wilbur Flanders how Cobb-busters worked. Same way he had explained it to her, how he switched out the payload for his special formula, left the stabilizer and firing chamber.

Tipping back in his chair, Sonny said, "Sounds like a pile of horse shit, you ask me."

"Shh, nobody is." Clara leaned close, her ear to the set.

Wilbur Flanders was asking how on earth Eugene Cobb was going to make it rain by blasting a mortar. Static stepped on Cobb's words, Clara tapping the side. Sonny waited on the rooster supper, the one he hit driving Clara to town so she could call her momma, inviting her out for Thanksgiving. Letting the tough meat simmer in the pot on the top of the potbelly stove.

Cobb was talking about mixing sulfur with black powder and peppering in secret makings he didn't care to mention. At least till the patent got passed.

Wilbur asked him when he was getting the show started.

"Did my calculations, and right around two's best."

"Sure gonna be something," Wilbur said, bubbling over. "You folks coming be sure to bring a slicker."

"You really gonna work with this nut, huh?" Sonny asked. "Stand there smiling with everybody we know watching, selling his dumb postcards. Not just gonna be this Cobb making a fool of himself."

"Doubt it all you want, now *shh*."

More static pealed through the speaker cone, Clara rapping on the set and twisting the antenna.

"Try the other way," Sonny said. "Here, let me get it."

"I got it." Clara slapped his hand away, saying, "'Least you can do is show up. Support me, same way I would you."

"That what you were doing, supporting me by running off?"

"Held the shotgun on them two, didn't I?"

"Except you didn't load it."

"You know, Sonny, you got the nicest eyes. Trouble is, sometimes you just don't see shit."

He smiled, thinking it was the perfect time to hit the bank — Eugene Cobb firing his Cobb-busters with the whole town standing by, watching him do it. "When did you say, two?"

"Yeah, at two."

"Well, guess I'll be there. Drive you to town too."

"Well now, that's okay." She pecked his cheek. "Eugene's coming by later."

"Here?"

"Wants to go over a couple of things. Can use the time, I still got lots to do before Momma comes. Said he can give me a lift both ways, says it's no trouble at all."

"He thinks that, huh? Won't be no trouble?"

"Now, come on, Sonny, play nice."

. . . TWENTY

The same K-L-X broadcast relayed via transmitters, Eugene Cobb on the air talking about how he proposed to bring rain from the bleached sky. Willis Taggart hearing him tell the listeners he'd have postcards of the blessed event for sale out front of the courthouse. The reporter/photographer from the *Hoxie Sentinel* sat next to him, a fellow named Jimmy Evans, telling how he'd be there catching history in the making. Willis ready to go, Handy Phibbs calling from his Conoco station, Sonny wanting to do it today, Handy explaining it. The rainmaker giving them the diversion they needed. Had to be today. Willis happy to get on the road, saying he'd be there.

The light came soft through the curtained window, a glow coming from the back of the radio console. Willis used to feel safe in this house, never needed the pistol in the drawer. His den wrapping him like a cocoon, the Grant Wood painting over the mantel, the plain wife looking at the husband with the specs, him looking grim and holding the pitchfork and staring out.

The run-ins with Whitey Adler had Willis moving to the Airstream at the Happy Mustard camp, his temporary office when the show went on the road, parked at the encampment by the river. His people around him.

Eugene Cobb went on about his Cobb-busters, how he packed in some secret ingredients. Wilbur Flanders wrapped up the segment by saying the whole town was sure to turn out, get a good soaking, him and Jimmy Evans laughing, then he spun a new number by the Ink Spots.

Reaching the Philco's knob, Willis switched it off. His pinstripe looking ragged from the second beating, he slipped it on, pocketed the revolver, then reached the BlackHawk from the ashtray. It would take a few hours to drive to Hoxie, giving Willis time to work on an alibi, in case the soup hit the fan.

•

After the Ink Spots, Wilbur Flanders spun a Blind Blake platter, getting up from the controls, thanking Eugene Cobb and Jimmy the photographer for stopping by, showing them to the door, stepping on the porch, wishing Eugene luck with the rainmaking. A minute to go before the song ended.

"Hope you come out and watch the heavens unfold," Eugene said, tipping his straw boater, looking at the cloudless sky, thanking Wilbur for the interview.

"Wouldn't miss it." Wilbur looking down to his mailbox, seeing if the flag was up or down. The same Model A drove along the county road, a humpback truck following behind it. Both stopping by the mailbox, blocking in Eugene's truck, the men inside all looking their way, then clambering out.

"Shit on a shingle." Wilbur said he had to go make a call, hurrying back inside.

Down at the road, the knock-off squad donned their

hoods, two of them pulling a giant cross from the back of the humpback, wrapped in burlap, soaked in oil and gas.

"How's the light for a shot?" Eugene said to Jimmy.

Jimmy Evans looked at the sky. "Not too bad." Not sure what was going on, but sensing it was newsworthy, he looked through the viewfinder, two of the men digging a hole by the road, the others setting the cross in the ground.

Going to the back of his truck, Eugene pulled back the flap and climbed inside. One man held his arms wide and called up to the house, "Got news for you, Wilbur Flanders. The White Knights of the Great Plains ain't gonna let you stand in the way of free speech and our God-given right to take our country back. Let this cross serve as warning to those who stand against us." The man struck a match and stepped to the cross.

Guessing at the calculations, Eugene set the mortar's angle at eighty-five degrees, picked up a Cobb-buster, this one painted red, white and blue, torpedo-shaped with fins at the back. And he dropped it in, twisting away as it struck the firing pin. The blast shook the truck. The Cobb-buster arcing past the men, tearing a gash in the earth like an angry gopher.

"Bet I get the next one right," Eugene called, adjusting the angle down, lifting another Cobb-buster, this one with his name on it, letting the men at the cross get a good look.

The four of them scrambled, leaving the burning cross, the one who made the speech yelled they'd be back, getting in the Highboy, the others jumping in the humpback, both vehicles roaring off.

Setting the Cobb-buster back in its crate, Eugene stuck his head around the side of his truck, calling to the porch, "You get that?"

"You bet. Gonna make the front page for sure," Jimmy called back.

Eugene smiled, counting on it, watching the trucks take off along the road.

Wilbur stepped out the door with his old Navy Colt, saying they'd been by before, had a couple of friends run them off.

Crossing the yard, Jimmy adjusted his shutter and photographed the burning cross. Saying he wouldn't mind getting one of Wilbur next to Eugene holding his Cobb-buster, get the burning cross behind them.

"Not afraid of them shit-heels." Wilbur showed the pistol, standing next to Eugene, putting a hand on his shoulder. "They come back, they'll catch hell." Smiling for the camera.

Jimmy moved to get the truck in the background of the next shot. Eugene smiling too, declaring, "I came to make it rain, ended up putting out the fire. And you can quote me on that."

. . . TWENTY-ONE

Humming "Pennies from Heaven," the tune from the last picture show Sonny took her to, Clara went inside the house, walking barefoot. Sonny and Handy sat across from each other at the table. Going quiet when she came in. Thinking they looked like they were up to something, she said what a striking fella that Bing Crosby was, adding, "Guess that's lost on fellas like yourselves." Saying to Handy, "The film's about this fella gets out of jail, Bing, who meets this gal —"

"Clara?"

She looked at Sonny.

"Can see we're talking, huh? Thought you was getting your wash-up done."

She looked from one to the other, picked up the wash basin, butted open the screen and edged out sideways, the dainties floating around in the water. Setting the basin on the porch, she wrung a pair of knickers, slinging them over the railing, wringing the next one, then the next, lining them along the rail. Seeing the Nash drive up and turn at the mailbox and pull in.

A mustached fellow got out. Kind of handsome, with the kind of smile like he wanted to sell her something. Walking to the steps. "You got to be Clara." Willis took his hat from his pomaded hair, the welts and bruises showing on his face as he got closer. Introduced himself.

A name she'd heard. Looking him over, she took the basin and tossed out the soapy water, some splashing in the yard at his feet. The parched earth sucking it down, leaving a soapy rim. Saying, "All the hot water and rubbing you want, and you still can't get all the sand out."

Willis Taggart gave a smile, saying, "Expect Sonny's waiting on me."

Setting the basin on its end, she sized him up, the bruised face, a beat-up suit. "Usually it's government men and bankers come out wearing suits. I got to tell you, we had it up to here with them fellas."

"Bet you have," Willis said. "I'm with Happy Mustard's Traveling Show, from over in Topeka. Maybe you heard the name, seen us roll past town, maybe caught the show?"

"Can't say so, no."

Pulling a fancy case from a pocket, he took out a business card, offering it to her.

"Not much rolls past here, Mr. Taggart." Ignoring the card, saying, "Can put that away. I know who you are. Clowns you want to see are inside." Just wishing she knew what they were up to.

"Thank you, ma'am." Coming as far as the bottom step.

"Knew a fella worked a show like that, maybe you heard of him," she said, not moving aside for him. "Name's Hanson, fella with two thumbs on the one hand."

"Two thumbs, huh?" Willis turned his lip, considering. "Well, lots come and go. Not exactly the kind of act Happy Mustard signs on. You want freaks, could try Mike's Midway. Ringling's bought most of them out, one at a time, taking over one clown step at a time."

"So, what kind of acts you got?"

"Got some showstoppers." He named some, adding, "Was me that discovered the Flying Farnsworths back when they was starting out, starring Trixie Ambrose. Maybe you heard of them, or how about the Rinky Dinks, out of Wichita?"

"Don't hear of much out here." Clara shook her head. Hearing a chair scrape inside, she eased aside and picked up the last pair of the dainties, wringing them, doing it like she was choking life from them. Telling him, "Best watch that bottom step. Sonny being too busy to fix it." Fixing Sonny with a look.

Coming to the door, Sonny held open the screen, letting Willis in, saying to her, "How about you go hang 'em on the line?"

Smiling at him, she slung the dainties in the basin, then going around to the back of the place, hanging them on the line, back to humming "Pennies from Heaven."

•

The Lamar Hotel was worn but clean enough. Wall coverings faded, its wood floors scuffed. Long time since the ceilings had seen paint. The second-floor window looking out at the main strip dulled by pelting sand. Hays was a town with nothing much going on, nearly as dead as Hoxie, the next hole in the wall. Only difference, Hoxie had a bank, the one they planned to rob.

Willis topped the bathroom glass, swishing it around, sipping and feeling the whiskey course down. Sitting on the hotel bed. Thinking Clara Myers was some dish, and Sonny a fool for treating her like the help, guessing the two had patched up more than one fight. The meeting with the mayor of Hays went well, Willis arranging for the Happy Mustard show to swing through town next season, set up by the historical park. Setting up his alibi.

Lifting the hotel room phone, he asked the girl at the desk to connect him to another line. The girl was Agnes, Willis learning her name when he checked in. Remembering it from the tag pinned over her chest. Agnes wore her hair in that small-town way, simple and tied back. No wedding ring on her finger. Unlike the big-boned and corn-fed gals in sack dresses usually found in these one-horse towns, Willis bet behind that front desk and under the blue-checked gingham with the bow at the neck was a body like Myrna Loy's.

He told Agnes the call was to Florida, a place called Sarasota.

"A call like that, sir, oh, that's gonna run you . . ."

"Mayor'll cover it, so let it run, Agnes. It is Agnes, isn't it?"

She said it was.

"Well, Agnes, this call's to the Ringling Brothers, you heard of them?"

"That like the Barnum Baileys, greatest show on earth?"

"Something like that, yeah."

"One of them shows came trucking through here . . . mmm, few months back. Trying to recall . . . had a funny name . . ."

"Betting that was my show, Agnes. Happy Mustard's."

"That's it, yeah sure."

"We been through Hays a bunch of times. Fact, why I'm here. Planning on coming back in the spring."

"That's you, huh?"

"The one and only."

"Sure love seeing the little fellas. Makes me laugh, the way they jump around."

"Little fellas, huh? Tell you what, you jot down your address, drop it in my pigeonhole, and I'll see you get tickets."

"Oh, that'd be swell."

"And, uh, Agnes, shall I make it two tickets?"

"Oh, it's just me, Mr. Taggart. Of course, there's Mother."

"And you say you like the little fellas, huh?"

"Yeah, the way they jump around."

"And how you feel about a full-size man?"

"Oh, now . . . best you give me that number, Mr. Taggart, let me hook you up."

He rhymed it off, hearing the blips of connection being made, Agnes sounding far away, talking to another operator. Sitting back against the pillow, he sipped his whiskey, thinking about the robbery. Sonny and Handy agreeing to lend some protection once they were done with the bank, keep Whitey Adler off his back.

A couple more clicks on the line, then Agnes told him to go ahead.

"Mr. North, Willis Taggart. How you doing, sir?"

A sigh, followed by, "What is it, Taggart? Got another freak?"

"Wanted to get back to you on that offer."

"What offer's that?"

"Selling the show."

"After this long . . . I don't know . . . need to rethink it, Taggart. This is the off-season, you know. Times are lean."

"Saw your first offer as a dim start, figure if we can kick it north a bit, we might get it settled."

"Playing eighteen in the hour, Taggart. Offer's the same, except I'll throw in one minute to decide, then I grab my clubs, and the deal's dead."

"I got some solid acts, make your eyes pop. Worth more than a couple thousand, but you want me to go to —"

"Tell you what, I got a Kansas man. You call him up, let him look things over. He says it's like you say, then maybe . . . You got a pencil?" North rattled off a name and number, then hung up and went to get his clubs.

Frowning at the dead line, Willis downed his drink, saying into the phone, "Agnes, you still there?"

"Pardon, sir?"

"Thought maybe you held an ear to the line, make sure we didn't get a disconnect."

"They call it monitoring, sir. Hotel's way of making sure our guests stay patched."

"And I thank you for it."

"You're welcome, sir."

"There a place around where a fellow can get supper, one that's decent?"

"Let's see . . . got the café end of the block, coffee's hot, and they make a nice sandwich, but if you want a sit-down kind of place, my favorite's the one just west on the 24, a bit north, a place called the Plainville Grill. Puts out a Sunday spread any day of the week."

"Sounds good. Oh, one other thing, Agnes . . ."

"Yes, sir?"

"What time you off?" Willis gave her a moment, let her put it together.

"I'm off at six."

"Nothing more sorrowful than a fellow dining alone, wouldn't you say?"

"Well, guess we wouldn't want that."

Willis telling her he'd had one busy week, was going to nap this afternoon, didn't want to be disturbed. Said he'd see her later.

A little later he snuck down the rear stairs to his Nash out back without anybody seeing him leave.

. . . TWENTY-TWO

Jimmy Evans was at the *Sentinel* office. Swishing the tray in the darkroom, the image of Eugene Cobb standing before the burning cross, his mortar in the background. Jimmy knowing he was on a hell of a story, one sure to run above the fold. Thinking of a headline: "Cobb wages war with more than the sky."

Cobb's truck was parked around the side of the court-house in Hoxie. A bench set up with his charts and supplies. A folding table next to it. Eugene loaded up a Cobb-buster, removing the fuse, opening the projectile body, switching the shell and bursting charge with the Cobb-buster pack, then replacing the cartridge case and rotating band.

Clara stood there, feeling silly in the outfit Eugene kept in a trunk in back of his truck, red with white and black cuffs, gold buttons, epaulets and tails. Except for the tights she wore underneath, she had the look of a ringmaster, the outfit with the whiff like it had been packed in mothballs. She told him where he could put the matching feather hat. Standing on the lawn, she smiled and waited for a crowd to form. Another unusually warm day for November, so the folks would come. Looking over at Eugene packing his rockets. Wondering what in hell Sonny was up to, the way he'd been sitting at their kitchen table and talking in low voices with Handy Phibbs and Willis Taggart.

A couple walked by the courthouse, the man accusing Cobb of playing God, and how he heard Cobb got hired in Tulsa, and all he left was a yellow trail and a sulfur smell. "Then went and shot the Cowtown windmill up in North Platte. Blew off its hopper chute. Got no rain there neither."

"Brought rain to Denver, just a few weeks back," Eugene called, watching the couple stroll off.

"Top of that, this town ain't got a windmill," Clara said, smiling over at Eugene. The shoes with those heels felt strange and pinched her feet.

"Like to hear about that, and the time in Amarillo." Jimmy Evans walked over to the table, took a printed article from amid his notes, showing it to Eugene. "Says you were mortar-pounding the sky when this duster howled up." Jimmy pointed to the caption, the photo of folks scattering as Eugene stood by his mortar. "Man with not enough sense to run."

"Wouldn't run, stood and faced it," Eugene said. "Laid my hand on the mortar, and the static electricity building up laid me out cold."

Jimmy read on. "Saved by the men who hired you. City council running out and dragging you to safety." Jimmy grinned. "See it made above the fold."

"You forgetting I ran off those hating sons of bitches."

Jimmy Evans nodded, holding up his hands, framing imaginary headlines with his fingers. "Cobb runs off the haters, then calls down the rain, commands the heavens." Jimmy thinking if he didn't do it, they could run a page-four exposé on the fool mayor who hired Eugene, the town getting a soaking. A good story either way.

Clara looking over as Sonny walked past, giving her a nod, then stepping into Grainger's. He was up to something, Clara watching him as he went.

•

Tipping the soda bottle, Sonny slung his jacket over his shoulder, felt the weight of the pistol in the pocket, and glanced out Grainger's window. Clara talking to the gathering crowd just past the twelve-pounder.

Tyrell looked up from the checkerboard, saying, "Hey, Sonny, you hear what happened to Bennie Dickson?"

"The bank robber?"

"Yeah, feds shot him back in April. Now they got an eyewitness says FBI surrounded him coming out of that hamburger place and just gunned him down."

"FBI," Albert spat. "Reminds me of that time they caught up with Creepy."

Sonny guessing he meant Karpis, feeling uneasy, not sure why they were telling him.

"Yeah, feds bagged him coming out of some joint in New Awlins, '36 it was, just getting in his car. FBI surrounds him, pointing guns like it's the Alamo."

"They shoot him?"

"Nope. Creepy was smart, threw up his hands. All them fed guns in his face. J. Edgar peeks from where he's hiding by his parked car, strolls over and tells his boys to take him in custody. Except none of them morons brung handcuffs. Had to bind Creepy with a necktie. The man in charge posing for pictures, acting like he knew what he was doing. Ask me the J's for jackass."

"Karpis did okay not getting shot," Albert said.

"Considering the way the feds did the Barkers, and the Parkers too."

Tyrell studied the board and said, "Old Ma never had a hand in nothing her boys did. Feds knew it, shot her anyway, someplace in Florida." Shaking his head, he hopped one of Albert's blacks.

"Got to lean over me like that?" Tyrell looked up at Sonny, striking a match to his pipe bowl, sucking on the end and making a wet sound, looking across the table at Albert, asking whose turn, then hopping a red over a black, crowning himself a queen.

"Nice talking to you boys," Sonny said, going over to the counter, Emmett Grainger wiping the wood top. Sonny saying, "Why they telling me that stuff?"

"All they talk about, robbers and dinosaur bones." Emmett giving him a sour look.

Sonny looking back out the window, seeing what was going on over at the courthouse. "So, what do you think?"

"Think I just as soon not have you asking about more credit." Emmett glanced at the soda bottle.

"Meant about the rainmaking." Sonny dug in a pocket, setting a nickel on the counter.

"Think that Eugene Cobb's a fool, and the mayor's an even bigger one, hiring a man like that. Not thinking bad of Clara, mind you. A job's a job, I guess. Just not sure it beats the picking we talked about."

"Get no argument from me." Sonny looked back out the window, then checked the Mr. Peanut clock on Grainger's wall.

"How long she gonna be working for him?"

"Have to ask her. All I know, we can use the money. Pay you off soon enough."

"You put that Moon on the books with Handy Phibbs?" Emmett said, his eyes narrowing.

"Handy and me got it worked out." Sonny smiled, thinking everybody knew your business in this town.

•

Another glance at Grainger's clock, Sonny took a swig from the soda pop, saying he didn't want to miss the rainmaking, going out the door, looking across the street.

Clara stood dressed like a ringmaster, talking up the locals. In her element. Cobb was setting his mortar, adjusting the base plate and tripod.

Sonny watched Town Marshal Blake come out of the courthouse, hurrying to his official vehicle and driving off. "Right on time." Sonny said, walking off the porch, sipping from the bottle, surprised his hand wasn't shaking, watching the marshal drive out of town. Strolling away from the Moon Roadster out front of Grainger's, he headed down Main and took the first right. Slipping on the jacket.

•

Willis Taggart pulled the Hudson Eight out front of the Sheridan Loan and Trust, Sonny's old truck had been reported stolen, Handy keeping it hidden down by the old bridge going over the creek. The grill missing, the radiator patched up. Sitting casual behind the wheel, Willis tugged the work cap low, letting the engine chug. The revolver under the seat, his hands and armpits sweating, his heart pounding.

Handy Phibbs crossed the street ahead of him, whistling and coming toward the bank, not wearing his mechanic's coat, just plain jeans and an overcoat, acting easy. You couldn't tell he held a sawed-off down the right sleeve. He winked at Willis and turned down the alley, going around the back of the bank.

Once he got past the crates lining the alley, Handy put cotton in his mouth, hoping it disguised his voice enough, flipped up his collar, took the gun from the sleeve and slipped on one of the hoods they took from the Knighthawks. Going in the back door, he switched the lock, then yelled past the cotton in his cheeks, "It's a robbery. Everybody on the floor." A half dozen customers and Vicky the teller behind the counter. Racking the slide, he told them again. "All but you, sweetheart." Looking through the eyeholes at Vicky.

Drinking his soda pop, Sonny came from the direction of the courthouse, walked past his truck, handed Willis the bottle through the open window, stuck the cotton in his cheeks, donned the hood as he went in the front door of the bank, pulling the pistol.

Handy already had everybody down on the floor. Coming around the counter, he stepped over to Vicky. Knowing about the alarm button by her wicket. Didn't matter it was wired to Town Marshal Blake's office, but it also ran to the Kansas Highway Patrol, a fleet of '31 Plymouths with silver tops and black bodies and gold shields on the doors. Some seasoned boys on the force who knew how to shoot.

"You think I'd hurt a woman?" Peering through the eyeholes, Handy made the look hard, talking around the cotton, putting a twang to his voice, going for Texas. "Better believe it."

Vicky was nodding, her hands trembling.

"You go on believing it, you'll be fine." Handy seeing Sonny step past him and into the office, sticking the Detective Special under Henningan's double chin.

The fat man took his hand away from the phone.

Pressing him backward in his swivel chair, Sonny put some Texas to his voice, saying, "You get one chance, fats. Open the safe or I put one in your neck." Cocking back the hammer. "You believe it?"

Henningan nodded.

Sonny guessed by the smell, the man just pissed himself. He nodded in the direction of the vault, the other side of the bank. Swallowing hard, Henningan shook his head, no, like he wasn't going to do it.

Sonny swept the ledger, name plate and phone off the desk, making it look convincing. "Good a day to die as any." Pressing and twisting the stubby barrel into the turkey neck, helping the banker make up his mind.

"S-state troopers are gonna hunt you —"

The boom sounded from the courthouse, Eugene Cobb assailing the sky. Shoving the barrel against Henningan's nose, Sonny said, "One of us ain't got all day, fats. You wanna guess which one?"

The banker put up his arms and tripped out of his chair, blood at his temple, a wet circle at his crotch. Going ahead of Sonny, he kept his hands held wide, crossing the floor. Sonny poking the pistol at his back.

Handy stood over the people on the floor, all of them on their bellies, their hands folded at the back of their heads. One eye on the front door, the other on Vicky emptying the cash drawer into a bank sack.

The vault was an old Mosler walk-in with its heavy door painted black, gold lettering across the steel front, a lever and combination. Henningan leaned close like he didn't want Sonny to see, spinning the dial right, left, right, turning the lever and pulling it open. Sonny pushed him inside and made Henningan fill the sack with the bundled bills from the drawers, then he nodded at the lock on the door, saying, "Anyone else know how to open up?"

Henningan shook his head, and Sonny stepped out, shoving Henningan back inside, and closed the door. Checking it was locked, he walked back into the main room. Another boom coming from over by the courthouse.

"Everybody stays down. First one gets up, gets shot. You believe it?" Sonny yelled through the cotton. Then they went out the door, Sonny sliding onto the front seat of the truck, Handy jumping in back. Willis drove off, tossing his cap on the floor, making the first right, then cutting down an alley between some stores.

Pulling off the hood, Handy spat the cotton on the floor, left the shotgun and overcoat and jumped out as Willis slowed back of the Conoco. At the next corner, Sonny did the same, shrugging out of the jacket, spat the cotton and jumped out, leaving the sack and handgun, taking the soda bottle Willis handed him. Then he was walking back toward the bank, looking casual. Watching Willis head for the county road, the spot outside of town where Sonny told him to wait. Sonny walking up the street, taking sips from the bottle, going back along the main drag, walking like he had all day, just a guy waiting on his wife to finish her day of rainmaking. Drive her home in the Moon and wait on supper.

The alarm started clanging as he walked abreast of the bank. Sonny looked surprised when Vicky came running from the front of the bank.

"Heck's going on, Vicky?"

"God, oh, jeez . . . we been robbed. Oh my. It's awful."

He put a hand on her arm, steadying her. "What are you saying?"

"We been robbed, and poor Mr. Henningan's locked in the vault. Can hear him pounding."

"Jesus, he alright?" Handing her the soda bottle, telling her to take a sip. Leading her to the front of the bank.

"Just hear him yelling and pounding." Vicky swigging from the bottle. "Poor man's got high blood pressure."

"Anybody hurt?" Sonny looking through the window.

Vicky shook her head, sobbing now, her knees going weak. "Don't think so."

Keeping her from sinking down, Sonny comforted her. "You see who done it?"

"Don't know. Two men, just run out. A truck out front. All of them wearing masks. Went so fast, I don't know. Cleaned us out and just drove off." She looked one way, then the other. "Who does something like that?" Another boom from the courthouse. Vicky falling into his arms, her whole body convulsing.

Comforting her by tapping her back, Sonny told her to go ahead and finish the soda. Feeling bad for her.

Downing the pop, Vicky tried to reel in her nerves, not in a hurry to pull away from him. Feeling safe in his arms.

Sonny saying they best get to the courthouse, let the marshal deal with it, the sooner the better. "Can you make it?"

"Just hold me." Vicky clutched onto him, saying, "What kind of man does that?"

"Don't know." He helped her along, kept his arm around her, heading her for the courthouse. Sonny knowing Marshal Blake was out at the K-L-X, taking care of a complaint. Wilbur Flanders swearing it was the White Knights of the Great Plains, coming back and wearing masks and driving past in a Hudson truck, uttering threats and waving pistols.

"What's going on?" Clara said as Sonny led Vicky through the onlookers.

"Bank got robbed."

Those within earshot all drew breath, everybody forgetting about Cobb and looking at Sonny. Jimmy Evans asked him to repeat it, and when he did, a few depositors went running for the Sheridan Loan and Trust, their life savings inside the vault. Somebody else yelling where the hell was Billy Joe Blake.

Waving his arms for order, Mayor Flint took charge, trying to avert a town panic, ordering Eugene Cobb to cease his rainmaking this minute. The man standing by his smoking mortar, holding a Cobb-buster in his arms as if it were an infant.

"Nothing, huh?" Sonny said to him, looking up at the cloudless sky. Most of the gathered heading for the bank.

Clara shook her head at him, tugging him aside, her hand squeezing his, whispering, "How much you get?"

He just looked at her.

"How we ever gonna be close, way you keep things from me," she said, not letting go of his sleeve.

"Didn't exactly stop to count it." He tapped a finger at her upturned nose. Funny, he wasn't thinking of getting away with it, just looked in her eyes. Then he turned and called to the mayor, "Where in hell's the marshal?"

Mayor Flint turned in a circle, looking for the lawman.

Somebody saying Blake went on a call, pointing in the direction the marshal drove. Somebody else saying they ought to go fetch him.

"I'll do it," Sonny said, telling Clara he'd be back for her. Then walking to the Moon parked out front of Grainger's. The graybeards looking out the window, wondering what was going on.

. . . TWENTY-THREE

Rolling out on the 24, getting on the county road, Willis Taggart saw it, slowed enough and lined the front wheel of Sonny's truck with the wrecking pothole, jumped out as he rolled it in, the front wheels swallowed. The truck bucked, a few parts falling off, the wreck resting on its frame in the middle of the road. Willis walked back up to it, tossing the hood on the seat, setting down the bank sacks, putting all the cash in one, dropping the empty one on the seat and leaving the truck with its door hanging open. He walked back to the adobe shack. Laughing away the nerves and telling himself they pulled it off.

Waiting an hour till Sonny drove up in the Moon. Willis walking over to him, Sonny looking down the road at his old truck in the big pothole.

"You had to do that, huh?"

Willis shrugged, saying, "Looks convincing, the kind of thing those robbing White Knights do to a stolen jalopy." Saying he left the klansmen's hoods and empty bank sack on the front seat.

Sonny nodded.

"Split it up while I waited," Willis said, shrugged and

glanced at the three bags on the ground by the door of the shack. "Count it if you want to."

"No need." Sonny pulled the pistol from inside Willis's pinstripe and pointed it at him.

Willis frowned and put up his hands.

Patting him down, Sonny pulled a bundle of twenties from the top of his boot.

"You got no idea of the hell I got after me," Willis said, making a long face.

Tucking the pistol back in Willis's jacket, Sonny shoved the stack in after it, took two of the bags and turned for the Moon.

"Oh, uh, you mind dropping me off?" Willis said.

Sonny just looked at him.

"I got a date."

•

Noting the black streaming from the tailpipe of the mayor's Zephyr, Handy guessed the engine was running rich, the choke needing a tinker. A finicky twelve-cylinder symphony going on under the hood. Handy grinned, thinking how he replaced the radiator on the Hudson after Sonny shot it out front of Wilbur Flanders's radio station, the man killing his own truck while chasing off the White Knights, assholes calling themselves the Knighthawks. Sonny getting Wilbur Flanders to call the marshal's office, claiming some men drove by in the truck, making more threats. Laughing as he pictured Sonny driving to the K-L-X, reporting to Billy Joe Blake the bank got robbed, Vicky the teller saying it was a couple of men in hoods, describing the old wreck parked out front. The same truck Sonny reported stolen a couple days back.

"Woohoo." Driving to Dingle's Diner, Handy put his foot to the floor. The needle rising past fifty, the sun warm on his arm hanging out the window. Thinking he'd hide his share behind the toilet tank at the Conoco, all but a couple hundred Sonny said they could each keep, called it walking-around money. Thinking he might sell the place, get a Zephyr like this one and drive it to Florida, lie in the sun till the money ran out. The speedometer closed on seventy. His foot mashed the pedal, the back end swaying on the gravel road, the exhaust not so black now. Nobody on the county road, just Handy tearing it up. Sure felt good. Slowing and crunching his wheels on the gravel out front of Dingle's, no other cars in the lot. Guessing Sonny was driving Clara home, just another face watching the rainmaking at the courthouse, and Willis sneaking in the back door of the hotel in Hays. The waitress smiled at him when he stepped in, going for the carafe, the apron matching the collar and cuffs, Nora printed on her name tag, her curls dancing behind the long neck. Looked glad to see him.

"Hey, Handy, how's things?"

"Pretty good, Nora. How about yourself?" Sitting on the swivel stool, he drummed his fingers and waited for her to fill a cup, thanking her, nice she remembered he drank it black. Making eye contact. First time he'd been alone with her in the diner, the place usually jumping. Watching her go set the carafe back on the gas burner. Always liked the way Nora O'Mara fit that uniform, her hips with a nice swing. "Keeping busy, huh?"

"Well, had a regular crowd in at lunch, but been quiet since." Nora good with the small talk that got her tips. "Suits me fine."

Taking a bill from a pocket, Handy folded it lengthwise

and set it down next to the cup. Searching for something to say. "Ol' Ed Dingle still own the place, huh?"

"Man's got me on my feet six days a week, breakfast till supper. Says I don't want to do it, plenty girls around who will." She rolled her eyes and gave a smile, though it looked tired.

"Guess folks like Dingle get a leg up, they figure they can treat folks poor. Shame you working for a fella like that." Handy knowing the Dingles. Edwin being a sorry bastard whose wife left him years ago, kids who didn't come around to see him but at Christmas.

Nicking her head to the window, she said, "Sure a nice car, Handy. Whitewalls, huh?"

"Yeah, she's got the bells and whistles. You want, can take you for a spin sometime."

"Oh, that'd be swell." Swinging the curls, she went along the counter. "I get you something else?"

"Well, what kind of pie you got today, Nora?" Handy liked saying her name.

"Got the banana cake."

"Banana cake, huh? You bake it?"

"When you suppose I got time for baking?" Again the smile.

Shrugging, saying he guessed she didn't, but sure wouldn't mind trying a slice.

Setting a fork next to the plate, she piled a mound of cream by the slice.

Handy stabbed in his fork. "Mmm, mmm. Man, that's good. Sure you didn't bake it?" Getting cream on his lip, cupping his hand and wiping it, saying sure to a second slice, eating well past needing some Pepto. Looking at her and smiling, thinking he had enough money to keep himself in pie for the rest of his life. "And what say to catching a show sometime?"

"Mean like you and me?"

"Sure."

"Well, what kind of show you got in mind?"

"Hear they got one coming up called *Gone with the Wind*. Read about it in the *Movie Mirror*. Guessing you'd like it."

"Think you know what I like, huh?"

"Figure you're not gonna say no to Cracker Jack and any kinda soda you want. Hoping you won't, anyway." Smiling, thinking up the next ailment for the Zephyr. Could tell the mayor he needed to keep her on the SkyHi lift overnight. Realizing he now had enough money to not bother with it. Could get his own car, maybe a Zephyr. Handy seeing himself driving with Nora next to him on the bench seat. Anytime he wanted. Sliding his arm around her shoulders.

Then he saw Sonny pulling the Moon into the lot, parking next to the Zephyr.

•

Back at the house, Sonny stepped out the screen door when Cobb pulled up in his truck, dropping Clara off down by the mailbox. Sonny walked down, eyeing the way she thanked Eugene, putting a hand on his arm, giggling about something.

"Don't look much like rain," Sonny said, throwing a look at the sky, cloudless and pale.

"Bank getting robbed messed things up, you know that," Clara said.

Sonny nodded, saying, "How about you run in and fix supper." It wasn't a question.

Raising a brow, she wondered on what stove he wanted her to fix it. "Inviting Eugene to supper?"

"Wasn't thinking that." Sonny turned to Eugene.

"Sorry, Eugene," said Clara. "Seems my man switched

138

places with his jackass. Maybe another time. But I thank you for the lift."

Sonny waited till she went up the porch, then leaned on Eugene's window. "Sure nice you rescuing her when the truck broke down, putting her up and hiring her on, giving her a lift home . . ."

"Well, sure, anybody would. And could see she needed the work."

"Yeah, about you giving her the business . . ." Sonny raised a hand when he started to protest. "Thing is, Eugene, she quit."

Looking offended, Eugene said, "That'd be for her to say, don't you think?"

"Let me try it another way. You come around again, Eugene, I'm gonna do my own Cobb-busting. That plain enough?" Following it with a smile.

Eugene looked at him, then threw the stick in gear, saying, "She got that part right, about you being a jackass." Then he was rolling.

Clara stood on the porch, folding her arms, watching Sonny walk back, looking pleased with himself. "Not bad enough you messed up his rainmaking."

"Not working for that fella no more."

"Yeah, well, so, how much we get?"

"We, huh?"

"For better or worse, remember?"

Lifting his leg over the busted step, he put his arms around her. "Got something better 'n money." Kissing her.

"That right? Robbing banks brings it out, huh? Thought you wanted supper."

"Supper can wait." He went back to kissing her, hooking the screen door with his shoe he took off Stonewall, getting them inside.

. . . TWENTY-FOUR

Two vehicles drove east from town. Near dusk, a black mass showed along the western horizon behind them. Second time Hollis Capp drove out here. The first was to collect the repossessed property, taking the stove, churn and sewing machine to his shop, sell them for whatever he could get, the proceeds going to Henningan's bank. This time, he was on different business, driving the DeSoto, figuring they had time to do what they came for before the duster swept through. Didn't want to go back and tell Grand Wizard Braxton Early the Nighthawks didn't get it done. Again.

They topped a crest, the peak of Sonny Myers's barn came into view. Hollis telling the Mulligan brothers to get set, Jesse sitting next to him, Levon in back. Slowing to a stop, he waved his arm out the window. Dale Telfer hauled up in the Highboy, the cross wrapped in burlap sticking out the back of the truck. Hollis took his shotgun and the hood from behind the seat. Jesse sliding behind the wheel of the DeSoto.

"Let's get the son of a bitch." With that, Hollis hoofed it across the dead ground, coming at the place from the back.

The DeSoto and the Highboy drove to the T intersection, coming around it from the front.

Setting his newsboy cap low, Hollis Capp moved down the ditch and across the barren field. Halfway across, he turned and saw the duster bearing down, coming faster than he first thought. He hurried across the hard-packed ground, nothing but the odd weeds poking up where the earth lifted along the cracks. Wanting to get to the barn at the same time the others arrived out front.

The wind was picking up, still he heard the rattling, making him freeze mid-step. No mistaking the prairie rattler colored like the land, coiled, its eyes ugly and its head up, black tongue flicking out. Reversing his step, Hollis moved slow. Would have shot it if it wasn't for the noise.

The shaking tail stopped as Hollis walked a wide arc. He kept going, flipping up his collar, his hand holding down his cap. A boiling wall as dark as tobacco and as high as a city building was bearing down and coming fast. The sand pelted him, and he started to run for the back of Myers's barn before the duster wrapped itself around and swallowed everything. The sand stinging like hornets as he got past the backhouse, a mule whinnying in its corral. Getting up against the lean-to at the side of the barn, he edged to the front corner. Couldn't see down to the mailbox, the sand blowing harder. The Moon Roadster sat out front of the porch. Slipping into the dark of the barn, Hollis hoped that Dale Telfer and the others were down at the front, getting that cross ready.

•

Sonny set down his empty tin cup. "Moonlight Serenade" finishing on the radio when the static started.

"That got a place?" Clara looked at the offending cup, then at him, drawing her lips tight, saying, "And no need for that man-of-the-house look."

"I got no such look."

Annoyed that he hid the bank money someplace and wouldn't say where, Clara just wanting to see it, run her hands through it. Never seen more than a hundred at one time. According to him, his share looked like about five grand, enough to make her whistle.

Sonny set the cup on the counter, saying he was going to tend to Pearl, get her settled for the night.

"Sure, her you care about. How about you spend the night in the barn? Talk nice and maybe she lets you cozy up."

Sonny grinned and shook his head.

A Ziggy Elman number came on, the static cutting hard into it. Tapping the side and fiddling the channel knob, Clara cleared the static, got up and tried to waltz him around the table. "Oh, come on, Sonny. One minute we're plum busted, next we got all this money. Fifteen thousand, you figure?"

"Third of it's ours."

"Never seen so much, is all. Come on, let me have a look." Pecking him on his cheek, she held his hands in hers, skipping on the floor, her hip bumping the table. "And, you know, I been thinking about splitting it three ways."

"Is that so?" He looked surprised.

"Well, it hardly seems right. There's me in the mix too, doing my bit at the courthouse. Talking about rainmaking, everybody watching me in my outfit, while you fellas rob the bank. You ask me, that ought to be worth something."

"I wasn't asking you, but I pulled two hundred off for now, enough so nobody raises eyebrows, the rest stays hid like I said." He reached in a pocket, took out the money and slapped it flat on the table.

Again she whistled.

"Get the rest when things settle."

The music became lost in more static, and Sonny glanced to the window, snapping from the hindrance. "Holy Jesus!"

Letting her go, he knocked into the table and was rushing for the door, grabbing the lantern on his way out.

"What in hell . . ." Clara watched him go like a crazy man, then looking out the window to see where he was running. And she saw it coming too.

•

Narrowing his eyes against the gust of cold. The air crackling. A boiling wall of sand coming over the flat land. Lightning flashing like hellfire inside the mass, static electricity churning. The lantern was ripped from his fingers, sent smashing against the porch. The farmyard a frenzy of whipping sand and debris.

Leaning into it, Sonny forced his steps, forearm shielding his eyes. Getting to the corral, calling Pearl's name into the howl, leading the screaming mule past the Moon and into the barn. Struggling to get her into her stall, the yard birds rushing around his feet. The wind shrieking through the slatted boards, swirling hay into the air.

Watching he didn't get kicked, telling Pearl it'd be alright, he grabbed the burlap sack from the post and slung it over her head, cinching the ties so she couldn't get it off with her rearing and stamping. Pearl kicked at the stall, braying her terror.

Nothing more he could do for her. He went out and got in Moon and felt for the keys, cranking the engine to life, flipping on the headlights, and rolled into the barn. Sonny pried the barn door off the outside wall, pushing for all he was worth till the wind caught it like a sail and banged it shut. Getting the latch on the door, leaning near horizontal into the force, he lead-footed back across the yard. A bucket bounced off his back, the wind sending him stumbling up the steps. The kitchen shutter ripped from its dog, flapping against the clapboard. Turning dark as night, the wind a scream in his ears, the sand biting his exposed skin. Edging along the planks, eyes near shut, he got the slapping shutter, latched the dog and slid the bolt in place. Feeling his way along the porch. A fence picket struck his thigh, spinning against the house and away. The triangle clanging against the post like it was mad.

Sonny saw the two sets of headlights, realized they'd come for him, watching them pull up at the end of his property, several men getting out. Going to the door, he grabbed the shotgun, told Clara to stay inside, her stuffing soaked burlap along the base of the kitchen window. He tugged back the screen, the wind stealing it from his grip, tearing it off its hinges. Spinning off like a pie tin out across the side yard. And out he went.

•

Using his thumb like a plug, Hollis Capp snorted out what was caking his nostrils, first one side, then the other. Tripping around in the dark, he knocked over a sickle and flail leaning against the wall. When Sonny Myers brought in his mule, Hollis hid behind a musty tarp, crouching at the back as Myers got it in its stall. Waiting till he rolled in the car, then closed up the barn.

Grabbing the tarp, he felt his way to the car, twisted the corner of the tarp and shoved it in the Moon's gas filler hole, smelling the fuel, then going to the barn door, getting it open.

Could barely see to the house, but he could make out the flickering cross down near the road. Going back, he struck a match and lit the tarp, dropping it on the straw. Getting out of there at the same time Sonny Myers came from the house with his shotgun, calling down to the Knighthawks like he was Tex Ritter doing "High Noon." Blasting the shotgun. Likely the same one he used on banker Henningan. The tarp and hay caught behind Hollis, sending a glow, putting him in silhouette. The mule stomped and kicked, hee-hawing. The sands whipping and fire spreading across the floor. Hollis Capp coughed dust and drew his pistol. Turning back, he lost sight of Sonny Myers somewhere ahead of him in the yard.

•

Sonny had told her to stay put, wrapping his kerchief around the doorknob saved him getting jolted by static electricity. Checking the shotgun's load, he went back out. Leaving Clara to shut the door.

Standing in the parlor, she recited the Lord's Prayer over the wind's roar, "Forgive us our trespasses . . ." Practically yelling out the line about delivering us from evil. The sound of shingles and tar paper peeling off the roof drowned out the rest. Thinking, if that fool gets himself killed without telling me where he hid the five thousand . . . And she went for the door.

Holding the barrel level, Sonny forced his steps across the yard, looking for movement down by the burning cross. Looked like a car and a truck down by the road. The smell of gas and oil filling his nose. He heard the gunshot, not sure who was shooting. Ducking low, he blasted a shot where he guessed they were, fumbling in his pocket for another shell.

Somebody fired again, showing a muzzle flash. Then he saw the truck lights as it drove off. He fired after it. Then more lights as the car started pulling away. A man went running from the barn, yelling something. Sonny seeing the flames inside, fumbling in another shell, taking a wild shot at the running man. Looked like he winged him, the man stumbled and kept running.

Then Sonny was moving for his barn, already knowing he couldn't save it. The flames licked at the slats, up to the rafters, boards toppling, the wind driving the flames, sparks flying to the house. Pearl's braying was like a scream.

•

By the time it blew over, Clara looked like she'd aged a decade, her hair and skin dusted gray. Leaning next to the door, Sonny guessing he looked the same, his face and body scraped raw, feeling worse than sunburned. His hair thick with the sand.

Dipping a towel in the bucket, she draped it over her head, lay on the parlor floor and after a while, she drifted into a fitful sleep, letting the candle burn to a stub.

Sleep didn't come to Sonny, mostly he paced the parlor, going from the door to the kitchen window, keeping watch. The men could come back. Toward morning, he found his Bull Durham pouch and rolling papers in a pocket, stepping out as the morning light started to show to the east, the sky acting like nothing had happened. Rolling up a smoke, he looked at the pile of smoking ash that had been the barn, the debris everywhere. Puffing, he took stock of the wreckage.

Clara stepped next to him, took the cigarette from him and took a drag. "Good thing we got that money. We can head off and start over, count ourselves lucky we didn't get shot."

"They burned my barn and killed my mule."

"Yeah, you hear the part about starting over?"

He shook his head, saying, "Can't."

"Can't or won't?"

"Can't." Pointing to the rubble where the barn had been. "I hid it at the back."

... TWENTY-FIVE

Morning brought that washed-out sky, the kind that always followed the dirt storms, the sun coming up angry red. A pair of buzzards winging slow and lazy circles above the burned-out barn. The porch rocker was gone, the screen door too, its hinges hanging from the splintered jamb. Sand wedged between the slats and boards along the front of the house, looked like it had been packed in. A couple of small birds stuck beak-first like darts in the siding, their bodies hanging limp. Sand drifted up the steps and porch, along the rail fence, burying it in places. Everything sifted colorless. The garden fence pickets were gone. The weather vane laying in the yard. Scattered scrub and tumbleweed, the backhouse on its side, the field beyond scoured down to its hardpan. This Sunday morning looking worse than it did after Black Sunday.

Kicking at some tumbling scrub, Sonny crossed the yard, the shotgun in his hand, looking up at the circling buzzards. Stepping by where the barn had been, looking at what was left of the Moon. Tires flattened, headlights and windows busted, paint blackened and blistered, interior burned out, barn rafters on top, crushing down the roof. The sack gone from Pearl's head, the mule on her side, her yellow teeth in a kind of grin, eyes wide open.

Resting the gun against some fallen boards, he squatted next to the mule and brushed sand from her muzzle and withers, stroked the long ear. Hoping the fright of the storm took her ahead of the flames. Would have been better if she died like the rest of the stock, sand lacing the hi-gear feed that filled their guts.

He pointed to the spot where he'd hid the money. Looking at the wrecked car, Clara told him how she wanted to drive into town and pay Emmett Grainger some of the money they owed, use some of the two hundred he showed her last night. The whole five thousand was gone. Covering her eyes, turning away from Pearl, she faced where he'd hidden the money, racked by sobs.

Feeling bad, having to tell her. Thinking how happy she'd been last night when he told her about the five thousand, the woman dancing round the table. Leaving her standing there, he found a bucket and tipped sand from it, seeing one of the yard birds standing next to the body of the other. Checking the pump, he filled the pan with water, set it down for the bird, wondering how it survived.

Hearing a car coming, he looked to the shotgun, but it was Handy. Sonny watching him pull in, driving the mayor's Zephyr. Getting out and looking at what was left of the barn. Walking over, he looked at the mule, then the destroyed Moon Roadster.

"Hid the money over there." Clara barely got the words out, pointing to where the corner of the barn had been.

"All of it?"

Nodding, Sonny lashed a foot at a beam, ash drifting up.

"Say we go find them sons right now," Handy said.

"How about you gimme a hand, help bury my mule?"

Clara went and brought an old blanket from the house, and they wrapped the body in it. Handy tied a rope to the frame of the mayor's Zephyr and dragged the mule from the ruin. Hard going through the drifts, the wheels spinning, engine getting hot.

Mopping sweat with his cap, Sonny looked up, more buzzards up there now. He found a spade among the rubble that wasn't too bad, and he chopped into the cracked earth as best he could. Thinking about Doris Grainger's biscuits. The three of them not talking much and not stopping till the hole was deep enough. Handy looked at Sonny, tightened his lips and shook his head. The two of them taking turns digging. The buzzards kept up their lazy orbits out of shotgun range, but close enough to show the ugly red heads and pin feathers held out like fingers. Nothing as dogged as a turkey vulture.

Hauling her with the Zephyr, they got Pearl into the hole, covering her with the blanket. Filling it in and tamping down the earth.

Then, rigging a fulcrum from a plank and stump, they used ropes and got the backhouse righted over a new hole they dug. The duster having filled in the old one. By the time the sun climbed halfway to noon, they had the yard cleared. Tucking the dead bird in her apron, Clara went about fixing a fire in the yard, getting a pan from the house and making a makeshift lunch of fried dough and gravy. Adding the little meat, she passed out the plates. The three of them sat eating on the porch, the acrid smell of burned wood, the burned cross hanging about the yard.

"Seen the rocker?" she asked.

"Likely in the same place as the screen and the triangle," Sonny said, glancing to the horizon.

Clara looking dejected, her throat so raw she could hardly eat.

The three of them hearing another engine, looking out at the road, the town marshal's car stirring dust along the county road, turning in at the mailbox.

"The hell's he want?" Handy said.

"Guess we're gonna find out."

Getting out, Billy Joe Blake adjusted his cap the way lawmen did and walked up, having a look around. "The hell happened here?"

"White Knights of the Great fucking Plains. Ones I already told you about." Sonny pointed to what was left of the cross. "Squad of them, believe they call themselves Knighthawks, come out just ahead of the blow, took some potshots at me and torched my barn. Think I mighta winged one."

"You identify any of them?"

"You're kidding, right?"

Blake took the place in. "Came about Henningan's bank getting robbed . . . got some questions."

"Right now I got bigger things than your questions. No offense, Marshal." Sonny gave him a level look.

"Maybe so, but I got to ask them anyway."

Sonny kept looking at him.

"Vicky's sure it was your truck by the bank, the paint nearly gone, the grill and windshield missing. Wilbur claiming the same truck drove by the K-L-X, three fellas with hoods on, making more threats."

"Sounds like my truck alright, one I reported stolen."

"Hold on," Clara said. "You think Sonny had a hand in the bank getting robbed, how about you come out and say it."

"Not saying anything, just asking."

"Him being the one who went to fetch you, consoling poor Vicky right after."

Blake looked at Sonny. "Say you walked by the bank right after, huh?"

Sonny put up his hands, like what could he do. "Came to watch Clara talk up the town while that Eugene Cobb took on the sky. Waiting for him to do it, I got a soda at Grainger's and stretched my legs, happened by the bank. Vicky comes running out, says it's been robbed. Two, three men in a truck. Yeah, guess it coulda been mine, one that got stole. I don't know, all over by the time I walked by."

Blake nodded and looked at Handy. "How about you?"

"Was under the mayor's car, getting her road-worthy." Handy nodded at the Zephyr.

"Let me ask you one, Marshal," Sonny said, pointing to where the barn had been. "How's shit like this go on in your own town?"

"Saying I'm not doing my job?"

"You come out here with your questions. Meantime you got haters running around, setting fire to barns, shooting and threatening. Bank happens to get robbed, and here you are asking us questions, 'stead of them."

"You see anybody out there when you went strolling by the bank, anybody at all? Something I can go on?"

"All I can tell you, look for a bunch of chickenshits hiding under pillow cases, and go ask them."

"I already put a call to the highway patrol, asked them to weigh in. Told me these White Knights got a parade planned for Topeka next week. All of us gonna be keeping a close eye."

"You catch up to them, you ask your questions, likely to tell you they were busy building a parade float. One alibiing the other."

"Telling me how to do my job again," Billy Joe said, looking at Sonny, then Handy, tipping his hat to Clara, turning for his car. "Sorry about your barn."

•

It took some doing, but Sonny convinced Clara to ask her momma to come for that visit, it being Thanksgiving and all, just while he was gone. On top of possessing an acid tongue, the old woman was a crack shot. Handy drove Clara to Grainger's to make the call, then drove her back. Sonny explained that Willis Taggart had a problem out at Happy Mustard's, and he was driving to Topeka with Handy to help him out, something he'd get paid for.

While Clara and Handy were gone, Sonny packed a change of clothes and his shaving kit in the old suitcase, got Pearl's plow harness, sawbuck packsaddle and gear, all of it smelling of the smoke but otherwise undamaged by the fire. He piled everything in the back of the Zephyr. Taking along the spade to deal with any sand drifts along the route.

Not happy about the burned smell getting in the mayor's car, Handy swung under the chassis and checked the petcock for oil. Climbing in behind the wheel, he rolled down the window. Sonny getting in the passenger side.

"Shame about the money." Handy looked at him, waiting for Clara to come from the house. "Split what I got with you."

"Can't let you do that."

"Didn't think so." The reason Handy slipped Clara some of the money he had on him. Pushing in the choke, he shifted, retarding the spark, giving it some throttle, choking and priming.

Clara came from the house, eyes still red, but not crying, walking alongside the passenger side as Handy backed down the drive, telling Sonny she was real sorry for Pearl, "Was a good mule."

"Yeah, you bet." Sonny leaned out the window, told her he left half of the two hundred for groceries and such and left the shotgun. Saying sorry he was missing Thanksgiving.

The two of them kissing. Clara putting a hand around back of his neck, making it one that would last. Adding what Sonny left with what Handy handed her.

Handy rolled down the drive, bumping over a sand drift, turning at the mailbox.

Watching them go, Clara went to the house, stepped over the busted step and onto the porch. Not sure what they were up to now, knowing it was more than they were saying, guessing it could be another bank, she waved as they turned at the mailbox, saying, "Just this one time, Sonny. Get it right."

·

"So, you gonna tell me?" Handy said, driving toward Hoxie.

"Tell you what?"

"What you did with it."

"Did what I had to," Sonny said. "That woman thinks we ought to cut her in."

Handy looked like he sucked a lemon, saying, "On account of what?"

"Distracting everybody in front of the courthouse, wearing that outfit."

"You think that?"

"What's it matter, the money's gone. 'Least she thinks it is."

Handy turned, looking at him, smiling. "You gonna let her know?"

"Maybe when I get back."

Taking his canteen, Handy said, "Wouldn't have left you flat."

"Woulda shared, huh?"

"Woulda robbed another bank." He sipped while steering with his knees. Driving Sonny to the Deal 'n Wheel, selling Pearl's stuff. Meantime Handy would go to see the mayor, telling him he had a clattering of the worst kind, the Zephyr in need of more road testing. Drive to Topeka and help Willis out with some loan shark and the White Knights of the Great Plains, planning to parade and threatening to bust up Happy Mustard's show. Sonny feeling eager for another run-in, a chance to even the score.

"Ain't Flint gonna wonder where his car went?" Sonny said.

"Why, you got feelings for the man?"

"Never voted for him."

Both of them grinning.

"Man's carburetion's off, chugging and blowing black smoke. Got me worried." Handy making a two-hand motion like he was fishing. "Top of that, I got to wait for parts, all the way from Chicago."

"He gonna buy it?"

"Man's lucky I don't charge him overtime."

. . . TWENTY-SIX

Handy drove into Hoxie and pulled up behind Hollis Capp's DeSoto Airflow. The wood siding on the shop was faded around where the old signboard for Polly Rupp's pie shop used to hang. A sign leaned in the window:

Capp's Deal 'n Wheel
Fair price for scrap metal

Hollis Capp, proprietor, underneath in script. A faded notice had been pasted by the door: cotton pickers wanted in California.

Sonny grabbed the stuff from the back: arms full of the plow harness and sawbuck packsaddle. Shops like this had been springing up in other Kansas towns. A cents-on-the-dollar kind of place. The graybeard geezers playing checkers at Grainger's talked about the honest men who couldn't hang on, having to stop in places like this. Croppers, sharers and owners alike. Selling anything they couldn't haul away. Sonny guessed the first mistake was thinking it didn't cost anything to ask a man like Hollis Capp how much he'd give. Guessing nobody was getting to California on what he was willing to pay.

He pushed the door with his backside. Stepping in, he

set the harness and saddle in the middle of the floor, waiting for Hollis Capp to come from the curtain in back.

Deep-set eyes and a long jaw, a wrap and a sling around his arm. Looking at the stuff on the floor, he gave Sonny the up and down. "Packing her in, uh?" Capp sounding matter of fact about it.

"Got some things need selling, yeah. Got the haines and tugs out the door." Pulling the old hackamore from his back pocket, Sonny laid it on the saddle.

Pushing the toe of his boot at the packsaddle, Hollis Capp said, "Looks like you had a fire." Knowing who Sonny was, having repossessed his stuff the other day. The one who fired birdshot at him last night.

"Stuff's still good." Sonny gave Capp a look. "Hurt your arm, huh?"

Looking down at the packsaddle, Hollis said, "How's two-fifty, counting what you got outside?"

"Two-fifty, you mean hundred?"

"Two dot fifty."

"A fella jokes like that, expect him to be wearing big clown pants." Sonny corked his temper. On the one hand, he was hoping to get enough to cover the gas and cost of a few truck-stop meals. More important, he wanted to meet the man face to face. Had a hunch he was at the radio station the day Sonny ran them off, hiding under a hood. And from the look of that arm, he'd had a hand in burning down Sonny's barn.

"Got my offer, friend. Take it or haul your stuff." Capp walked back to the curtain and said, "Gimme a shout, you want to deal."

Knowing it was worth two, three times that, even smelling of smoke, Sonny looked around the place. A Sears Roebuck walking plow next to a hand plow, a seeder, a wood stove and a pot stove, a three-burner like Clara's, mattocks, axes and wedges on a bench, a couple of bedsteads leaning against the wall, one table stacked on another, chairs around them, farming gear piled by the walls, more stacked under the tables. Sonny called to the curtain, "You the kind of fella that don't want to chew, just wants to swallow, that it?"

Hollis Capp came back out, sizing Sonny up. "What do you mean by that?"

"Go and strip folks' places clean, like a vulture." Sonny stepped around the harness, getting close to Capp. "What happened to your arm?"

"Ain't your business." Staring back. "And I don't force nobody, pal. Same way nobody's forcing you. They come all on their own."

"Don't matter they're hungry, their kids too. Moving on 'cause they got nothing else. You not giving enough to buy the gas to get there."

"You heard my offer," Hollis said, scratching his chin. "Stepped in here on your free will. Didn't make you do it. You don't like what I got to say, then pick up and go."

"You don't know these folks and what they been through."

"We all got a story. Mine's I look out for me and my own. Now, I'm gonna tell you one more time to shove off."

Sonny looked at him, then the wrapped arm. "You torched my barn." Expecting Hollis Capp to call him crazy.

Capp just grinned, saying, "You prove it?"

"Was you at the radio station too. One of the fuckers we ran off."

"Day you shot your own truck." Hollis grinned, shaking his head.

"And you running like a rabbit. Same as last night."

"Ought to come out to a meeting, get to know some of the boys. Get a better understanding."

"Heard the grand wizard charges you fools five bucks for pillowcases worth fifty cents. The ones you cut holes in and stick over your heads, hiding and singing 'Onward, Christian Soldiers.'"

His fingers closed to fists, Hollis wanted to sock this dirt farmer and heave-ho him out the door. And he might have tried, except for his injured arm, still smarting from the three bits of buckshot he dug out himself, that and the want-to in Sonny Myers's eyes. Not big, but the man looked wiry enough from working his land, planting government trees. Something else the White Knights had made Hollis aware of, the way FDR pissed money away, doling out to these fool farmers. Knowing there would be a better time to deal with Sonny Myers, Capp pressed his hands in his pockets and said, "You come in hoping to sell or get in a set-to?"

"Can see the notion just passed you by," Sonny said. "Came in for the one, but wouldn't mind settling up like Kansas men."

"Except I'm from Boise."

"Yeah, that don't surprise me, like that other fella we run off . . ." Sonny thinking of the name, saying, "Stonewall, he called himself. You know him?"

"You think you know something, the marshal's right over at the courthouse."

"Billy Joe Blake, sure, known him since the Bee Hive school, both of us from around here." Sonny looked around the place, catching sight of a Winchester leaning by the far wall, a Model 1890 with hand carving on the stock. Recognizing it as Amos Bragg's, he went and picked it up, working the lever action. Saying, "Belongs to a friend of mine."

"Folks come in, they got stuff to sell." Capp showed his hands, saying, "And I'm here to buy."

"How much you give Amos?" This fellow Capp sure reminded him of what was circling over his barn.

"Mean how much I'm asking, it's seven bucks."

Sonny set the rifle down.

"Look, mister, grab your gear, take it someplace else. Not doing business here."

"Except there's no place else, and you know it." Sonny took his time, pulled his pouch and papers, twisted up a smoke, saying, "Now, I set the gun down so there's no mistake."

"Mistake about what?"

"About you and me settling up. My stuff for the gun." He flared the match, puffing the smoke to life.

Hollis Capp watched the match burn down to the man's fingers. Sonny dropping it on the floor, not stepping it out.

"If it gets you out of here, let's call it a deal."

Sonny took the rifle, slung it over his shoulder and stepped around the harness and packsaddle, angled through the door, saying, "That's how it's done in Kansas. I were you, I'd remember it."

Hollis Capp watched him go out the door, then called after him, "Hey, how about the haines and tugs?"

. . . TWENTY-SEVEN

"What took you?" Handy said, filling the Zephyr's tank.

Sonny walked to the Conoco, the carbine in his hand. "Got to dickering," Putting the Winchester in back.

Locking the garage doors, Handy got in and started the car, the two of them driving off.

Sonny asked him to pull in at the stone orchard, and Handy steered the Zephyr between the double row of trees of heaven, waiting in the idling car while Sonny paid his respects, keeping his ears on the symphony of the cylinders.

Kneeling by Orin's plot, Sonny tugged up some new weeds, telling the old man he got another line of trees in, still had the west side to plant. Brushing sand from the cross, going on about the land being as dry as a nun's gusset. "But the rain'll come, and we'll get in some seed this spring." Then he turned and brushed sand from his ma's grave. Knowing she wouldn't like what he was getting himself into. Robbing a bank and hiring out as a tough, butting heads with the White Knights of the Great Plains.

They rode the 24 east past Tasco and Hill City and Stockton, that stretch of road tabletop-straight out to the sky-line. Both looking out at the road that ran along the Solomon

River, low on its banks, the road veering to the south after they passed Cawker City. A truckload of Okies passed them, hands waving as they rolled west. Swerving his wheels, Handy missed a gopher snake sunning out on the hot road, said it was bad luck hitting them. Sonny said Indians figured everything was good or bad luck. Handy saying it was about honoring the four-legged along with the two-legged, something a white man wouldn't understand.

"You know a snake's got no legs, right?"

Handy shook his head and said Sonny was just plain ignorant. The Zephyr passed a road crew, Handy taking the posted detour around the section the crew was cobbling together, the interstate expansion part of Roosevelt's New Deal. A mile farther, drifted sand crossed the lanes like dunes. Handy slowed and wheeled to the shoulder and made it around a felled utility pole without getting stuck, the wires knocked off its cross-members.

A road stand as neglected as the land stood abandoned next to the highway. A line of shelterbelt saplings lined the opposite slope coming off a ridge. Looked like the same green ash Sonny had been planting. He took his makings and rolled a smoke, saying, "The new boss's got every man jack planting government trees and fixing holes in roads."

"And yet the shit keeps happening." Steering with his knees, Handy took the makings and rolled his own, Sonny striking a match off the dash.

A billboard came into view, both men dragging on their smokes. A smiling gent telling them it was cider time, holding up a bottle of the stuff. The sign's upper corner was peeling, the sun and blowing sand had dulled its color. Past the billboard, another windbreak of trees stood a half dozen rows deep.

Handy saying, "Roosevelt's serious about getting his rows of trees planted."

"All the way from Texas to Canada, keeping the loam from blowing off. Same soil Hoover said the farmer can't exhaust. Even got the army boys pitching in digging holes, giving them something to do while they wait to get in the European theater."

Handy shook his head, saying he couldn't figure it.

"Well, sure hope the new boss's got more 'n damned trees up his sleeve."

Handy raised his canteen, taking a warm swallow. "Here's to coming up with new acts to keep us from starving. The whole country set to go bust or to war, and you and me got this fella smiling at us with his nice cider."

A mile down the road, a sign tied to a fence post off the shoulder told them to repent. Peppergrass and shortgrass stuck up in patches past the ditches, scatterings of thistle and scrub. Trucks rolled past, going the other way, loaded with scroungers and loungers, rounders and bounders, all giving a wave, and all their worldly goods tied up on the back. Sonny thinking about Amos and Katey and their kids picking fruit someplace, hoping they didn't end up in one of those Hooverville camps.

"Someday, gonna hand the Winchester back," Sonny said. "The two of us'll laugh about it, go out hunting jackrabbits."

"Soon's you learn to shoot," Handy said.

Passing an old farmhouse of stone, its roof beam sagging and the barn withered. No sign of life or livestock or vehicles, wind witches tumbling on the porch. Sonny nodded off, thinking of his own parcel, been in the family for three generations. Seeing himself handing Henningan the cash, the money they stole from the man's own bank. Remembering how the man wet his pants. Sonny smiling about the money he didn't hide in the barn.

And he dreamed how the rains would come and the farm would be rich in wheat and alfalfa once more. And Clara would be smiling. Sonny letting the years peel back like curtains, liking the way the two of them were, back when he first brought her to the farm, back when Orin was out working the fields.

"How you want to handle it, this loan shark beating on Willis?" Handy interrupted his thoughts.

"Only one way with fellas like that."

Handy nodded.

"How about the cross burners and their damned parade?"

"As it comes, I guess."

"Know there's just two of us, right?" Handy said. "By parade, I'm guessing there's gonna be more 'n two."

A couple of pikers trudged single-file along the opposite shoulder, their bindles across their backs. Both looking straight ahead, one giving a tired wave. Another westbound truck heaped with belongings slowed for them, steam sneaking from its radiator, the pikers getting on its running boards and holding on.

Another sign on a post flew past, telling them to get saved. A line of mud cropper shacks stood near the road, a buried hayrake with just the tops of its iron wheels showing. A tank house at the back of the property. A mile marker called it two hundred and fifty miles to Topeka. Past it, a man with his hat in his hand stood by a rusting Plymouth angled off the shoulder, looking like he was giving it last rites. Handy slowed, and Sonny called out his window, offering a lift. The man, about Sonny's age, walked to the door, saying he wouldn't mind. Looking back at the lifeless

Plymouth, saying, "Nothing much works, but anything you fellas can use, help yourself."

"Not much'd fit a Zephyr," Handy said, looking out the back. "Those tires any good?"

"Fronts are down to the paper, ones in back maybe got some ply left. Guessing a gallon or so of ethyl if you wanna suck it out. Oil in the crankcase is black as molasses, not much good, but you're welcome to any of it."

"Won't say no to ethyl," Handy said, working the shift and backing up.

They got out, and the man stuck out his hand. "Crawford Miller. Obliged for the lift."

They all shook hands. Crawford pitching in and working the bumper jack, Sonny getting some rocks from the ditch and piling them under the Plymouth's rear axle, taking a wrench to the nuts, pulling off the wheels, tossing them in the Zephyr's trunk.

Eyeing the mayor's car, Crawford said, "Curse myself for going Plymouth. Zephyr, huh? Sure a sweet-looking ride. First one I seen. She any good?"

"The one thing old Henry Ford got right," Handy said, taking the jerry can from the back, getting a length of rubber hose, unscrewing the filler cap, shoving in the hose and sucking on the end, getting what he could from the belly of the tank. Careful to pour it in the Zephyr's filler neck, not wanting to spill any down the side.

"Times ain't bit you boys too hard." Crawford looked the car over, smiling. "'Less you stole it."

"Belongs to the mayor of Hoxie," Sonny told him. "Taking it on a test ride."

"For a minute I figured you boys for bank robbers. Them and bankers the only ones got money for this kind of car."

"Well, we sure ain't bankers." Handy and Sonny laughed, Crawford joining in.

They left the Plymouth jacked on its axle and drove off, Crawford sitting in the back, pulling a pack of store-boughts, offering the pack around. Sonny and Handy reaching.

"Funny, first fellas to come driving east, everybody else going west," Crawford said, then asked how far they were going, adding, "Stood there more 'n an hour watching half of Kansas with everything they own piled up and driving the other way, off to some promised land. From the look of it, gonna have the 66 lined with cars all the way to the ocean. Just hope them handbills are true, ones I seen about enough work out there. Seen 'em for pea pickers, some for peaches. Last year was mostly for cotton."

Sonny saying he'd seen the handbills. Talking about the trees he planted and holes he dug for the phone company. "Lucky I got water down my well. Letting me hang on. Sure ain't been the bank helping us."

"Was the bank sent a fella round telling us to get off our land," Crawford said. "Man looked like he'd never been out in the sun. Told him we weren't going no place. Next day, they sent a couple more fellas on a tractor. Can't argue with a tractor. Stood by and watched them two put their blade to the place, the place I built with these hands. Sheriff deputies come and run the family off the next day. Off our own land."

"Where they at now, your family?"

"Sent the wife and kids to live with her sister, Fayetteville down in Arkansas. Kid brother owns a couple roadside joints. One here, one in Florida. Gonna work for him a while." Crawford drummed his fingers on the seat back, rolled down his window and flicked the butt out. "Brother's down at his place in Florida, and my Aunt Cricket's running things up here. Putting me to work sweeping, frying, whatever they got. Place I was heading when the Plymouth quit on me. Paradise Arms, up the road twenty miles or so."

Handy said they'd get him there. Then they talked of the parade in Topeka. How they got hired on by Happy Mustard as security.

"And the city lets it happen, huh, a parade like that?" Crawford shook his head.

"'Less some act of God shuts it down." Handy glanced at Sonny, both grinning.

Crawford guessed it was one of those Kansas jokes born of hard times, like the banker turning the farmer down for a loan on account his land was blowing past the banker's window. Grinning along.

"They come along, try to bust up the show, we'll be there to stop 'em."

"Got to be more than just two of you." Crawford looked from one to the other.

"See how it goes," Handy said. "Sure be fun to mess up them white sheets they like to hide under."

"Pay to see something like that," Crawford said, laughing.

"Yeah, how much?" Handy turned and looked at him.

...TWENTY-EIGHT

The place had a rundown yet clean look about it. The waft coming off the grill drifted out the door, held out its home-cooked promise. The three of them got out of the Zephyr, looking at the heart-shaped marquee that hung crooked over the door, the sun paling it near colorless. Valentine's was one of those corrugated pre-fab affairs evoking the look of an early railroad dining car, topped with a barrel roof.

Crawford Miller had seen these places popping up, only thing he knew about it was the food was cheap, saying, "Wish I could say lunch is on me, you boys giving me a ride and all ..."

Sonny and Handy said that's alright, following him in and looking about the place. A cash register with its side crank anchored one end of the counter, a glass-domed cake stand on the far end, a couple of pies on display. Paneled walls, tiled floor, a row of swivel seats bolted to the floor, a trucker at the far end, his ass spilling over the seat, a swabbie in uniform sitting on the middle stool, a J.P. Seeburg Audiophone angled in the corner. A ceiling fan whirled round slow above the white-and-red checked oilcloths that covered the three tables by the window. Sonny taking the seat next to

Crawford and watching the fan moving the air, knowing Clara would be sure to admire blades like that turning in her kitchen, stirring a breeze. Sonny thinking about the electricity running through wires behind the walls. Something about it running in the walls didn't feel right to him. Maybe something he could get used to in time.

The pass window framed the line cook behind it. A rough-looking mulatto with a boxer's nose and three days of scruff on his chin stood in a grease-spattered apron, taking a couple of patties from the icebox, scooping lard from a tub with his spatula, letting it melt and sizzle on his grill, scraping, then laying on the patties, pressing them down, the fat sizzling. Tossing some sliced onion and mushrooms next to it, moving it around with the spatula.

The waitress might be the cook's woman. Had some shape under her uniform, a name tag calling her Elsie, her black hair tied up in back. Quail-puffing air at the wisp of hair falling to her eyes, she came with her pad.

"How you fellas doing?"

"Doing fine." Rubbing his hands, Crawford sat and ordered up a one-eyed Sam.

Both eyeing the menu board, Sonny and Handy said that sounded pretty good, cheapest thing on the menu, neither sure what it was.

"And coffees all round," Crawford said.

Jotting the order, Elsie puffed at her hair, went and stuck the ticket on a peg. Calling the cook by name, "Order's up, Zep."

Sonny asking Crawford, "What's a one-eyed Sam, anyways?" Watching Zep pull the order off the peg, making out Elsie's scratchings. Flipping the patties on his grill.

Crawford explaining, "You take a slice of bread, see, hollow out the middle, set in it a pan with butter, clap an egg in the hole. Trick's not to bust it. Fry it up nice, and you got yourself a one-eyed Sam."

"Fry an egg, put it on bread, huh?" Handy said.

"Got to be inside, or it's not a one-eyed Sam."

Sonny watched Zep through the pass, the man plating the patties on a waiting bun, setting the plate in the window and slapping a bell, turning to get some eggs.

"Heard a fella say, 'Anyone's been in a Valentine's knows to leave room for pie,'" Crawford told them, looking like he was hoping their pockets were deep enough for pie. "Sure hope it's pumpkin today."

Stepping down the counter, Elsie delivered the burger to the trucker, calling him Curly, coming back with the coffee urn and filling their cups.

Crawford asked about the pie, looked disappointed it was cherry. "Well, put me down for it. How about you, boys?"

"How you say no to pie?" Handy said.

The trucker pushed himself up, a big man going about two-fifty, a good deal of it hanging over his belt. He called to Elsie to plate up a double slice before it was all gone, then shuffled to the J.P. Seeburg Audiophone over in the corner, sticking his nickel on the coin slide, pressing the selector, the tonearm lifting and dropping down. The record crackling, and then Shirley Temple was singing.

The navy recruit sat to Sonny's right, tending his bowl. His swabbie hat next to his plate. Gray dungarees and hobnailed Munson Army Last boots. A short-barreled build, the crewcut making him look prim, trim and ready for his Purple Heart. Thick arms and a neck like a stump. Glancing at Curly by the juke, he said, "'Good Ship Lollipop,' huh? Like, where's your kid, Curly?"

"Damn thing played the wrong one." Thumping a big palm, Curly frowned, declared he was pressing for some Fats

Waller. Curly said he didn't have no kid, calling the swabbie Malcolm, asked if he ever got tired of running that mouth.

Grinning, Malcolm hummed along, looking up from the day's special, saying, "No offense meant, Curly, but it's sure kinda catchy." Digging a spoon at his stew.

Telling them both to behave, Elsie went about fixing a fresh pot of coffee. Malcolm had an eye on her, not the stolen kind Curly had been giving her, doing it like he was daring her to do something about it. Zep the cook built the one-eyed Sams in a line on far side of the pass window, not paying any of them any mind.

"What say you, Elsie, you think it swings?" Malcolm asked.

"You mean the song? Like it well enough, I guess." Going to the register, she cranked the handle, coming around the counter, giving Curly back his nickel, saying, "You want your slice of pie now, hon?"

"Yeah, a double with cream." Casting a dark look at Malcolm, Curly took the nickel and stuck it in the Seeburg, pushing more buttons.

Hearing Zep's bell, Elsie got the plates and set down the one-eyed Sams, asking if they wanted anything else.

"How about a Kist?" Malcolm said, grinning at Sonny next to him, leaning forward, setting his arms on the counter, puckering his lips at her.

"Told you, we ain't got Kist, got Crush or Sun Spot. Same as always."

"Well, Crush me, then." Malcolm said, winking at Sonny. "Along with better music, this joint could do with some Orange Kist." Then he told her, "You know, Els, you kinda remind me of the gal they got on their signs, that Kist company."

"Whoopee for me, huh?" Reaching in the cooler, Elsie pulled a dripping bottle and snapped the cap on the opener, setting it in front of him, saying, "Hope it cools you some."

Laughing, Curly wagged a finger for her to come around the counter, the Fats Waller number coming on.

Smiling, Elsie said, "What the heck." And she crossed the floor. Curly taking her hand in his paw, other hand lightly on her hip, saying, "Pie's a dime, song's a nickel, but the dancing's free." Wheeling her between the stools and tables, clomping his boots to the beat. The man showing he could move his feet.

Having fun with it, Elsie put some back and forth into it, didn't matter her dogs were aching, her apron stained and she hadn't lathered her hair in a week. She cut a rug, her hand in the trucker's, letting him dance her around to Fats doing "Numb Fumbling."

Swiveling his stool, Sonny watched the dancing and thought of Clara, the woman dancing anytime she heard music, something that had always eluded him.

When she broke off, Elsie came back around the counter, puffing at her hair again, slicing up the pie, setting a plate in front of Curly, saying he earned it, then coming along the counter, saying, "How're the Sams, fellas?" Setting down their pie.

"Best bread and egg I ever ate," Handy said.

Elsie asked if anyone needed a java top-up, going for the urn.

Digging into the pie, all three of them washed it down with coffee, catching the swabbie's chatter. Malcolm eyeing Elsie, saying to Curly, "Sure like to shake them peaches."

Curly pointed to Zep behind the pass. "Man looks like he could go ten rounds with Tom Heeney."

"Zep? Oh, he don't care. 'Sides, wasn't you just dancing with her?"

"Dancing's not drooling," Curly said. "I expect you touch them peaches, Mal, you gonna find out." He grinned past a mouthful of pie. "'Sides, the woman'd turn you flat, Zep or no Zep."

Malcolm lifted a hip for his wallet, told Curly to put his money where his mouth was. Slapping a bill on the counter.

"You boys know I'm right here, huh?" Elsie cleared the plates, took the urn off the bottle gas, swung along with the fresh coffee, topping cups.

Sonny put a hand over his, saying, "No, thanks."

"Refills is free, hon," she said, pouring when he moved his hand, asking, "How was the pie?"

Sonny admitting it was good as any he'd ever had. Handy and Crawford nodding around mouthfuls.

Malcolm held out his cup.

Splashing it to the brim, Elsie took his dollar and tucked it in her top, thanking him for the tip. Sliding the urn back on the gas.

Curly laughed at Malcolm, practically choking on the pie.

"Was gonna leave a tip anyhow," Malcolm said.

"Nobody tips at the counter, just at the tables," Curly said.

"How about you go play your Shirley Temple and mind your own." Elsie saying, "You boys start another fuss, you can go eat someplace else."

Tapping Malcolm's shoulder, Sonny said, "Mind me asking, you active or on leave?"

"How you mean?"

"Navy, right?"

"Yeah. Training exercises over in Fairfax," Malcolm said, swiveling to him. "Been some talk about shipping us down to Porterfield, though."

Lost count of how much sugar he'd scooped into his cup, Sonny took a taste. Next song came on the Seeburg was about a Latin from Manhattan.

"Itching for action," Malcolm said. "Yeah, get into that European theater. Any luck we gonna get sent over, help out with the Maginot Line. You hear of it?"

"What part's that?"

"French part," Malcolm said. "Bunch of rifle droppers, the way I heard it."

"Name's Sonny." Offering his hand, he introduced Handy and Crawford.

"Nice to meet you fellas." Saying he was Malcolm. "Buddy at the end, that's Curly."

All of them leaning and nodding hello.

Crawford saying, "Went to sign up, had this navy doctor put one of them things on me, you know?" Tapping his chest, saying, "Next thing, he's putting me down as four-F."

"Four-F, huh?" Malcolm said.

"Some kinda thrombosis he called it," Crawford said.

"That's a bitch." Finishing his double slice of pie, Curly pushed himself up and dug more nickels from his pocket. Separating them from the lint, he headed back to the Audiophone.

"We get the call, you can go try again," Malcolm said to Crawford. "Won't be so choosy once we get in the fray. Meantime, somebody's got to mind the farm, right? Plus, us flyboys got to eat."

"What you flying?" Sonny sipped from his cup.

"Sport trainers for the time. Got barely enough juice to give lift-off. The kinda beaters you fellas use for dusting crops. Me, I got the itch to sit my keister in one of them Wildcats. You ever seen one?"

Curly saying, "Bet the medics got a powder for that itch."

"Tell you this, Wildcat's got enough whiz to kick some Heinie cans, that's for sure. And soon as old Houdini in the White House gets the kahonies to send us over . . ."

"Don't go disrespecting the boss, now." Curly pointed a sausage finger at him. "Fella handed us the New Deal and booted out that damned pro'bition. Said it was good time for a beer."

"Well, I guess he got that part right," Malcolm said.

"Keeps me hauling and putting food on the table." Curly looked out to his truck.

"You got beer in your rig?" Malcolm said.

"Wouldn't say so if I did."

"Well, I give the boss my vote, just sayin' he's sure taking his sweet time. Got troops planting trees from Mexico up to Canada, biding his time." Looking at the others. "No offense, case any you fellas voted the other way."

"We get dragged in, I'm going with the marines," Handy said.

"Marines, huh?" Curly said, looking at him. "Trouble there, take your code red situation. Marines is the first ones in, going up on the beaches, all that. Laying in muck up to here. Holding the fort till the navy shows up. Meantime, you got more sons of bitches named Fritzie running at you, and none of them boys gonna be pointing bratwursts, promise you that."

"To hell with the Fritzies," Curly said, watching the tone-arm lift and scrape on the platter, the strain of Glenn Miller's trombone. "In the Mood" playing from the Audiophone.

Elsie set down their tab. Crawford picking it up. Sonny and Handy chipping in.

"Not much doing till we get shipped to England," Malcolm said. "And all the action's in France."

Curly said again there was a cure for his itch when the door opened.

Hollis Capp walked in, smiling when he saw Sonny and Handy at the counter. A half dozen of his Knighthawks coming in behind him, all of them holding axe handles.

. . . TWENTY-NINE

"We hit the jackpot, boys," Hollis Capp said, stepping up behind Sonny and Handy, both swiveling their stools around. Behind Capp stood Dale Telfer, the Mulligan brothers, Stonewall Bradley and a couple others — none wearing their hoods this time.

"Finding you two in this nigger-looking joint." Hollis looked at Zep behind the pass window. Zep looking up, taking up a cleaver and going about disjointing a hen, never taking his eyes from Hollis.

"Won't have talk like that," Elsie said, pointing to the door, telling them to get out. "Not getting served here."

Hollis grinned, hefting the axe handle. "Didn't exactly come to eat, girlie."

"Be better you run your feet instead of your mouth," Sonny said.

"Way I see it, it's seven to two this time." Hollis slapped the axe handle in his palm, grinning back at Dale Telfer.

"Three," Crawford said, turning around.

Malcolm swiveled on his stool, saying, "Sounds like that action we was just talking about."

"Count me for two." Curly shoved up his two hundred and fifty pounds, glaring at the Mulligans.

"How about we take it outside," Sonny said, looking at Capp. "And we make it just you and me, way I wanted it back at your shop, back when you weren't putting on a show."

Handy looked at the others holding their axe handles. "Any of you stick your beaks in, you're gonna get them bent."

Not waiting on an answer, Sonny moved through Hollis Capp and his Knighthawks, going outside, past Capp's DeSoto, half expecting to take a blow from behind.

Without a word, the Knighthawks filed out the door. A semicircle forming around Sonny and Hollis, the two of them facing off between their trucks. Passing his axe handle to Stonewall, Hollis shoved up his sleeves, looked easy, rolling his neck and shoulders, shaking his arms to loosen up. "So you know, did some bare-knuckling back in Boise."

"There you go, throwing Boise around again." Sonny spat and stripped off his shirt, thinking he could have done without the pie. Not a scrapper by nature, but he was strong from working the farm, and he had the iron will Orin passed down to him. What he didn't do was waste time talking. Stepping in, he snapped a straight right in Hollis's face. The man's eyes watered and his nose bloodied.

Shaking it off, Hollis smiled and nodded. Putting up his hands, he waded in. A feint and follow, he threw a solid hook into Sonny's ribs. Pressing it, he sent an overhand loop, connecting with Sonny's ear. Ducked a wild punch and shoveled a right for Sonny's chin.

Burping up pie and tasting blood, Sonny saw double but kept after him, knowing not to give him room. Taking one on the shoulder, Sonny countered and missed. Hollis coming over Sonny's shoulder again with a short right.

Sonny's teeth cutting into his mouth. Then Hollis caught him with an elbow to the ear. Sonny staggered backward, gaining himself. Thinking he hurt him, Hollis followed, overconfident, and stepped into a second straight right.

Breathing hard, Sonny clubbed with his left, Hollis blocking it, trapping the arm and slamming his ribs with a solid blow. Ignoring the pain, Sonny pressed in and shoved his palm under the man's chin. Then sending an uppercut, he put Hollis on his ass. He didn't shake his hand out, didn't want Hollis to know he'd hurt it.

Hollis pushed himself up, didn't matter he was puffing hard. Throwing a fistful of gravel, he jabbed for Sonny's face, then landed a right that didn't have enough behind it. Trapping the arm, Sonny bulldogged him down, getting fingers round his throat, punching with his hurt right hand.

Hollis Capp not sure where he was, thinking he was the better fighter, squirming to break free. Man, this hillbilly sure could scrap. Shaking his head, he tried to push up, but the ground shifted and he stumbled, landing against one of the trucks, grabbing an axe handle from one of the Mulligans. Gripping it like he was stepping to the plate.

Sonny rushed inside the wind-up, taking some of the blow across his back, clutching Hollis by the throat again and driving his knee into his groin. The axe handle dropped, and Sonny let go and Hollis sunk to his knees, folded up, his mouth dropping open.

Reaching for his shirt, Sonny yanked and stood him up. In spite of the pain in his hand, he threw one for the nose. Somebody grabbing him from behind, pulling him off. Dale Telfer and Stonewall saved Hollis from falling, the Mulligans looking like they might jump in.

"By God, I wish you'd try." Curly ripped the axe handle away from one of them and stepped in front of Sonny.

Handy and Crawford looked ready, and Malcolm pulled a tire iron from his trunk. The Knighthawks backed off, saving it for another time, the Mulligans carrying Hollis for the door.

"Not coming in here." Elsie said, her arms folded, standing in front of the door, Zep behind her with his cleaver.

"The man's hurt," Dale Telfer said.

"Looked to me like he just took his medicine," she said.

Nothing to do but turn around, put Hollis Capp in the passenger side of his DeSoto. Going around to the driver's side, Dale Telfer saying, "Won't forget this place anytime soon. And some night, we'll be back —"

And Zep was past her, raising the cleaver. Telfer slamming the door shut, getting it started, trying to back out of there, as Zep swung the cleaver down, burying it in the hood. Telfer driving off with it like a new hood ornament.

Wanting some of that, Curly swung his axe handle at Stonewall and the Mulligans as they jumped in their Model A. Malcolm swinging the tire iron, bashing out a headlight.

When they were well down the two-lane, Elsie said, "Zep, how about you go dust off a jug." Holding the door, she said to the men, "We been saving it special."

"That come with pie?" Malcolm said, tossing the tire iron back in his trunk, winking at her.

"Rest of the pie's on the house, even for you, Mal," she said.

Curly put his hand out to Sonny. "Like the way you done that, son."

Thanking him, Sonny shook his hand, wincing at the grip, thinking he might dribble some of that whiskey over his bleeding knuckles, make a fine disinfectant.

... THIRTY

Had to be the mayor's Zephyr parked out front of Room 6. Black and sleek. The only one in the state. Insects swirled around the lit sign of the Paradise Arms. Vacancy blinking on and off. Leaving his patrol car next to the phone box, Town Marshal Billy Joe Blake watched the duster blowing off to the north, could hear its howl from there. This damn tornado alley.

Walking along the line of rooms, he didn't see lights on in the office. The place shut down for the night. A single light on behind the curtain of Room 6. Blake guessing the elected head drove out here for a tryst, some place far from the wife and any town eyes. Not why Blake was here, but it had him curious, and having something in his back pocket on Mayor Flint could come in handy. Blake was investigating these Knighthawks. Witnesses putting them at the top of his list of suspects. Blake fixed on solving who robbed the Sheridan Loan and Trust. Sonny Myers's old truck was used, the wreck left on the county road, its axle busted in some pothole, hoods and a bank sack left inside. Maybe it was too tidy, but he'd catch up to the White Knights of the Great Plains, converging for a parade in Topeka this coming weekend.

The porch ran the length of the motel, his heels sounded hollow on the planks, Blake stopped at the window and had a peek, the curtains parted enough. Bracing himself for the sight of Hoxie's elected official in the midst of humping his pasty haunches up and down.

Instead, Sonny Myers sat on the bed. Handy Phibbs paced and muttered. A lamp on the nightstand lit the room. Blake wondering what they were doing here, with the mayor's car. Something not right about these two. He considered whether they might be mixed up in the robbery, but couldn't see them throwing in with the Knighthawks, especially with Phibbs being part Kickapoo.

Blake had been sitting with his feet up on his desk. Could hear that rainmaker Eugene Cobb out on the courthouse lawn, with most of the town waiting on the nut to shoot off his Cobb-busters. Clara Myers worked for him, dressed like she was set for the circus, talking up the crowd, a good-looking woman with not enough sense to know better than to work for a guy like that. The phone rang with an excited Wilbur Flanders on the other end, aflutter about three White Knights outside his place making threats to burn the place to the ground. Same ones who'd come wearing hoods and burned their cross on his yard midweek, shots being fired. Blake told Wilbur to stay put, hurrying out and sticking his gumball on the roof of his patrol car and gunning it over to the K-L-X. No sign of any White Knights when he arrived. Wilbur Flanders ready to swear on a bible they drove off in Sonny Myers's old truck. Around that time, three men in hoods walked into the Sheridan Loan and Trust, cleaning out the cash drawers and vault of fourteen thousand dollars. Locking Henningan in his vault, the man wetting his expensive suit, Vicky the teller and a couple of customers scared half to death. While the rest of the town

181

stood on the courthouse lawn, three armed men making a clean getaway as Eugene Cobb fired mortar rounds at the sky. Vicky getting a look, giving a pretty good description of the getaway car, the front grill and windshield shot out. Billy Joe played back how Sonny Myers drove out to the radio station in his new Moon Roadster, saying the bank just got robbed. Something just not right about it.

Leaning close, trying to listen, Billy Joe looked past the window, Sonny stretched on the bed, saying to Handy, how about they get some sleep. Wide in the shoulders, muscles like cords in his arms, the dirt farmer was hard-boiled and likely desperate enough to rob the bank. Plus he had a hate going for the banker, but then many did. The graybeards at Grainger's contended how Handy Phibbs had been mugging customers for years, the pumps at his Conoco rigged and the ethyl likely watered down.

"Something I can help you with there, Tom?"

The voice had his hand dropping to the pistol butt as he turned. Blake was looking at a stout woman, her creases marking her age, a trash poker in her hands, wielding it like she was Bucky Walters taking to the plate, showing her intent.

Holding up a hand, Blake pointed to the badge on his jacket.

She pointed to herself, said she was Cricket, adding, "I run this place. Now you . . ." Didn't seem to matter about the badge, she kept the trash poker at the ready. "Wanna tell your business, Tom?"

"First off, ma'am, I'm not Tom. I'm the law."

"Well, if you ain't Peepin' Tom . . ." Her hands tightened on the handle. "Then you'd be Gawkin' Gus. Come around with your nose pressed to the window of paying customers."

"You go swinging that at me, you're gonna spend the night in the slam." Billy Joe not sure where the nearest jail was.

Handy pulled back the curtain, looking out at him and grinning, saying through the open window, "Well, Town Marshal Blake, what a surprise."

Looking in at Handy, it dawned on her that she never rented out Room 6. The man in the window was hoboing. Not the first of his ilk to come sneaking in after she closed up, jimmied the lock and helped themselves to a bed.

"Need you to lower that stick, ma'am."

"And I want to know is why you're looking in a room with somebody already in it. Yeah, you got a badge, but you ain't no highway patrol. You got no jurisdiction, and you ain't got no warrant?" Showing she knew something about the law. Looking to Handy in the window, seeing another man in the bed. "What the hell's going on in there?"

"Just trying to get some sleep," Handy said, grabbing at the curtains.

Cricket saying, "You want sleep, you got to pay for it."

"We're friends of Crawford's. Told us it'd be alright."

Cricket looked sour, still not lowering the poker.

"See, the office was dark when we pulled in. And was a duster blowing up, and your nephew guessed you were asleep, not wanting to bother you about it."

"You pay him a dollar rent?"

"Let it slide on account of us sharing the road and turning into pals."

"Being pals don't pay no bills. Top of that, I'm particular who I let in. Let down my guard, next thing we got tramps with their graybacks and pants rabbits. Had one fella tried bringing in livestock. You just try and get something like that out in the wash."

"She saying we could catch something here?" Sonny said, sitting up on the bed, pulling on his pants, stuffing his feet in his shoes.

"Only thing folks catch here's a good night's sleep," Cricket said, still looking set to swing. "It's what they pay for."

"Like me to escort them off, ma'am?" Blake looked like he'd take pleasure in it.

Sonny buttoned up his pants, coming to the door and opening it, no shirt on, the welts showing on his ribs and face, asking, "What the hell you doing way out here, Blake?"

That's when Cricket started swinging.

Dodging the stick, Sonny shrugged into his shirt, getting past her to the Zephyr, Handy going past him and jumping behind the wheel. Town Marshal Blake enjoying the show, watching Handy start it up, peeling out of there and heading east.

Cricket Miller scowled as they drove off, then left Town Marshal Blake standing there and went into Room 6, scouting around for pants rabbits.

"The hell was that?" Handy said, laughing behind the wheel.

"Suspect Crawford's gonna be doing some explaining at breakfast. Far as Blake, I'm wondering about that."

"You mean, why he's tailing us?"

Sonny nodded.

"The hell with him," Handy said. "Right now I'm finding a place to pull over, sleep till morning." When he pulled down a dirt track a few miles down the road, he reached under his seat, pulling the Colt he used in the robbery. "Had enough of folks dropping in on us middle of the night."

. . . THIRTY-ONE

Off the two-lane, tucked back of a dune on some forgotten wagon track, the Zephyr sat partly hidden in a pair of tractor ruts nearly up to its whitewalls, its chrome nose against a stand of buffalo berry. A coyote yipped in the early morning, a shaft of early sun skimmed the terrain, moved up the hood and lit on Sonny's face. He opened an eye, the early warmth feeling good after he'd shivered through the night, the damp getting in his bones. He pushed out the passenger door, the hinges rasping.

Waking from the sound, Handy looked around, remembering where he was, saying, "Fuck me." Then grinned, remembering how they got run off from the Paradise Motel. "That a nail on the end of the stick she was swinging?"

"Was a trash poker."

"Calling us trash."

Both of them standing on the dry ground, stretching away the numbness from sleeping on the bench seat. Sonny rolled a smoke and offered the pouch. Handy rolled one and cupped his hand around the match. Puffing on it, he went looking for kindling, building a small fire. Sonny got the cooking irons from his pack, Clara insisting he bring them in spite of the weight. Pouring water from his canteen, he hung the black pot and brewed the chicory she packed. Busting an old board over his knee, Sonny grimaced through the pain, guessing he had a bruise there too, not remembering getting hit in that spot. Setting in the pieces and watching them catch. Heating the last of his Van Camp's beans, the label turning black. Wondering how Clara was doing, guessing her momma was talking her ear off back at the house. At least she wasn't on her own, seeing the town marshal wasn't dropping in like he said he would. Sonny wondering what the man was up to.

"That old gal sure put up some rhubarb, huh?" Handy said, laughing and stamping out his smoke.

Squatting down, Sonny held his palms to the heat, looking at his swollen knuckles, saying, "Tougher than Hollis Capp. Looked like that nail was rusting."

"Bet she's gonna lay some hell on old Crawford, maybe chase him around with it."

Sonny grinned, adding scrub to the fire, holding his hands out to it, the heat feeling good. "Figured us for hobos, bringing pants rabbits. Guess I sure got the look." Sonny went about pouring brew in the tin, blowing across the top, taking a sip, scorching his lip and passing it. Saying, "Careful, it's hot."

Handy checked for chicory bits floating around. "You think Blake's got something on us?"

"Wondering the same thing."

Handing back the tin, Handy shrugged and stepped from the fire, saying, "Sure a keeper of a morning." Squaring himself before a sagebrush, he unbuttoned his fly, going about his business, looking at the rising sun, saying, "Be a nice country again, if the good Lord'd water her once in a while." Buttoning back up, he stretched, walking past what remained of an old buggy mostly buried in the sand, pulling a couple of wood spokes from its rotting wheel sticking up, coming back and setting them on the flames. "You think them sons of bitches figure they got God on their side?"

"Who we talking about? The krauts?"

"White Knights."

"Bet they believe it."

Going to the driver's side, Handy dug a canteen from his pack, uncapped it and had a sip. Held it out to Sonny.

"Don't want no water."

"You'll like this water." Handy passed it to him, saying, "Just don't hold it near the fire."

Then Handy told how he convinced the mayor his car wasn't running right. "Easy enough, one bullshitter to another. Pride myself at dishing up maladies."

Sonny grinning, taking a drink.

"Told Flint, 'Shh, you hear it, the clattering? Could be pistons, maybe the crank.' Leaned an ear close to the hood, shaking my head, going, 'Hmm. That pinging under the hood, you hear it?' Flint was sure he did, asking me what could be done." Handy slapped his thigh, laughing about it, taking the tin back, having some. "Said, 'Well, could wait and see, Mayor, you don't mind pushing your luck. Of course, could end with you pushing your car.' Told me mebbe best I keep her in the shop a day or two. Told him I'd run her on the highway and blow her out, do some diagnostics. The man seeing the sense in it. Told him I was giving him a price cut. The mayor walking back to the courthouse, wishing he had more constituents like me. Didn't matter I was part Kickapoo."

The sound of engines got them looking toward the two-lane, a caravan trundling into view over the scrub. Jalopies dulled by dust, a Chandler in red dust, a Chalmers in gray dust, the truck towing a makeshift trailer behind them, the wail of a child coming from inside. A squealing coming from under the Chandler's hood.

"You hear it?" Handy said. "Distributor shaft's shot. Fool likely thinks his fan belt's doing it. Be lucky it holds till supper." Handy sipped chicory, feeling bad for the tenant men and women with the kids piled on top, heading for a better life, more likely to end up busted in some Hooverville.

Raised on the Kickapoo reservation, Handy was a runaway at fifteen. Rode some boxcars, stole when he had to. Looking out for himself ever since. Had hoped his split from the bank would turn things around. Had imagined sitting with Nora O'Mara at the pictures, watching Errol and Vivien light up the screen. Dared to wonder what Nora was like under that waitress uniform. Likely take more than a couple of picture shows to find out. She sure was different than the low-minded gals he paid his hard-earned dollars. Thinking how he'd call her up at that diner. "Hey ya, Nora. Know who this is?" Not sure the diner even had a phone.

"How's that?" Sonny looked at him.

"Nothing, was thinking about that car drove by. Won't make it to sundown. Poor bastards."

"Said that already."

"Guess I did." He handed Sonny the tin.

Filling it with the last of the chicory, Sonny drank some, then tossed the grounds at what was left of the cook fire, kicking sand over it, saying, "Come on, still got some miles to put on. You want me to take a turn at the wheel?"

•

Billy Joe Blake had tailed the Zephyr from the Paradise Motel, saw their taillights where they pulled in. Stopping his patrol car a quarter mile back. Sleeping on and off, playing it though his mind: how Sonny Myers and Handy Phibbs could have pulled the Sheridan Loan and Trust robbery. Knowing there was a third man, he had a hard time thinking of them mixed up with the White Knights.

He leaned over the hood, held up his field glasses, adjusting the focus screw, making out the mayor's Zephyr poking from behind a dune. Could see Sonny tending a fire. The two of them having breakfast, rolling smokes and sharing a tin. Blake thinking he sure could use something hot to shake off the early chills.

. . . THIRTY-TWO

The Phillips 66 was abuzz, everything black and orange, the attendant no more than a boy in coveralls with the company patch on the pocket, working the twin pumps, fueling a Chevy at the ethyl pump, with the anti-knock, and a Ford at the 77 pump. Both cars packed with belongings, the Ford with a mattress roped across its roof, hanging halfway down its windshield. A fuming panel truck rolled in from the east, Handy waved the driver ahead of him, waiting with the sun on his cocked arm out the window. Sonny was sleeping, his head tipped to the side window. Handy guessing he was sleeping off the fight.

"Swell car," the boy said as Handy rolled to the pump, then saying he was supposed to ask to see the money first.

"Thanks, kid. Busy place, huh?" Showing him some bills.

"Mostly folks heading through, few locals getting set for Thanksgiving, and truckers now and then," the boy said. "How much you need?"

"Depends how far a stretch to Topeka."

"Well . . ." Squinting an eye, the boy considered. "Just

passed a mile marker if you come in that way. Can't remember exactly."

"Maybe was one before the last dirt storm, nothing there now. Least nothing I saw."

"Yeah, don't surprise me. Not the first one blown off, and that last blow was a doozy alright." The boy grinned, showing a gap waiting on a front tooth to grow, saying, "Fact, my pa spied a tree chasing some mongrel dog."

"That so, huh?" Handy said, "Over in Hoxie, I saw a rattler sneezing sand. You believe it?"

"Yeah, that's a dinger." The boy was grinning. "Let my pa know it."

"Any other fill-ups between here and there?" Handy pointed a thumb east.

"There being Topeka?"

Handy nodded.

And the boy twisted his mouth, thinking before saying, "Don't think so, but three, four gallons be my guess. Ought to get you there."

"Well, let's play her safe, see how we make out on fifty cents." Handy got out, showed him the filler cap on the rear fender. "And make it ethyl, huh."

"Yes, sir." The boy set the pump, unscrewed the cap and shoved the nozzle in the filler hole, watching the numbers spin.

Handy looked at the car coming from the west, stirring dust as it pulled in. Tapping on the passenger window, he said, "Hey, sleepy, we got company."

Opening his eyes, Sonny watched Town Marshal Billy Joe Blake pull around to the far side of the pump.

"A greenback of ethyl and pull the dipstick, will ya, son?" Blake said, getting out, walking to the Zephyr.

"Sure thing." The boy said.

"And check the tires while you're at it." Blake said, putting his foot on the Zephyr's bumper, nodding at Handy, then Sonny.

"Didn't know better, I'd say you was tailing us," Handy said.

"I bet the mayor's wondering about his car. You two out road testing some ailment you dreamed up?"

"Ain't stolen, if that's where you're going."

"If I thought it's stolen, you'd know."

Handy looked in at Sonny and grinned.

The boy racked the pump handle, saying, "You want me checking your oil, mister?"

Handy telling him no thanks, giving him the fifty cents.

"How much you after, officer?" the boy said.

"Already told you, a buck, ethyl, and check the oil, tires too."

"Suppose to ask to see the money first on a tank-up," the boy said.

"Can see I'm a lawman, can't you, boy?"

"Yes, sir, still . . ."

"You can't trust the law, you can't trust nobody." Blake looked at Handy and shook his head.

The boy shrugged, then went about running the hose around the lawman's bumper.

Blake called to him, "And best not scratch the paint."

"Well, you mind turning her around, sir?" the boy said, pulling the hose tight, "Not sure I got the stretch."

"You got plenty, just don't go rubbing against my paint." Blake turned from the boy, looking back at Handy, taking his foot off the bumper, coming close, saying, "Suppose I call the mayor, see what he says?"

"You a mechanic before you took to the law, Marshal?"

"I know it don't take two to road test no car."

Sonny grinned at him, rolled down his window.

"Got something to say, Myers?"

"Yeah, you find who torched my barn?"

"Right now, working on who robbed the bank."

"Well, if you're looking at us, then you got us wrong, Marshal," Handy said. "Just two guys checking for pings and clatters."

Blake tapped his knuckles on the Zephyr's hood, turning to the boy. "Told you to watch my paint. You got any idea of the cost of chrome?"

"No offense, sir, wish you'd just turn her around."

"Jesus Christ," Blake said, going to turn his car around, telling the kid he was interfering with law business.

Handy got in and pulled the handbrake, engaged the transmission to neutral, pulled the choke, adjusted the throttle and turned the key, adjusting the spark advance. Pulling out to the road, he winked and called to the boy, "Watch out for them trees, the ones chasing the dogs."

"And you them rattlers, sir." Setting the nozzle back, the boy waited till the marshal got turned around.

Angry that Handy drove off, Blake asked the boy, "What's wrong, you some kind of goof, can't do a simple job?"

"Tried to explain to you, sir, the hose can't reach, asked you couple times to turn her around."

"I'll give you sassing me." Blake went to grab him.

The rack of a shotgun stopped him. On the covered porch a woman stepped past the Howdy Soda sign, the side-by-side barrels of a Winchester looking at him.

"You see the badge on my shirt, ma'am?" Blake said.

"Yuh, make a fine target," she said, then to the boy, "Scooter, tell the nice officer how far to the next fillin' station."

"Not so sure exactly," the boy said. "But I bet they got the pump on the side you want . . . sir."

Blake got in his car and rolled out, looking at the fuel gauge, hoping he had enough in the tank to make it to the next place, the Zephyr gone from sight ahead of him. Thinking the women in this county sure were hell on wheels.

... THIRTY-THREE

"Chicory be damned, Momma. The kind of money I'm talking about, I ought to be drinking the coffee comes in the red can." Clara pulled the door on the potbelly, looking at the pie's top crust, deciding it needed a few more minutes. Hadn't used this stove for baking in a year; she loved that three-burner Westinghouse. And the churn and the sewing machine. Damn that Henningan, taking it all away from her, served him right getting locked in that vault, proud it was Sonny who did it.

"You got a bit of money, guess I don't see what's all this fuss," Mildred said, guessing she meant the money Sonny left for groceries.

"Just thinking what it's like to come into some, real money, I mean." Clara couldn't help herself. All that money Sonny hid in the barn, saying it all got burned up. She'd been so close to having some.

The minute Sonny and Handy drove off, she got the shovel and started poking around. Kept the old shotgun next to her. Wanting to see for herself. Not sure he was being square with her. Did it till her momma showed up.

Turning from the pot stove, she hopped on one leg, tipping her head, trying to get the water from her ear. Sometimes happened when she dunked her head in the tub, washing her hair with the bar of Lux her momma brought. The hop turned it into a kind of dance, the music on the radio playing a swing number. Memories took her stage center of the Alice Tully Hall back in Kansas City again, a bouquet of white flowers in her hands, Guthrie bowing to her as the audience applauded.

"Landsakes, girl, careful of your bunions."

"Oh, bunions be damned, Momma." Clara doing a ball-heel, a shuffle then a heel-step. Her toes glancing on the boards.

"Second time you blasphemed." Mildred folded her arms. "Taught you better than that."

Making a half turn around the table, Clara hummed along to the song on the radio. Telling herself there were other banks. Sonny could go rob another one. Maybe the National over the state line in McCook, or the Security State in Lawrence. Take his buddy Handy with him, go on a spree. Sonny hadn't said Handy was in it with him, but she guessed he was. And that beat-up one with the mustache from the Happy Mustard show, one showed up the day she washed her undies.

Watching her, Mildred drew a breath, saying, "Best keep checking that pie, girl."

"It's not my first pie, Momma. Just getting good 'n golden on the edge."

"Well, if you just want to hum, dance and dispute everything I say, may as well go have my nap till the pie cools. That is, if it survives."

Ignoring her, Clara went from her toes to her heels, catching a childhood fancy, the one where she saw her momma dead, the image of a steer skull in the desert sand, same hair as Mildred's. Knowing she'd feel bad for thinking that way later. This being Thanksgiving and all.

"Always got your head off woolgathering. Tell you, sometimes it causes me to fret."

"Nothing wrong with a little daydreaming, Momma." Opening the pot stove's door, Clara glanced at the crust. Closing it. "You know, Momma . . . all these years, scratching a living out of dirt, knocking up against hard luck. I'm just getting a sense things could be changing. It's like I can feel it coming."

"Well, high time your luck changed, I suppose." Mildred looked to where the Westinghouse had been. The sewing machine not in its corner either.

"Sure feel prouder than punch to walk into Grainger's and pay what we owe. Just to see the look on Doris Grainger's face. You got no idea."

"Said last week you owed more than you can ever pay. The reason you were heading west, you said."

"Well, that was then."

"So, what's changed?"

"Well, Sonny's digging his holes and planting his trees, guess, faster than ever. Plus we been socking it away pretty good." Clara glanced out the window, looking for any cars on the county road. Troubled about these White Knights coming back. The Cooey loaded hanging over the mantel. First thing she did when Sonny and Handy drove off, she checked it was loaded.

"Well, sure didn't raise my girls to end in no poorhouse, tell you that." Mildred glanced around the walls of the place, thinking it wouldn't be so bad if Sonny would splash on some paint. "I tell you, had my frets about you living out here, middle of squat. But, then, at least your sisters —"

"Oh, Momma, don't start with your Lizzie this and Irenie that. Not this day."

"Just making a point, is all. Now, you just take that boy Thomas, providing for Lizzie. Causes me no worries, that one. Never has. Always got a hand in his pocket for that girl."

"Got more than his hand in her —"

"Just hush that talk."

"Well, it's true, Momma. You know as well as me."

"And Irenie's gonna get herself hitched to her pharmacy beau. Be any day now."

"When's it my turn, Momma?" Clara opened the oven door again, reaching in with her apron, half pulling it out, deciding it could use just one more minute, get real golden.

"Someday, you might be a mother yourself, then you're gonna see."

"Oh, for Pete's sake." Folding her arms, Clara looked out the window again, remembering those times living at the house by Silver Lake, her time in East Drucker feeling like a sentence, all those years dreaming her mother dead, just a steer skull in the desert.

"And don't know what gets in you, denying your own flesh and blood their poke at happiness."

"How about my poke, Momma?"

"Tried to tell you, you get hitched to a dirt farmer and you end up with dirt, nothing to show but a man talking to his livestock. Can't lay that on nobody else. Now, I grant you, Sonny puts his back into it. Just too bad he don't know when it's time to quit and hitch the wagons."

"There you go, running him down." Looking at her weathered hands, Clara held back the tears, looking out the window again. "Thought you were gonna have a nap."

"Know what? We got this wrong. Should be you coming out to see me. What say first thing tomorrow, we drive to civilization?"

"Topeka?"

"'Course Topeka. Have a fitting time, just you and me, maybe go shop and find you something nice to wear. Always cheers me up."

Clara thinking of the money Sonny left her, just enough for groceries, no more. Had dreamed all night about the money that got burned, what it would be like to get one of those player pianos, the kind she could dance to. "You know, maybe that's not a bad idea." Clara thinking they could drop in at the Happy Mustard show. She'd like to ask Sonny again what happened to the bank money.

"Would do me good to see you coming up flush just once, have the good Lord smiling down on all my Sweeney girls."

Tipping her head to get the water from her ear, Clara glanced out the window and saw the truck coming along the county road, stirring dust behind it.

·

"Step's still busted," Eugene Cobb said, getting out of his truck, looking at where the barn had been. No sign of the Moon Roadster. Looked like Sonny Myers was gone, the old-timers hanging around Grainger's got it right — the only reason he dared show his face.

"That what you come to tell me, my step's busted?" Clara waited on the porch, folding her arms.

"How about you ask me in for a cup of coffee or something?"

"You guess or sniff that Sonny's not here?"

"Drove over, just needed to see you." Eugene grinned.

"Driving down a blind alley."

He pointed to the burned cross tipped at the front of the property. "Can tell me what happened to your barn over that cup."

"Sonny told you I was done."

"Rather hear it from you."

"Well, I'm out of coffee."

"Whatever else you're serving's fine."

"Cold shoulder it is."

"Like we never meant nothing. Come on, still got the perfume lamp back of the truck." He smiled.

"That thing scares me."

"Don't believe much scares you, Clara."

"Bet Sonny scares you." She glanced inside, over her shoulder.

"But he ain't here. Heard he rode out of town, him and the halfbreed from the gas station, in the mayor's car."

Must have been the old-timers at Grainger's telling him, always making everybody's business their own. "And maybe we got things patched up."

"And maybe you don't know which way your wind's blowing. Come back and work for me. Can always use a good hand."

"Think to you, one hand's as good as the next, Eugene. So, just go find somebody else." Movement up the road got her looking, another car coming, raising dust along the county road.

Eugene looked relieved that it wasn't Flint's Zephyr, saying, "Expecting somebody else?"

"You bring your cannon?"

Eugene watched as the car slowed down by the mailbox, a man inside looking their way. Then the car drove on.

Creaking pine boards announced Mildred coming to the door, saying, "Who's this?" Watched as the car drove on, then looked back at Eugene and his truck. "This the rainmaker, huh, one who shot that town windmill?"

"Yeah, the fellow I was working for. Eugene, Mildred."

Mildred gave him a curt nod. "Gonna invite him for pie?"

"Oh, shit, the pie!" Clara rushed past her.

"Already took it out." Mildred smiled, holding the door for Eugene, asking him, "How about you, son, you like pie?"

"Who don't like pie."

"Yeah, I can tell." Still smiling, she let him in. "So, I got to know, how you do it?"

"How I make it rain?" Eugene smiled, stepping in and looking around.

"How you get folks to believe you can," Mildred said, smiling at him and shutting the door behind him.

. . . THIRTY-FOUR

In better times, Happy Mustard rivaled the Ringling show, always decent turnouts in the Joplin district. Willis managed to keep the fleet to eighteen trucks. Most of the Fords and Studebakers ailing now, rust and patches showing age and ailment. A converted Bedford ambulance, an International bus and the big Whites that hauled the trailers and served as quarters for the performers. Some pitching tents. The red-and-black lettering had faded to pink and gray, bleached streamers hung and flapped.

Wearing his top hat, Deacon Leathers, the show barker dressed like an undertaker, piped notes and steam from the calliope, calling it his steaming piano, sitting himself in the open lead truck anytime the show rolled down the main drag of a new town.

Back in early November, coming back from the last tour, they got caught in a black roller and had to batten down along the side of the 24, waiting out the blow. The deacon stuffed sacks into the whistles and over the brass keyboard. The drivers rigging chains to drag behind the bumpers to keep static electricity from shorting out the electrical systems. When they were forced to stop, they swaddled the carburetors and stuffed the grills with burlap sacks, the blasting sand finding its way into everything. Respirators were passed out, the men and women covered their faces and waited in the trailers and trucks. Afterwards, they dug the wheels and axles free from the drifts, the women shaking out the sacks. Carburetors were taken apart, soaked in gasoline, and crankcases were drained.

That storm claimed one of the older Fords, the crew having to leave it at the side of the highway. Fifty miles on, the motor blew on the Diamond T, and the transmission on the REO Speedwagon was sounding like it was about to go. Handy Phibbs was called out from Hoxie, doing what he could to get the REO running, towed the Diamond T back to Hoxie and went back with a flatbed a day later, hauling away the Ford.

The show limped into Topeka, waiting on the trucks to be fixed, Handy Phibbs having to scrounge for parts. Willis greasing city palms so they could pitch the camp in City Park. Going through the money he borrowed from Whitey Adler, the loan shark, charging five points a week over the nut, handing over the cash with a smile. No choice about robbing the bank in Hoxie.

Willis was in as soon as Handy told him about it. Sonny insisting they only take two hundred each and hide the rest till things cooled down. The others seeing the sense in it, going along. Spending a little at a time avoided suspicion. They agreed to split it, and each hide all but the two hundred for the time being.

Posters and handbills were printed for the upcoming weekend show and upcoming circle tour, the winter months taking them south through Oklahoma, to Dallas, Houston, San Antonio, El Paso. Then they would wind their way back. Willis paid for new yellow-and-red and pennants, and posters promising the best of shows. Outfits were sewn up and patched, the performers working on new acts while they waited to get on the road and roll down the main drags of these prairie towns, performers smiling and waving to the dwindling crowds.

Used to be Willis Taggart would press a banknote into a palm, and some smiling official granted Happy Mustard prime parkland, back when he had folding money to press. Whitey Adler's money covered a lot of debts, along with the repairs and back salaries. And the two hundred wasn't much, but it would spark the upcoming circle tour to Wichita, Tulsa, Oklahoma City, Amarillo and Springfield, then back.

Maybe that Taggart luck he used to feel was as dried up as the land, but he was savvy and dogged by nature, Willis keeping the show alive by any means. And the money from the bank would put things back to what they were in '27. That time the caravan rolled into Topeka in time for the county fair. Heralded down Jackson by Mayor Rigby himself, the Knights of Pythias Band played on the State House steps, both sides of the streets lined with every man, woman and child from Shawnee County, all cheering and waving. Folks drove from as far as Colorado and Nebraska, cueing and craning their necks, eager to lay their dollars down. Willis Taggart showed them all what they'd never seen before, and the folk were happy to turn their pockets out, and Willis was happy to rake it in — was enough to make a grown man weep.

Black Tuesday hit in '29 and brought on a different kind of weeping for Willis. Wall Street crashed and the lined streets vanished. Topeka's shop windows got soaped one after another as places went bust and emptied, not just in Topeka, but in every colorless town across the wheat belt.

Townsfolk more interested in feeding their families than entertaining them. Hardly anybody came out to see tattooed women and strong men. Those who did likely showed up hoping to see someone worse off than themselves.

A canvas sign now fluttered between the wooden stakes, announcing the Saturday matinee. A tractor wheel leaned against a rusting harrow, half-buried barrel hoops with thistles growing among the spindles. The performers swept and raked, others checking guy lines holding the patchwork tents and lean-tos against the trailers. Half a block east of the insane asylum over by the tracks of the Rock Island line. The Happy Mustard show had been allowed to camp as long as Kiwanis members got free day passes. Willis Taggart making concessions, and doing it with a smile.

Handy and Sonny pulled up in the Zephyr, coming to help with Whitey Adler and his two goons. Willis saw it as the least they could do after they talked him into hiding the bank money. He could have paid Adler off and hired enough miners from Fifty Camp, have them form a skirmish line when the White Knights parade passed by City Park. Their soot-faces and hollow-looking miners' eyes enough to dissuade any thoughts of cross burning and busting up his show. The White Knights of the Great Plains were set on ridding Topeka of Happy Mustard. Grand Wizard Braxton Early proclaimed there wasn't a true and decent Christian among the performers and crew. Braxton called them a nest of niggers, freaks and gypsies.

Top of that, Adler's goons would be back, the reason Willis moved from the house to the Airstream in camp, keeping his Colt in his desk or sliding it under his camp cot. Never shot a man, but Lips or Milky Eye could be the first. Maybe he'd even go after Whitey Adler, teach him some good business. Before hitting the bank, there were a couple times when he'd been drinking and had chewed on sliding the barrel under his own chin.

"How's that?" Sonny said, looking at Willis, the man walking between them, showing them around. The yellow-and-red pennants flapped in a line, performers practiced their acts and worked about the camp. The Kansas River flowed slow and muddy out past a grove of trees. Beyond the trees, they could see the bricks of what looked like a hospital to the northwest.

Willis shook his head, saying, "Know you're getting old, you starting talking to yourself." Nothing happy behind the smile he put on, turning to Sonny, the man looking punched out, almost as many bruises on his face as his own, his knuckles swollen. Handy had told him what happened at the diner. Willis thinking these two would likely be enough to get him out of the jam with Adler, but Morticiah Jones, the show's remaining midget, had been to town and seen dozens of the haters gathering for their parade through the streets.

"Read in the paper, farming's supposed to keep taking a kick in the pants," Willis said to Sonny. "Between the drought and blowing sands."

"Nothing grows when she's dry as a bone," Sonny agreed.

"More fruit in hitting banks," Handy said, keeping his voice down.

"Not much good, you can't spend it," Willis said, giving Handy a sideways glance.

"You gonna keep chewing on that?" Sonny said. "Told you, you start spending it when it quiets down."

"Not that I don't agree, just don't mind fuming about it."

They were quiet a moment, then Sonny saying, "It'll rain soon enough, and things'll turn around."

"Hang on long enough, sure everything'll turn green," Willis said, thinking a different kind of green.

"Serious, why not hit another bank?" Handy said.

"'Cause we're letting things cool."

They stepped alongside a tandem-axle White, the show's name sun-bleached down the side. A bullseye on a plank leaned against its side. A second bullseye on a spinning platform behind it, harness straps for wrists and ankles hanging open.

"This here's Tigor, the Great Throwzinski." Willis said the name like it should mean something. The man's hair straight up and gray like he just had a bad scare. Tigor readied a throwing blank, testing it for balance, a red shock cord wound round its handle. Willis pointed to Tigor's wife, Lupe, standing against the bullseye in a sequined outfit, red and twinkling silver, her arms up in a pose, smiling a hello. "Tigor and Lupe are tops in the impalement arts."

Without a glance, Tigor flicked the blade left-handed, flashing steel thunking center of the bullseye, the red grip shaking inches from Lupe's pretty face. The smile in place, the woman hadn't flinched. "You the extra security, huh?" Tigor said with a Slavic accent, shaking hands with Sonny, then Handy. "Good to know you gents."

"Man's never even nicked himself shaving," Willis said, clapping Tigor on the shoulder.

"Not him I was worried for," Handy said, still looking at Lupe, tipping his cap to her.

Tugging at Handy's sleeve, Willis said, "Ought to see them do the wheel of death." Pointing to the spinning platform opposite the big bullseye. "Or the devil's door, or cutting the straw. Stops your breath every time."

"Why you need us when you got him?" Handy said, looking at the next knife Tigor drew from the sheaf.

Sonny said he'd sure like to catch their act, thinking of the times he'd swung his maul and tried for the eye of a stump, the wood splitting to either side, the way the maul would sink through.

Willis steered them past the White tractor trailer, telling them about a tomahawk tosser he hired on one time, couldn't recall the fellow's handle. "Names don't matter much. Danger's what folks pay to see, waiting on that one in a million times somebody misses. Recall when I worked for Barnum and Bailey, hiring performers for the trapeze. Rare time one missed a rung and dropped in the net, everybody in the joint going oooh, holding their breath. If it hit the papers, the show'd be sold out rest of the week." Willis clamped his cigar in his mouth, careful he didn't split his lip again.

Past the White stood a Ford Flatbed, a Model B with its back end jacked on blocks, tandem wheels off on the one side, a guy in overalls patching the tire. Four trailers with the Taggart show name down the sides formed a box, making a kind of windbreak for the campfire flickering in the middle. A thin line of smoke rose between the cooking irons. Willis walked up to Hagar the strongman. Mid-twenties, a shock of blond hair, big arms and heavy through the chest, his head bigger than it should be on his body, wide nose, ears that stuck out like they belonged on a good listener. He gripped an iron horseshoe in his hands.

"Take Hagar here, man's mighty as all get out, wraps a chain across his back and snaps it," Willis said, puffing his cigar. "Hey, Hagar, you need a hand with that?"

Growling, Hagar clenched his teeth, the veins and cords in his neck sticking up like tree roots. Muscles bulging on his arms, across his back and top of his shoulders. Smiling like he was pleased with himself, he offered the twisted steel to Willis, swiping a wrist across his forehead. "You bend it back, you can keep my pay."

"Just drained all the luck out of it." Willis smiled, handing it back, knowing he hadn't paid any of them in weeks, introducing him to Sonny and Handy.

Grinning his horse teeth, Hagar offered a big paw.

"Ask me, between the one with the knife and him, you got plenty security." Handy said.

"Told you, they got to keep focused on the show." Willis led them away, saying, "Tell you one bent Hagar ain't got, the man believes he's blessed with the pipes for singing."

"He sings too?" Handy said.

"What he calls it," Willis swung an arm around Handy's shoulder, feeling the boniness under the shirt, sinew like rope. "You fellas versed in the tale of Achilles?"

"The fellow with the heel?"

"Mighty as all get out, the same as Hagar. Point is, his singing voice's like that fella's heel. He brings his guitar out and does kumbaya by the fire, you gonna find out."

"There a point?"

"The man's family, and none of us got the heart to tell him. One looking out for the other." Willis relit the cigar, puffing smoke.

"That include us?" Sonny said.

"We get trouble from the White Knights, everybody's gonna jump in. Not gonna leave it to you."

"All for one, huh?" Handy said.

"Something like that," Willis said, then introduced them to the Hovey twins, identical down to the shoes. One of them balancing on what he called a rola bola, a board balanced on a tube. Then they met Orville and Greeny, the show clowns.

"Both grads of Clown College," Willis said, turning from the twins to the company midget. "And then we got Morton here, goes by Mort for short."

"Never get tired of that, huh?" Smiling like he was wincing, Mort said howdy to the new men, looking like he wanted to kick Willis in the balls. Setting jacket potatoes among the coals.

Tattooed head to foot, Thelma Hart tended a pot hanging over the fire, her raven hair pulled back, showing a neck of inked paisley. A stem rose ran up one arm to the shoulder, the stem disappearing under loose denim, coming down her other arm.

Behind her, a trio of women set out folding chairs. Their giraffe necks were ringed in brass, colored scarves wrapped their tied-up hair, sandals on their ebony feet, barely a word of English between them.

"Come all the way from Burma," Willis said, nodding and smiling at them, getting the same back.

"How they get their necks like that?" Handy said, couldn't help staring.

"Kayan women add a ring every year from their awkward years on. It's kind of a status thing where they live."

Willis introduced them to the others around the fire, the show folks busy fixing Thanksgiving supper. Deacon Leathers told them supper would be an hour, told them to come back hungry and meet the rest of the crew.

"The deacon plays a mean calliope," Willis said, leading them from the squared-up trailers, crossing the row of trailers to his Airstream Clipper, the show office and sleeping quarters.

"Guess we ought to get down to it." Willis ushered them inside, sitting behind the cramped desk, leaving them to decide who sat in the only other chair, Handy letting Sonny take it. Filling whiskey glasses, Willis slid a couple across, saying, "Won't kid you boys, any of these shows — traveling, tent, wild west, vaudeville, medicine, freak, circus or carnie, don't matter — all of us are drying up like the land. Give folks something chancy, what they never seen before, or some freak who's landed on harder luck than their own. It just ain't enough anymore. So if you want to do another bank . . ."

Handy saying, "Or how about we take it to the White Knights, kidnap their grand wizard, demand a shitload to get him back."

Willis downed his drink, pouring more. "You know, that's not bad."

Handy looked at Sonny. "Kind of payback for your barn and mule."

"How about the cops?" Sonny said.

"There's no crime in talking. The two hundred takes care of some pressing business, but even with a decent turnout, what we scratch up'll barely get us on the road," Willis said, looking at them, then going on, "Put a bug in an ear over at the *State Record*. Getting them to send a reporter for a story. Gonna make the same call to every newshound and stringer in the county: *Weekly Gazette*, the *Appeal*, the *Reason*. Any man that puts ink on paper. But, in the end, I need more than what we took, a lot more."

"Well, I ain't gonna have to lay under no chassis for a long time." Handy looked sheepish, then over at Sonny.

"Hardly need to stick in any more trees. Got plenty to last me, long as Clara don't find it."

Willis sighed, the three of them quiet a while. Then Willis looked at their glasses and downed his shot and said, "I say you're both drinking like girls."

. . . THIRTY-FIVE

To be strange is to be real. The words had been scratched into the supply trailer's wall, their digs stood parked past the trucks making the square. Standing on the top step, Sonny poked his head in, the trailer smelled faintly of kerosene and like it had been locked up a long time. Paneled walls painted glossy blue, a stack of crockery jugs marked bleach next to crates of soap powder. Spools of electrical cable, boxes of glow lamps, a couple of push brooms and a mop leaning in a corner with some tent poles. Lengths of rawhide hung off hooks, a roll of canvas and cans of paint on a rickety shelf. Most of it had been moved to the round end of the trailer, leaving room for two slim cots to either side of the tiny window.

Bumping his way in, Handy looked at it, saying, "A bit tight, but guess she'll do. I'll take this one." Tossing his pack on the far cot.

They stowed their gear and stood outside smoking till somebody clanged a dinner bell back by the fire, both of them hungry.

Some wore dungarees, some in khakis, a couple sporting newsboy caps. The camp was busy setting out folding chairs, tending the festive supper, a couple of the men gathering wood for the fire. Thelma Hart rolled her sleeves past the tattoos, stirring a blackened pot of stew hanging over the fire, telling Sonny and Handy to make themselves at home. Handy pulled up a folding chair, Sonny sitting on a turned-up crate, both offering to pitch in.

Trading her show outfit for what ladies called a Hooverette, a reversible dress, Tigor's wife, Lupe, wore the red percale side with the ruffed sleeve, coming into the square with a big smile, her mouth painted red. Tending a coffee pot balanced over a grill, getting jacket potatoes from the coals. A three-legged cauldron of corn steamed into the evening sky.

Welcome smells, the men and women exchanging pleasantries, fixing plates. Nobody letting Sonny or Handy pitch in, treating them like guests. Sonny watched them, a contrast to the gravity of the times, not a beaten-down look among them. Not like the folks living back in Hoxie, most of those left wizened.

The giraffe-necked women smiled, fixing plates and sitting together on the folding chairs, plates in their laps. Sonny wondering about them swallowing, trying not to stare.

Lupe turned over a bucket and sat by Handy. Handy offering his chair. The deacon said grace, everyone around the fire, digging into their stew and beans. Accepting plates and tins of canned milk, Handy thanked Thelma. Sonny setting his down and flapping out a folding chair for her, the canvas sewn and patched in places. Sipping from the milk, furrowing a brow. Never had it condensed or from a tin before.

"Armored heifer's what we call it," Thelma said, nodding at the tin. "Only milk we take on the road. Packs up light and doesn't sour."

He took another sip and said it was pretty good.

"And when you get done with Mort's beans, we got some rag soup coming up."

"Rag soup, huh?" Sonny said.

"Spinach and macaroni in a broth, if we're lucky."

Forking a mouthful, Handy said, "Well, the beans sure hit the spot." His eyes falling on her porcelain skin, her dark hair curled and tied back, showing the pattern of ink on her neck and arms, an indigo rose amid paisley. Thorns and leaves wrapped her neck, ending in another rose behind her ear.

"One thing Mort does well," Thelma said, lifting a lid and stirring a pot, "Got a way with the pintos, calls it his secret. You ask me, it's just blackstrap and lard from side-meat, and a handful of salt. Oh, and he slices in wieners. Not much of a secret, but you're right, it's good."

Handy smiled, back to sneaking looks at the tattoos. Thinking she was no man's parlor ornament, comparing her looks to Nora O'Mara's.

"It's real," she said, catching him looking.

"What is?"

"First thing folks ask, if it's real, meaning my ink."

"Sorry, guess I was looking."

"Staring more like it." She smiled, pushing her sleeves up, showing her arms.

"Got to admit," Sonny said, "it's not what a fella from Hoxie sees on a wheat farm."

"Or at a filling station," Handy said.

"Not something you see anyplace," Hagar said, gesturing with his strongman's arm. "When our Thelma steps from that curtain and waves that oriental fan the way she does, you ought to see all them gawkers."

"Wasn't for that, I'd likely forget it's there," she said.

"How long you had it, I mean, if I can ask that?" Handy said.

"I did it to hide the scars." Holding her arm close, showing scar tissue under and around the paisley and flowers. "To a girl of fifteen, burn scars can be a chilling fright. Was asleep on the top floor when the boarding house went up. Couple of lodgers pulled me out. Fireman told me I was lucky and I should get on with the fortune of living. For a while, it was hard to understand that, with nothing but pitying eyes on me. Went like that till I got to the World's Fair. Where I met Betty Broadbent, covered neck to toe in ink. A fine-looking woman, never had a scar in her life. She told me the tattoos made her special. Let the frock off her shoulders, let me see the Madonna and child across her back." Thelma pushed down her sleeves and picked up her plate. "Still write when we get the chance. Last time, she told how she entered this beauty contest. Can't say how she made out, but that Betty sure opened my eyes."

"And not a show from here to Texas won't sign Thelma up." Hagar nodded like he was proud to know her.

"Guess you're doing alright," Handy said, spooning up the last of his beans.

Deacon Leathers stepped over and fished tongs into the cauldron, pulling a dripping cob onto a plate. Setting on an upturned bucket next to Lupe, saying, "So, you two got hired, like show bouncers? Keeping an eye on those damned White Knights?"

"Something like that," Sonny said.

"Was in town picking up supplies," Mort said. "Seen a bunch of them. Robes and hoods, one on horseback, said he'd talk to anybody who ain't Catholic, Jew or Black. Looked over at me and called me a freak of nature. Pointing right at me."

Tossing the nibbled cob under a wheel, Hagar called them sons of bitches, lifting the lid and dipping the tongs into the pot, pulling another cob, dripping water.

"Well, they come around looking for trouble," Mort said. "We won't leave it to you two. You can bet on that." Mort frowned at Hagar, kicking the chewed cob into the embers. Cutting a tobacco plug with a clasp knife, he stuck it in his cheek, folding the knife away.

"Can see what's in the cards," Minnie Plum, the show's fortune teller, said to Sonny, taking tarot cards from a pocket.

"Not the time for a hustle, Minnie," Thelma said. "These fellas are with us."

"I say I was going to charge them?" Letting the cards back in the pocket, Minnie's eyes traveled the circle. "Anyone hear me say that?"

"But you were thinking it," the deacon said, bending over the pot, helping himself to beans, saying, "Who scooped out all the wieners?" Looking at Hagar.

Sonny thanked Minnie, calling her ma'am.

"It's Minnie. Minnie Plum. Ma'am's more prune than plum and makes me feel old."

"Minnie's got the sight, no denying it," Hagar said. "Pegged every president-elect since Taft in '09. Could've warned us on Hoover, maybe, but she's got the sight."

"This one time in Cheyenne," Mort said, sitting cross-legged on the ground, taking a mouthful of beans. "Minnie stepped from her trailer, told me my stars was lining up. Said it was a good time to make hay. So I headed to Frontier Days, rodeo going on just out of town. Spread my bets on the dogging and barebacking. Won a bunch and plunked it on a quarter horse heat. Took a wild stab on a long shot named Aces Wild. And when that nag came in by a nose over the favorite, Lady Harebill, Aces paid five to one. Fletch can vouch. Saw me with my pockets full." Mort asked if Sonny met Fletch yet. "Head's as bald as a stone, man wraps himself head to foot in writhing serpents. Eats fire and charms anything that slithers. You ask him, he'll say a few words, ward away the crawlies from your boots and bedroll." Mort set a log on the fire, sparks dancing skyward. "Did it for me a while back, been sleeping easy ever since."

"Nothing'd crawl up your bedroll, all them beans you eat," Hagar said.

Everybody laughing.

"Well, you boys just be careful," Minnie said, looking at Sonny and Handy.

Sonny said they would.

"When I was with Freaks of Nature," Mort said, "Worked alongside Armless Martha and Zip and Pip and Koo Koo the Bird Girl, had a couple of them haters come up to us at the White Castle, middle of my sausage links. Told us to beat it out of town, chased us out. Well, that show went bust and we split up. Who knows what woulda happened. Only good thing come out of it, I got to work alongside Little Angelo. You hear of him?"

"Can't say so," Sonny said.

"Well, Angelo went on to play in a Cecil B. DeMille picture. Said if things didn't work out with the pictures, he'd turn to lawyering."

"Fella'd fall short when the judge says all rise," Hagar said, laughing and sputtering corn kernels, nodding to Amaziah the magician coming in between the trailers, getting a chair.

"What's that got to do with anything?" Minnie said.

"All foolishness aside," Amaziah said, nodding hello to Sonny and Handy, "you fellas watch your backs, and if Willis is paying you, take your cash up front."

Thelma busied herself with the coffee pot, passing steaming tins of it around. The deacon went to fetch a jug to go with it. Hagar going to get his guitar.

"The deacon with the Baptists?" Sonny asked. Thelma gathering the tins, Minnie boiling a pot of water for the wash-up.

"Not sure which way he's affiliated," Thelma said. "The deacon just wandered in after that Black Sunday. Kind of guess he lost his way, same as lots of folks. Why, you want him to say some words or something?"

"Hoping it don't come to that," Sonny said.

THIRTY-SIX

Thelma raised the lantern, casting its yellow glow, the gas hissing. Handy snagged his shoe on a tree root, nearly spilled the bottle. The shoe spitting a couple of the shoe nails he'd just pounded in, the toe flapping again. Bumping into her saved him from tripping.

"Guess you had enough to drink," she said.

"Ain't me, it's my shoe." Lifting a foot and showing the flapping sole.

"Ought to get yourself a nice pair like I got," Sonny said, grinning, reaching the bottle from him and taking a pull.

The two of them grinning now.

Thelma shone the light over to the supply van, the old Trotwood with a door and small window. "Well, you need anything else, me and Minnie are right over here." She pointed to her own trailer, guessing from the seesaw sound drifting from the open window Minnie had turned in early. A motorcycle leaned on its kick, a big fender over the rear wheel, the lantern light showing on its red paint.

"That Minnie's?" Handy said, sipping from the bottle.

"Aren't you the funny one." Thelma smiled, the tattoos looking like bruises in the pale light. "Pell-mell and reckless if you ask Minnie. Figures if you can't ride it side saddle, it's no place for a lady. Guess I never figured myself that way."

"So it's yours. Must be something, riding it, I mean," Handy said, looking over the bike.

"Indian Motoplane, good old American iron." Thelma walked by it and slapped the leather saddle. "Kind of like flying on two wheels." Taking the bottle, tipping it and handing it back, saying, "Don't know how you two're gonna keep lookout?"

"Handy starts seeing double, he just sleeps with one eye open," Sonny said.

Turning down the wick on the oil lamp, she wished them a good night and went up the steps, shutting the door behind her.

Sonny went in their trailer and found a couple of blankets next to the brooms. Going to the door, he shook out the mouse droppings. Most of the lights of the camp were blown out, the few voices drifting over from the fire giving way to the chirp of crickets and distant frogs.

Lying on the slumping cot, cupping him like a hammock with just enough room to roll on his side, its brace sticking in his back, Sonny wrapped the blanket around him. Ignoring the musty smell, he fell asleep, dreaming of rain falling and getting into the skin of the earth, rousing the clay and soil and bedrock from its ten-year sleep. Dreaming he was back home with Clara. Watching her dance in the yard as the rain fell. Fat, cold drops landing on her skin, soaking her hair and her shirt. She tipped her head to the heavens and laughed.

Sitting on his cot, hearing Sonny sawing logs, Handy drained the bottle. Leaned on the wall, he drifted to sleep sitting up. Not sure how long he slept, waking with his neck stiff and thinking he heard something outside, trying to decide if it was inside his own dream or if it was real. Could be mice scuffling around. Or better yet, maybe it was Thelma, coming to get him. Something about that woman. Handy blaming the booze for thinking like that.

Sitting up, rubbing his stiff neck, he took his makings from his shirt, looked over at Sonny sleeping on the cot by the door. Going out, he stood and rolled one, looking across to Thelma's trailer, the Indian motorcycle out front. Wondering if she was asleep.

•

Out past the camp, the top of the State House showed in the distance, the bridge over the muddy Kansas showed through the trees. Hollis Capp watched the midget called Mort, sitting against the wagon wheel asleep, just barely visible from there, his head nodding down to his chest. Guessing he was the lone sentry, Hollis moved to the edge of the encampment, low and quick, keeping to the shadows, going past the calliope, his cap tugged down. He gripped the gunny sack and went along the trailers.

A bank of cloud drifted past the half moon, the light showing the Zephyr by the supply van. He saw the glow of a man's smoke. Hollis waiting till the man went back in the trailer, giving it five minutes more. Then at the driver's side, he looked in, waited some more, hearing crickets, and somebody's snores coming from the trailer across the way, a motorcycle out front. Taking his time opening the car door, he lay across the seat, sticking his head under the steering column, taking his screwdriver and pulling the ignition switch. Risking it, he put the screwdriver between his teeth and struck a match, looking for the wire that cranked the motor, then he reached in the sack, taking the five-pound device and shoving it up under the column, wedging it in and twisting the wires together.

Sliding off the seat, Hollis stayed in a crouch, feeling the pain from the beating he took from Sonny Myers, guessing this evened the score. Easing the door shut, he started to move back the way he came.

"Something I can help you with?" A woman's voice. She stepped from behind the motorbike out front of the opposite trailer.

Keeping the cap down, he turned enough to catch the tattoos running up the woman's arms, up her neck.

"Asked you —"

His arm was already swinging, the fist catching her flush, putting her down. Leaning in, he rabbit punched her, making sure. Dragging her into the shadow of the Indian motorcycle, he told her, though she'd gone limp, "Want to talk like that, you better get a badge pinned to your tit." Looking up at the trailer window, hearing the steady snores from inside, he disappeared past the tractor wheel, the old harrow and the sleeping sentry, heading out of the encampment and back along the river.

. . . THIRTY-SEVEN

A man on the side had done her no good. Not a bit. Neither had the one in her head. It was Sonny who she couldn't get out of her mind. The way he told her the money was gone, all burned up. Clara not sure she believed him, guessing he had reason not to trust her. Then wondering if Sonny would do it again, rob another bank. Maybe with her wheedling a little.

Standing in the kitchen, she switched on the radio, tuning in the K-L-X. Keeping it low in case Momma was still sleeping behind that Pendleton blanket they strung on clothespins, the curtain her mother insisted on, spanning the parlor. "Steel Guitar Rag," with Bob Wills going *ah hah*. It got her swaying, dancing back the years, capering to that time before these damned dusters and drought, her feet featherlight on the boards. Feeling those castles in the air, she closed her eyes, a smile turning her lips. Clara letting go and whirling from the farmhouse planks to center stage of the Grand Theatre. The spotlights and fiddles of yesterday sweeping her along. After Bob Wills was done, a tune from *Gold Diggers* came on.

"Oh, baby what I couldn't do," Clara sang softly along, "with plenty of money and you . . ."

"You're in a rare mood," Mildred said, coming into the kitchen, cinching her robe.

"Fine enough, I guess." Clara caught herself and turned the radio down. "How about you, Momma, you sleep well?"

"Well enough. Dancing before breakfast, huh?"

"And singing too. Do it sometimes, gives me a lift."

"Thought you were done with all that."

Clara rolled her eyes. "You mean, you wish I was."

"That fellow yesterday, with his name on the truck . . ."

"Eugene Cobb. Told you, wants me to come back working for him."

"Rainmaking, well, I should say not."

"That'd be best, Momma, if you say not."

"No need for your sniping. Just hard to believe, the man drove all this way to talk business . . . and with that way he was looking."

"What look?"

"The devil-may-care look, no mistaking it."

"Oh, Momma, the things crawling round behind your eyes. Mayor hired him for another week, and he wants me back in uniform, is all. Talking up the folks while he loads up his Cobb-busters. Focuses on pounding the sky."

"Mattress pounding, more like it."

"Momma!"

"I may be getting on, but I know the look. And that man wants his ashes hauled, make no mistake." Mildred plunked herself into her chair. "Now, how about you fix your momma some coffee, and put some more beans in it this time."

. . . THIRTY-EIGHT

The whiff of side meat and coffee drifted from the cooking fire. Thelma Hart and Minnie Plum fixing breakfast. Hoping the coffee would give him a jump from the sleepless night, Sonny sipped it, black and hot, then took the axe out by the wagon wheel, turning up a log and swinging the blade for that eye, splitting it clean, putting up the next one, taking a breath and aiming for that spot and swinging down, thinking how Tigor threw his blades at his smiling wife. The Great Throwzinski did it as easy as tying his shoes. The woman playing with the dark angle, doing it in tights and with a smile on her lips. Sonny betting the woman didn't sleep around on a man like that.

He set the armload by the fire and looked at Thelma, seeing the mouse at her eye. "Happened to you?"

"Walked into the door." Too shamefaced to tell what happened, getting sucker punched like that, she went about stirring eggs, lifting the pan from the fire, telling him Minnie had biscuit pone coming up.

"Sure could eat." Sonny cupped his fingers around the tin, the heat feeling good against the morning chill. Sinking into a folding chair, letting the heat from the flames do the soles of his feet some good. Looking at Thelma, wondering what really happened.

Laying a split of wood on the fire, she got another pan spitting, layering in the pork belly. "Got porridge in the small pot, you want to start on that?"

"That like mush?"

"Some call it gruel. According to my grampa, it was convict chow. Had a bowl every morning for ninety years. His secret to a long life, long as it's thick enough to hang wallpaper, way he put it."

Minnie dropped lard from a tin and let it sizzle around the pan. Saying to Thelma, "Don't know why you care, riding round on that death trap on two wheels." She glanced at Thelma's eye, not saying anything.

Sonny accepted a bowl of the porridge, Thelma passing him a spoon.

Hagar and Mort walked between the trucks, dragging up folding chairs, sitting either side of him. Mort asking about her eye.

"Goddamn mind your own, Mort." Snapping, she looked at Hagar. "You two want porridge, or not?"

"That side meat I'm smelling?" Hagar said, showing the whites of his hand.

"Just getting it nice and crisp," Minnie said, scooping boiled eggs from a pot, setting them on a plate and passing it, rolling her eyes. "Don't mind her, she walked into a door."

Busy spooning cornmeal dough, Thelma scowled, pinched on salt and made the biscuits.

Deacon Leathers, the Hovey twins and Tigor filed into the square, getting themselves seated. Handy coming behind them, saying he sure felt like hell this morning.

"Happens when you drink corn 'stead of eating it." Mort told him. "Got to find that even footing."

"You boys set for the show?" the deacon asked, giving Handy a doubtful glance.

"Set as I'm gonna be," Handy said.

Not looking at them, Thelma passed out steaming tins, saying there were eggs, biscuits and side meat coming in a minute.

Handy saying he sure could use it. Then seeing Thelma's eye, asking about it.

•

Mort set the phonograph arm on the rest and shut off the platter, next to the small dancing stage set up for the giraffe necks. Looking at Willis tip up the bottle, the man drinking before noon. Sonny and Handy coming along.

Mort saying, "Was maybe a couple dozen of 'em, over by Washburn College. White Knights of the Great Plains. Don't know what's so great, going around in bedsheets, looking like the village bigots, hating anybody's different. Anyway, one doing the talking, calling himself the kleagle, said they got lots more coming from all over, joining this so-called parade. Going to end up in City Park Saturday for an open-air meeting on account that auditorium on Quincy ain't built yet."

"Except we're in City Park," Willis said.

"That's what I called to him. And the kleagle looks at me, said they're gonna rewrite history, and do it with lightning."

"What the hell's that mean, with lightning?" Willis drank more, offering the bottle.

"Wants to regain their foothold in Kansas." Mort taking it and tipping it. "Went on about reviving their heyday. Getting folks stirred up. Don't know why Kansas, maybe 'cause it's got a K in it. Talked about purifying, then the kleagle starts pointing at me, saying I'm what's wrong with this country. No place for freaks and how this show's a cesspool of Blacks, freaks and white trash. What happens when you mix your cow with a pig. Some of the folks started nodding along, a few walking away. Then the whole bunch start singing 'Onward, Christian Soldiers.' I was getting some ugly looks, nobody needing to tell me it was time to go."

"Can't believe the City handed them a permit," Willis said. "Money gets passed from a hating hand to a greedy one. City council's like a bed of snakes. You ask about it, and they call it a free country."

"Free to flog and hang who they want," Handy said, passing Sonny the bottle.

"We could shut down till it blows by," Mort said.

"We're going to be open," Willis said, taking the bottle back, just a sip left in it. He started for his Airstream, sure he had another one in his pack. "We'll take care of it, right?"

Handy and Sonny followed, Handy saying to Sonny, "Fifty against you and me, you see something wrong with them odds?"

... THIRTY-NINE

Making sure Sonny and Handy weren't around, Mort stepped to the evening fire, set his lantern down and pumped it, turning the lamp up, a rolled-up notepad in his hand and an idea in his head. Talking to the performers around the fire.

An uneasiness had rested on the camp all day. They opened without a hitch, not many turning out for the Friday show, word getting around how the White Knights of the Great Plains were coming to bust it up. The Hovey twins packed up that morning and walked off, the Burmese women huddling together on the far side of the fire, looking scared.

Thelma fed split wood to the flames, shifted the coffee pot at the edge of the embers. Fearing mutiny, Willis came by just before dark, said he scrounged what he could, doling out half the payroll for the week, paying it out of the bank loot he had stashed behind the Grant Wood painting back at the house. Had to get some to Whitey Adler later that night. Sonny and Handy didn't need to know about taking the money, but he needed them to come along.

The consensus among the performers was half pay was better than no pay, and there was whiskey instead of canned milk tonight. Hagar sipped from a tin, straining the canvas of his folding chair, turning the peg for the low E string on the battered guitar, getting it tuned. More a chord man than a picker, he strummed and sang a verse of "Down by the Riverside."

Stepping to the fire, Mort stopped Hagar between refrains. "Before you get to kumbayaing, listen up, folks, think I got something." Flapping the notepad open.

"Got what?" Minnie Plum said.

"I'm taking bets." Getting their attention. "On how much time we got before them sons of bitches come and close us down." Mort dug in a pocket for a stubby pencil.

"Can't be serious?" Minnie said.

"Already came, likely one of them hit you. And don't go telling us you walked into something," he said, looking at Thelma. "Maybe Sonny and Handy can handle the loan sharks, but no mistaking, even with all us taking a stand, we're no match for that swarm with their burning crosses, making folks disappear or hanging them from trees."

"And you want to make sport of it?" Thelma said.

"Sure, lighten things up. One who picks the time closest takes the pot."

"The hell's wrong with you, Mort, coming up with something like that?" Minnie said.

"Making the best of things," Mort said. "At least one of us gets enough kick for a bus ticket, get the hell out of here."

"Got to admit, that's low, even for you." Hagar strummed a chord, grinning, then setting the guitar down. "How much?"

"Much what?"

"What kinda action we talking?"

"Simple, we pick the day and time, say from right now," Mort said, giving Thelma a sore look. Then to the others, "One who gets closest takes the pot. Two land on the same time, we call it a split. Everybody can play, all except Minnie."

"Why the hell not me?" Minnie said.

"You got second sight and sixth sense and likely already know. Wouldn't be square, would it?" Mort said, looking at the faces in the firelight. "And course, anybody so much as seen talking to her forfeits."

"You ask me, it's dirty wages," Minnie said.

"No offense, I'm not asking you. Like I said, you're out."

"How big a bet we talking?" Fletch came to the fire, Mort having to re-explain it. "A buck a bet. Bet as much as you want, a buck for each time." Mort looked around at the faces, readying the stub of pencil. "Who goes first?"

Reaching in a pocket, Fletch said, "Put me down for a deuce." Counting out his money. "Say they either come tonight, or early tomorrow."

"Need the exact time, how it works."

Fletch thinking, picking eleven and eight in the morning, asking who keeps the bets.

Ignoring him, Mort tucked the bills away, scribbling the times on the pad. "How about you, Hagar, just gonna sit there blocking the heat?"

"Tomorrow morning." Picking nine, the big man rose from the chair, dug in a pocket and counted a dollar in change, handing it over.

Mort scribbled on the pad, looking around at the faces. "How about you?" Looking at Thelma.

"You run this by Willis?" she said.

"Nope, he's out of it too. Too close to it. And Sonny and Handy, not sure about them either."

Tigor and Lupe leaned their heads together, talking amongst themselves. Tigor reaching in a pocket for the pay Willis handed him, putting up five dollars.

Deacon Leathers looked at his money, peeling off some bills. Mort jotting dates and times in his notebook, thinking how much of a cut he'd take for setting it up.

Thelma and Minnie headed for their trailer, Minnie calling back to them, "Sometimes I just can't believe you people."

The sound of a car door shutting got the two women looking past the trailers, seeing Willis backing up his Nash, Sonny getting in next to him and Handy climbing in back, carrying something long in his hands. They pulled from the lot and drove off, heading for the bridge.

"Think they're bailing out?" Minnie Plum said.

"'Course I don't," Thelma said.

Both pretending they weren't thinking the same thing: the three of them were running out, leaving the rest of the crew to face the White Knights.

... FORTY

The moon tucked behind the cloud bank, the landscape looking ink black. No matter how much he licked, Willis's lips felt dry. He made a three-point turn on the dirt track so he'd be facing the way Whitey Adler would be coming. Switching off the engine, he watched past Handy out the back window of his Nash, felt the sweat rolling down his arms, inside the suit. Sonny sat low on the bench seat, leaning on his door and looking relaxed. Handy stretched across the back seat and tipped his cap low, the two axe handles on the floor. Said to let him know when they showed up.

An owl screeched somewhere on the back road. Willis had the Nash parked on the same spot by the muddy Kansas. Whitey Adler had told him to come alone, same as last time. Only this time he told Willis to bring the rest of his money.

"A country with nobody living in it ain't much use," Willis said, looking out the windshield. No lights showing from any nearby farms. The yelp of a coyote was answered by another farther to the north. Willis twisting the radio knob, the station playing a song by Jimmie Rodgers, the singing brakeman. Willis hoping the tune would calm him, his foot tapping. It took a couple more songs till he saw the

233

pale light past the rise to the east, the winding road they'd come in on.

"Here we go," he said.

Sonny opened his eyes, sat up and pushed open his door and got out, Handy doing the same, handing Sonny an axe handle, the two of them moving away from the Nash in opposite directions, disappearing into the dark.

Headlight beams topped the rise, Whitey Adler's Packard pulled up, the two cars facing each other, fifty feet between them, headlights to headlights. Willis feeling trapped, with none of the money he owed Adler. Sonny assuring he wouldn't need it. The Packard's headlights stayed on him, blinding him. The driver's door opened, and Lips got out. Milky Eye getting out the passenger side.

Sucking a lungful of air, Willis pushed his door open. Taking a step toward the idling Packard. Unable to see much past the silhouettes of the two men. Lips grinned at him, same fedora he wore the night they came and beat the hell out of him in his front hall, repeating it Tuesday night in this very spot. If he had to pull the pistol at his back, the first round was going through those grinning teeth. Not a shot he was likely to miss from this close, even with the shaking hand, the snub-nose tucked at his spine.

The rear window rolled down, and a hand reached out, palm up. Boney and old. Whitey Adler looked at him, eyes from a tomb. "Let's see my money."

Willis just stood looking at him.

"Okay, hurt this bum," Whitey Adler said and started to roll up the window. "Nobody gonna hear you scream, asshole, but go for it anyway."

His goons moved to grab Willis, Sonny and Handy rushing from either side. Lips and Milky Eye caught as the axe handles rained down.

Seeing the big men fall, Willis took out his pistol, went and tapped on the rear glass, waiting for it to roll down. Taking hold of Adler's shirt, he pulled him halfway out, pressing the pistol against the old man's cheek, saying, "You see this? Huh, you see it?" Adler not answering, Willis tucked the pistol back in his belt and took hold of one of the old man's hands and squeezed and twisted with both of his as hard as he could, making that face that Hagar made when he bent the horseshoe.

Whitey Adler screamed.

"Like you said, old man, nobody gonna hear it way out here." He let go, the scream turned to a moan, and he said, "Rest of that debt . . . we forget it, what say?"

Willis waited for a nod, then walked to where Lips lay face down and kicked his foot into the V of the man's crotch. The hollow eyes jumped and rolled like a Vegas slot machine. "Son of a bitch." He walked back to the Nash and got in. Feeling better as he started it up, waiting till Sonny and Handy got in. Shifting, he swung off the track and pulled around the Packard.

Raising his head from the dirt, Lips watched the tail-lights fade through the rising dust, disappearing over the crest. Then he was crawling to the Packard.

. . . FORTY-ONE

The Top City General Store had more aisles than Grainger's back in Hoxie. And the shelves were stocked up like the land of plenty. Tins of Hormel's and Heinz and Libby's, boxes of Persil washing powder and Chipso soap flakes, bushels of apples and pears, sacks of potatoes and onions. Fresh loaves. A Coca-Cola icebox with the opener on the side. Indian blankets stacked on a barrel stamped pickles, shelves of denim, flannel and buckskin. A rack of hats, poor-boys and porkpies. Another one with hanging leather belts. The rubbed-up counter lined with glass-stoppered jars of hard candy, licorice and cinnamon sticks. Tootsie Roll Pops, Krackel bars and Red Hots. A glass case displaying baked goods next to a cash register of brass with ivory buttons. An arrow pointed to the shoe shop in back, fashions from Paris and London. Everything folks could want.

The clerk pointed to the phone box, telling Sonny the call was six bucks a minute, Sonny asking if he was kidding. The clerk telling him nobody was kidding these days, and nobody was bending his arm either, saying the phone company set the rate. "Want to call somebody a crook, call them, complain about it."

"I call them, guess that costs six bucks a minute too, huh?" Sonny laid six bucks on the counter, telling the man he ought to relax, then going to the phone box in back, making good on his promise to Clara, feeling stung about the six bucks, but wanting to hear her voice.

Readying his stopwatch, the clerk followed him and put the receiver to his ear, told the hello girl the name of the town and the switching number Sonny had written down, then he waited through a round of clicks and buzzes. Somebody picking up at Grainger's. Handing Sonny the receiver, the clerk thumbed the stopwatch. Getting a look from Sonny like he might jam the Bakelite receiver up the man's backside.

Hearing her hello through the copper wires, Sonny felt a stir in his chest, her voice coming from all those miles away. "Hey, Clara, that you?"

"Hey ya, Sonny."

"Being told we only got a minute —"

"Yeah, alright."

"You alone?"

"Kind of question is that?"

"Mean is she there, your momma?"

"Momma's here, uh huh. I'll say hi for you."

"Everything alright?"

"Everything's fine. How about you?"

"Fine, look, something you should know . . ." Sonny glanced at the clerk, see if he was listening in. Saying, "About the barn burning, what I told you about the money."

"About it getting burned."

"Yeah, only it didn't."

"You lying sack of —"

"I hid it, it's safe."

She paused, then saying, "So, you gonna tell me where?"

"Not on the phone."

"Oh Sonny, we always got to have trust issues?"

"It's the phone I don't trust."

"How about a hint?"

"It'll keep till I get back."

"Jesus, show me where to spit," she snapped, then calmed and said, "According to the paper, Henningan claims twenty grand got took."

"You believe that crook?"

"Don't know who to believe . . ."

"Just wanted you to know." Sonny turned, the clerk waving that his time was almost up. "Be back soon in a couple days."

She started to say something, but he was already hanging up, realizing it as he put the receiver back. Walking down the aisle, he took a soda pop from the cooler, using the opener on the side, snapping off the cap.

The clerk looked at his watch, saying Sonny went over the minute. "Store policy's I got to charge a dollar extra. And be a nickel for the soda pop."

"Take off for you eavesdropping, I call it square." Flipping a nickel on the counter, Sonny walked out, heading for the Nash, Willis letting him take it after they got back so he could go make his call.

Just his luck. Hollis Capp pulled his DeSoto behind the Nash, the Airflow blocking Sonny from getting out. Dale Telfer sat on the DeSoto's passenger side, the Mulligan brothers in the back.

"Well, look who's having a soda," Hollis said, starting to get out.

Sonny wasn't sure he could get to the axe handles still on the back floor — Orin's knife was in his pocket, but it wasn't much — aiming to get in a few good licks with his fists before they stomped him into a black hole.

Another car rolled up, big star painted on the door. "Something I should know about?" Town Marshal Billy Joe Blake said out his open window.

"Just shooting the breeze, Marshal," Hollis Capp said, smiling. "Nothing wrong with that, huh?"

"Not if that's all you're shooting."

"No offense, Marshal, but you got jurisdiction here?" Hollis asked.

"A badge don't know no bounds, son." Billy Joe got out and walked around, taking a pack of Lucky Strikes from his pocket, taking his time, sticking one in his mouth. "Want to know where you boys were when it happened?"

"What's that, Marshal?" Hollis asked him.

"When the bank got robbed." Billy Joe stepped up, leaning in the window, looking at each of them. "One in Hoxie?"

"Yeah, one in Hoxie." He blew smoke at Hollis, took out a small notebook and nodded at him. "Start with you."

Sonny waited, having his soda, leaning against the Nash, enjoyed the show, each of them coming up with an alibi. Billy Joe Blake collecting his information. Hollis making a finger gun at Sonny as they drove off.

"Looks like I saved you some more bruises, Myers," Billy Joe said.

Sonny shrugged. "Except those mutts fight like girls. Nothing like that one at the motel with her trash stick."

"Yeah, she was something." Billy Joe laughed, then said, "Just talking off the record here, but it was either you or them, can't quite figure it out yet."

"You asking, or just passing the time? 'Cause it's one thing to say it, but another to prove it, huh?"

"Yeah, needs a little more police work, but I'm leaning to you and your grease-monkey buddy. Too convenient, I get a call from your buddy out at the K-L-X Radio same time the bank gets hit, two men in hoods like the White Knights wear, locked Henningan in his vault and made off, left the truck you called in stolen out on the county road, empty bank sack and hoods inside. Leaving clues for me to sniff."

"Really see yourself as a lawman, huh?" Sonny looked at him.

"Guess you're gonna find out." Billy Joe slapped the pop bottle away. "You know, Sonny, can see you're in no shape, but much as it'd hurt my hand, wouldn't mind taking a swing at you myself sometime."

"Guess that'd be off the record too, huh?" Sonny smiled, seeing the highway patrol drive up and swing into the lot next to the town marshal's car.

"Your lucky day," Billy Joe said.

The one driving cranked down his window, seeing the marshal star pinned on Billy Joe's hat, saying, "Got a call, somebody's causing trouble."

"Got it under control," Blake said.

The driver got out, saying he was Martin Fisher, corporal with the highway patrol. Coming over, he stuck out his hand. "You come to help with the parade, huh?" Guessing why Blake was there.

Telling him he was investigating a bank robbery, Billy Joe shook the man's hand, the younger officer getting out and coming over, standing off to the side.

Sonny picked up the soda pop, still had some in it. Getting grit in his mouth when he sipped. It hurt when he spit, the three others looking like they might arrest him. These good old boys with nothing better to do.

•

Driving back into the encampment, he nodded to Mort playing sentry by the harrow and wagon wheel. Sitting on the calliope, his feet swinging, not touching the ground. Willis putting him on duty on account Mort was the most sober back around the fire. Handy, Hagar, Tigor and the deacon tipping the jug and singing songs. Sonny could hear them from where he parked Willis's Nash behind the Zephyr, going to the supply trailer.

Getting out of his clothes, Sonny laid on the cot, every part of him still sore. Rolling himself in the blanket, he thought of Clara and tried to sleep. When he gave up, he sat up and took out Orin's knife, turning it in his hand. Getting the lantern going, he searched around the trailer and found a paint stick, "stir well" embossed into it. Shaving at it with the edge, he let the wood curl and drop, then he sliced its other edge, humming what he remembered to a Jimmie Rodgers number about all around the water tank, waiting on a train. Wondering what Orin's view would be on things, robbing the Sheridan Loan and Trust, all the trouble at home with Clara, and him out here at Happy Mustard's, saving Willis Taggart from a loan shark, getting mixed up with Hollis Capp and his Knighthawks.

The paint stick had been whittled down, and he wasn't any closer to answers. Folding the knife, he stepped to the door, getting a look at the stars. Opening it, he reeled back, looking at Thelma, her hand raised and set to knock. She looked surprised too. Her other hand holding a lantern, its circle of light casting inside the supply van, shadows along its corrugated wall.

"Some of us sitting by the fire, swapping stories. Was just about to put more corn in the pot. Thought you might be interested."

"Still can't chew so good." He put a hand to his jaw.

"The boys got corn in a jug, no need for chewing at all." Smiling, she held out her hand, obviously, she'd been imbibing.

"What the hell." Sonny shut the door behind him and took her hand.

. . . FORTY-TWO

A pair of tent flaps had been sewn into a curtain, and it hung in front of the stage Hagar had nailed together from the boards of a roadside fruit stand. An oilcloth had been tacked over its boards. Back of the curtain, Minnie sat with a pot of paint and dipped a brush, sweeping gold paint on a placard offering fortunes told and palms read, all for a nickel. Angry at Mort and that stupid bet, looking toward the street, worrying that the ones in the hoods would come, even in the morning light.

Both feeling the drink of last night, Sonny and Handy stood by the calliope at the edge of the camp. Deacon Leathers sat behind it, decked in his hat and tails, barking about the wonderments found within to the few folks gathered out by the makeshift gate. "Just two bits gets you in, folks. Stay all day, you want."

Nobody jumped to come in. Most of them looking nervous; everybody knew the place was going to be hit by the White Knights. Somebody said something about half the police force not showing up for work, a call going out to the highway patrol. Pennants flapped in the show's colors of red and yellow. One couple wandered up, coins in

243

their hands, asking the deacon if they still had Nellie the dog child.

"Nellie's all grown up, retired from the spotlight and raising a healthy family. But, if it's entertainment you're after, we got the Great Throwzinski, defying death itself. Sure you'll be amazed." He pointed between the rows of trailers. "Top of that, we got the Burmese giraffe girls, all the way from the darkest part, doing ritual dancing in copper neck rings, necks stretched to here. Garbed in their rainbow robes, like nothing you ever seen. And if that ain't enough, there's Minnie Plum down at the back reading fortunes. Thelma all tattooed head to toe. Along the way, you'll see Hagar, the strongest man alive. And yes, sir, we got midgets."

Show of Wonderments had been inked on the handbills passed out and pasted on the posts of the main streets of Topeka. In spite of the White Knights' parade, Willis stood his ground. The man knowing how to put on a show, spending his last borrowed dollar to do it. The performers feeling everything was riding on this weekend going well. Willis paying half wages using the money from the bank job. No way of explaining how he got it, but he had to pay them something.

Handy nudged Sonny, and they walked between the rows of trailers. Hagar grunted and lifted a boulder from the ground and set it in the back of a cart. Five hundred pounds painted in red across the stone. The muscles and veins in his arms and legs were pumped up. He'd do it every hour, in between straightening horseshoes and snapping chains across his back.

Fletch strolled down the row with the boa draped around his neck, the snake as docile as a necktie, a viper across his extended arm. Patrons who'd started wandering in parted for him. He loved telling them, "You want to touch it, you

244

go right ahead." Holding it out, winking and advising, "Just be sure you charm it first."

At the middle of the show grounds, Tigor had set the wheel spinning, wearing his red cape. Lupe smiling in front of a wooden board, her outfit in matching red with the sequins and tassels showing off her shape. She explained to the gathering crowd how Tigor fastened her wrists and ankles to the backboard, spinning her as he threw his knives, doing it every hour. Tigor stepped back ten paces, taking a blade with the red grip from his sheath. Lupe spoke of spinning round, smiling as his blade struck the wood backboard, inches from her head. Tigor kept doing it as she spoke, till the sheath was empty. The growing crowd loving it.

The Hovey twins had come back, performing at the end of the row: one juggling pins, the other eating fire. Focused, yet fretting about being attacked. A unicycle, some rings, balls and devil sticks set for their next tricks. Minnie Plum pulled back her curtain and sat behind the rickety booth, smelling the fresh paint of the sign offering fortunes. Straightening her turban with the brooch, the crystal globe and her tarot cards fanned in front of her. Hands on the table, a ring on every finger.

Amaziah Johnson worked at his card table, making one card vanish, another one rise. Orville the clown walked with a string of balloons, passing them to the kids, keeping a painted eye to the front, watching for the White Knights. Mort walked next to Greeny on his stilts, both dressed like Abraham Lincoln, both smoking cigars — one up high, one down low — ready for a day of shaking hands. The air filled with scents from the peanut cart, candy corn, candy floss and candy apples on display.

Handy nodded to Thelma coming from her trailer and stepping around her Indian, waving her fans, her sleeveless and backless outfit showing her ink. Handy watched her walk by where you could shoot a tin duck, then where you could try your hand at swinging the mallet and show your stuff.

Past the phonograph console perched on a rickety side table, The Victor Talking Machine Company stamped in black across its deck. A towhead boy with a gap where his front tooth ought to be pushed his way through a mishmash of adult legs, trying to stop the platter from spinning.

"Hey, knock that off, son." Mort in the fake Abe beard, top hat and tails, shaking a finger at the kid.

"You can't talk to my boy like that." The mother was a teapot of a woman with a plumed slouch hat. Her hands on her hips, ready to give Mort the business. "Not from the likes of you."

"The likes of me, ma'am?"

She glared at him, then back to her kid. "And you . . ." She took hold of his ear and steered him away. Turning to the father, asking what he planned to do about it.

"Do about what?" the man said.

"Your fussing boy."

The man offered she was welcome to shush the kid till doomsday if it suited her. "I'm of the notion a blind eye and deaf ear works best."

Giving him the scorching eye, she waited as father hoisted son to his shoulder, the woman saying she could tell him what his future held, didn't need Minnie Plum for that.

Sonny grinned at Handy, said he guessed he knew how the daddy felt, both turning back toward the entrance.

Mort, with his top hat, cigar in hand, gripped a rope and drew up a tarp curtain, it catching halfway, Greeny leaning and flipping the rope free, the curtain rising. Mort got on the small stage, taking a microphone, tapping his fingers on it to make sure it was on, his voice coming through the paper cone speaker by the stage. Saying hey to the folks, calling them ladies and gents. Leaning too close and tapping a tooth on the coil. The crowd laughing like it was part of the show. Greeny flicked a switch and swung an ellipsoidal spotlight on the giraffe-neck girls. Mort saying they were from the deepest, darkest part of Burma, stepping aside and making room. Greeny laid on a platter, the music playing. The three women stepped stage center and started gyrating. Folks gathered, the boy on the father's shoulders, his mouth hanging open. Saying, "Holy Topeka." His fist crushed his mother's hat, the teapot mother watching them dance, forgetting she was even wearing a hat.

Flashbulbs started popping. Some folks clapped, somebody in back yelled for the husband to set that kid down. "Folks trying to see."

Sonny spotted Jesse and Levon Mulligan moving through the crowd. He nudged Handy.

"Look at them turkey necks," Jesse called loudly over the crowd. "Coulda had one of them for Thanksgiving."

"How about we get them robes off, show some dark meat, give us a real show." Levon laughed, shoving past the man with the boy on his shoulders. "Here, let me help."

Mort put up his hands, protesting this was a family show.

"Time to send the kiddies home, folks." Jesse pushed by Mort, knocked Greeny off his stilts, and climbed up, saying, "Sure you girls won't mind a bit, huh?"

Sonny started for the stage, but Handy pulled him back, saying, "Rest your hand. I got this." Stepping behind Levon, sticking a finger in his back, he said, "Best get your buddy and go."

Levon turned, saying, "Gonna need more than a fing—"

Handy socked him on the side of the head, knocking him back. "Finger's got friends."

Sonny helped the women down from the stage. Then he kicked the stage and it caved in, Jesse toppling off. Sonny snatched him up and shoved him. Mort caught the rope and lowered the curtain over the busted stage. Sonny and Handy trucked the pair through the crowd, past Deacon Leathers at the calliope, and showed them off the grounds, warned them about coming back. The deacon piping his notes, welcoming the folks walking up. Two clowns collecting their money.

"Guess we had a warm-up," Sonny said, watching the retreating Mulligans.

"They'll be back, with friends," Handy said. "And we got to be nuts, two of us taking on the White Knights."

"Did pretty good so far."

"Only five at Wilbur's, seven at the diner," Handy said, watching the road, thinking he ought to catch a nap before the evening show, his hangover kicking inside his skull.

•

Willis was catching the scorch eye from the mother of the gap-toothed kid, the woman complaining about the security Happy Mustard hired on. Willis tussled the boy's hair, gave him a penny and told him to have some cotton candy at the peanut cart. Smiling at the mother, he made a quick turn toward his trailer, thinking he needed a drink.

Knowing they'd be coming, white hoods and sashes over white garb, parading behind their grand wizard on horseback, coming along Kansas Avenue, crossing the tracks by the Rock Island depot. Likely be a couple hoisting a big cross, waving rebel flags. Willis could almost hear them singing about standing and being counted.

"Come wreck my show, huh?" Going to his Airstream, Willis reached in his desk and set the pistol on the top.

Taking the unlabeled bottle and filling his jelly glass, he downed half the drink.

Glancing out the tiny window, he was thinking he should have fetched that squad of hollow-eyed, raw-boned coal miners from over in Fifty Camp, passed out the axe handles and used them like strike breakers. Letting the rest of his drink slide down.

The knock had him reeling. He put the pistol in the drawer. Saying, "It's open."

Ringling's man pulled back the door, looking in. "Willis Taggart?"

Ushering him to the seat across the desk, Willis offered him a drink. The Ringling man was Jack Spenser, a button-down type in a good suit, saying it was kind of early for a drink, tugging up the knees of his pants, taking a tight seat opposite the desk. Taking out some papers, saying, "Been going over your offer, made a few points, and I'm coming to you with a counteroffer."

Filling his glass, Willis looked at the papers, Ringling's man pointed out the last page, some red circles around handwritten numbers, some initials and a signature at the bottom. Jack Spenser saying, "Just needs your John Henry on the indenture. Your brother's too, and we're all set."

"Dentures are teeth, huh?" Willis grinned, looking at it, not surprised it was a poor offer, saying he best read the fine print. Trying to focus past the booze fog. Hearing a commotion out by the calliope.

"Pure boilerplate, the legal eagles insist it gets signed *tout suite*," the Ringling man said.

"Used to be you could take a man at his word, just shake his hand," Willis said. "Nowadays everything's in ink."

Jack Spenser said the trouble was ink and booze didn't mix, asking about getting his brother to sign.

"Walter, we been partners for years, the son of a bitch."
Willis ignored the question. "And worse than him's the wife,
Jesus, what a ball buster. The two of them . . . just be glad
you don't have to meet them." Glancing from the papers,
then out the window, Willis said, "Something I learned,
when a fellow in a suit writes one of these, it's best to get
another fellow in a suit to give it a look." Looking back at
the man, Willis sipped from his glass, thinking with the
bank's money and Whitey Adler out of the way, what did
he need Ringling for?

Ringling's man frowned. "It's your standard peek-and-
sign form. No surprises, I assure you, Taggart. Now if —"

Willis pushed the papers back across the desk. "Think
you can do better."

The man blinked, finally saying, "You understand, time's
of the essence, and if I can be frank, I got a feeling yours is
running thin." Ringling's man got up and made a show of
gathering the papers. Saying he'd give Willis twenty-four
hours to come around. Leaving in a flap.

Willis refilled his glass, saying to himself, "What the
hell."

. . . FORTY-THREE

Clara looked at the city, nothing much changed. Hadn't been back in a couple of years. The former home of the College of the Sisters of Bethany. The hustle and bustle on the sixty-some miles of paved streets just as she remembered it. Like any other place in the Midwest, the depression had kicked Topeka in the pants.

A streetcar passed. A delivery truck pulled to the corner, two men got out, going around back and unloading boxes in front of a shop. The sign on the light standard marked this road as the parade route for the White Knights of the Great Plains, giving the day and time. About a half hour from now.

Donned in her Mother Hubbard, Mildred wheezed to keep up, hooking Clara's arm, complaining about having to park three streets over and her walking too fast. Folks started to gather on the sidewalks, some with their kids. A couple of the brotherhood in their white robes were passing out pamphlets, the words to "Onward, Christian Soldiers" printed on the back. Telling folks everyone was welcome to join in with the grand wizard and sing when they paraded by.

"Long as you're white," Clara said, crunching up the pamphlet, tossing it down.

"Well, you're white, ain't you?" the man said, looking down at the balled paper.

"Can see I am," Clara said. "But you, why you hiding under a hood?"

"So we'll be recognized." The man pointed to the crunched pamphlet. "It's all there."

"Get recognized by hiding," Clara said. "That way nobody knows who's burning the crosses and tormenting folks. Like the one you assholes set on my yard."

"Ain't the chosen ones we're tormenting, lady. Just the ones don't belong."

"You're wasting your breath, girl." Mildred took Clara by the sleeve and led her away.

"Man's talking like I'm the fool," Clara said, walking on.

"Likely the hat," Mildred said, glancing at Clara's bonnet. "You come to town dressed like a pilgrim."

"Wore what I got." Clara pulled her sleeve free, then put a hand to her hat. Feeling her bunion throb inside the shoes she hated wearing.

"Well, it's high time for a new one, stretch silk up your leg while you're at it."

Untying the bow, Clara took off the bonnet, looked at it, then sailed it back at the member of the brotherhood, the bonnet sailing into the street. A Chevrolet swerved to avoid it, the driver cranking down his window and calling her crazy.

"Ain't a puppy, mister," Clara called.

"And the clothes you got belong on Fanny Farmer, not on a Sweeney girl," Mildred said, took her by the sleeve again, leading her along. "Not the look of somebody's got all this money you hinting you and Sonny got stashed."

"Well, this is Topeka. They got shops, don't they?" Clara starting to feel sorry she confided in her mother on the drive out there.

"You can see they do."

"Well, let's wander in then, could use something ain't packed in misery. And how about the way *you're* dressed?"

"Nothing wrong with the way I'm dressed," Mildred said.

At the next corner they saw a group of the White Knights hurrying up the street in their white robes.

"Bunch of crazies, that's for sure," Mildred said.

"Like to see the look on Sonny's face. I go over to Happy Mustard's, a new outfit and some powder on my face, cherry on my lips." Clara laughed at the notion, guessing the man would fear she'd found the money.

"Laugh if you want, but you can use it in the worst way." Mildred took her hand, saying, "Just feel that cracked skin. Can use some of that Palmolive."

"And some nail varnish, you know, the kind I seen in magazines. And maybe I'll have myself a Coca-Cola."

"Well, let's stop talking and do it."

Turning the corner, diagonally crossing Harrison, Mildred aimed her to the Silkville Hat and Dress, Clara catching a reflection of herself in the shop's window. The latest styles on the soulless mannequins in front of a curtain. Lingerie draped on a chair. A sign declaring autumn fashions had arrived. Never thought about it much, but decided that's what she wanted. The money from working for Eugene Cobb, and what was left from what Sonny left for groceries, would do the trick. Thinking of the bank money he hid somewhere on the farm, Clara got a sensation, anything behind that glass could be hers.

Mildred said, "After, we can go for tea at the Jayhawk. Case we get peckish. Read in *Movie Times* how the likes of Groucho Marx and Sally Rand liked taking tea. That is if the fools in the white hoods don't come by and smash out all the windows, turn cars over and start hanging folks from the lampposts." Mildred looking around, wondering aloud where the lawmen were hiding. Mildred old enough to remember the Tulsa riots back in '21.

"Tea, huh?" Clara pushed open the door, hearing a bell tinkle.

•

The proprietress was Elouise Cole, striking with auburn hair and an air of middle-aged sophistication. Sitting behind her counter, daydreaming of ways to deck the shop out for the holidays, needing the miracle of Christmas shopping to pull her through another tough year. Looking up when she heard the bell over the door. The smile veiled the dispirited feeling, these two coming through the door dressed like hayseed have-nots, mother and daughter, likely going to ask for directions to the Union bus depot.

Setting her lunch dish on the *Redbook*, Elouise stepped from behind the counter and smoothed her skirt, running her tongue over her teeth to get any bits of the pasta with chives. Pasting on that smile. "How may I help you ladies?"

"Like to see something," Clara said, glancing around at the racks.

"In fashion?"

"Wanna get fitted out, thinking maybe a dress or something."

Elouise smiled, wondering what the something could be, taking in this woman's sackcloth. The other one in a Mother Hubbard with the tiny print, covering her from head to foot, as little skin as possible showing past the ruffled cuffs and collar. Hadn't seen a rig like that in twenty years, at least not in town. For sure, these two were straight off the farm. Likely here for the parade. Still smiling, she pointed to a rack behind Clara. "Just got in the latest Schiaparelli." They'd take one look at the tag, and Elouise could finish her lunch.

Clara stopped herself from asking, the what?

"Also got some Vionnet, and Coco over here," Elouise turned to the other side of the shop.

"Coco, that the one with the little black number?" Mildred said, showing what she knew, going to the rack and checking a tag, her eyes flickering, cheeks puffing air.

"Coco calls it her Ford, meaning like her little Model A," Elouise said.

"Nothing little about the price," Mildred whispered to Clara. To Elouise, "Ask me, black's kind of for mourning, wouldn't you say?"

"That can be true." Elouise flipped through the rack, showing the little black dress. "The idea's to accessorize it from a simple expression, dress it up or dress it down, you know?" Pointing to costume earrings and necklaces behind a glass case.

"Or wear it to a funeral," Mildred said, going to the display of costume jewelry, checking more tags. Fifty cents for earrings.

Rifling through a rack, Clara pulled out a gray number, saying, "How about this?"

"The wool jersey suit — like that one myself," Elouise said.

"You got something more, I don't know, cheerful?"

"That just comes in the herringbone, but . . ." Elouise sized Clara up, started to take her serious, picturing her in a nipped waist and a dropped hemline. A pretty girl under all that country, with a nice figure and a turned-up nose. Maybe with the right hairstyle, this girl's hair looking like it had been shorn by sheep shears.

255

Holding a hem to her nose, Mildred said, "You don't pack them in mothballs, huh?"

"No, of course not."

"Best way to keep stuff from getting holes bit in."

"I've heard that, but it's never been an issue." Elouise smiled.

"How about I give this a try-on," Clara said, holding a patterned dress in front of her, looking at her reflection in the full-length mirror along the wall.

"You know your size?" Realizing it was foolish to ask, Elouise guessed her a 34, flipping through the rack, found one and showed her behind the change curtain in back. Reracking the Coco, she went through the motions, pulling out an Edith Head, then an Orry-Kelly, an Adrian, then a Mateldi and a couple by Lely and Julien. The sackcloth dress fell to the floor behind the curtain.

Elouise was thinking the girl likely came into some money. A deceased uncle maybe. The way she went on trying on different dresses, liking the styles, looking at herself in the mirror, behaving like she might revive the spirit of reckless spending single-handed. Elouise handed her dress after dress, reracking the ones she was handed back. Making conversation with the mother. If the girl would only say yes and buy something. Elouise's jaw was getting sore from smiling, her lunch wilting.

Stepping in front of the full-length mirror again, Clara fingered the material, twirling and looking at the reflection, liked the shape of her calves, been a long time since she felt pretty. Guessing this number would blow Sonny's socks off. Maybe not just his socks. Twirling again, looking at herself, saying, "This silk, uh?"

"Rayon . . . but, you're right, it's like silk, the latest thing."

"Rayon, that's like my hose?" Mildred lifted a few inches

of Mother Hubbard, showing her ankle above the scuffed oxford shoe.

"Yes, ma'am, though hosiery's leaning more to nylon these days," Elouise explained. "Especially since silk runs near forty-nine cents, you believe that?" Surprised how down-home she was starting to sound.

"Hardly makes sense, you see so little of them," Mildred said, smoothing her dress.

"That's true." Elouise smiled again.

"And this zipper thing . . ." Clara said, feeling in back. "It come with buttons?"

"Well, the trend's gone to zippers. One you're wearing's a Vionnet."

"No buttons, huh?"

"I'm afraid not." Elouise explained about a cross-cut bias, showing them one like Ginger Rogers wore. "Got a big write-up, you ladies know of *Good Housekeeping*?"

"Sure, but just try keeping the sand out," Clara said.

"Yes, bet it's just awful." Elouise ran her tongue over her teeth, guessing anything green on her teeth wouldn't matter.

"So, what say to this one, Momma?"

"Think I'm coming back round to the black." Mildred considered. "Maybe just add in some knickknacks, like the lady says. Just so you don't look like you're going to a funeral."

Agreeing, Elouise grabbed the Coco from the rack.

"You say it's silk or made out of that . . ." Clara snapped her fingers.

"Rayon, right," Elouise said.

Taking it behind the dressing curtain, Clara put it back on, liking the feel of it against her. Stepping back out, the empire waist showing off her form. Giving a whirl, she smiled at her reflection, getting a flash of dancing with Guthrie again, the man stepping up behind her in his tux and tails, with the white gloves on his hands, putting his hands on her waist. The two of them swaying back and forth.

Knowing the smile and that faraway look, Mildred gave her that look that said she guessed the girl was back on that long-ago stage, her make-believe man giving her a twirl.

Helping with the zipper, Elouise glimpsed the undergarment made of the same sackcloth, guessing it used to be a feedbag. Saying, "I've got a hat, think it could set the whole look off." Going to the storeroom in search, thinking she just might make her rent.

Keeping a low voice, Clara said, "Never putting on sackcloth no more, Momma."

"You're coming around, girl," Mildred said.

Elouise stepped from the back, a stack of hat boxes under her chin: a beret, a chiffon headband, a cloche with pheasant feathers and a couple more. Trying them all, Clara checked herself in the mirror. Elouise showing her how to tilt the Lilly Daché.

"Ooh, I'll take this one." No turning back now, Clara already smelling the sweet soap on her skin, the cream keeping it smooth, all the frilly things she'd slip into, liking the look of the girl in the mirror, the dress feeling dainty against her. Guessing with the money from the robbery, she'd hardly put a dent.

"You look like you just stepped out of *McCall's*," Elouise said, meaning it, going behind her register, smiling the way she remembered Jelly Roll Morton did that time she saw him get behind his piano, bringing his hot jazz to town. Tapping the keys, six dollars for the Coco and two more for the hat. Music to Elouise's ears.

"Feel just like when me and Guthrie danced the Palais Royale," Clara said to Mildred, getting her money and setting it on the counter.

"Pay attention," Mildred said, telling her to count it out.

Elouise watched Clara count loose change from what could be a sock, relieved the younger one didn't ask for a trade-in on the sackcloth.

"Hold up a second." Clara stopped counting in mid-cipher, Elouise looking like she might cry.

"You got any shoes?" Clara looked down at her dusty shoes, wiggling her toes.

"You know, I was thinking the same thing. Hold on," Elouise said, going to the back. Clara telling Mildred she was going to be a little short.

Mildred taking a big breath. "How short?"

Elouise called from behind the supply-room curtain. "Got some Mary Janes with a Cuban heel, just come in . . . and some dainty D'Orsays." Elouise coming past the curtain, her arms wide with shoe boxes, asking, "You know your size, hon?"

"Dainty, I guess." Clara slipped a foot from a shoe, lifted it, letting Elouise have a look.

"Yuh, I'd say so," Elouise smiled. Setting the boxes on the counter, moving her uneaten pasta on the lower shelf, taking out a pair of Mary Janes, saying they ought to fit.

•

Loving the feel of the rayon, Clara tipped her head, the breeze threatening to carry off the slouch hat. Taking no notice of the pinch of the new shoe leather. The power of money in every step. The shopping bag in her hand held the old dress and shoes, her old life. She was thinking what she'd say to Sonny; in the end it didn't matter. Maybe he shouldn't have lied about the money. Looking around for a trash can, Clara was done with that old life. The years and misery stripped right off.

"How about that tea?" Clara spotted the Old Prairie Town, a restaurant with an awning and planters flanking its entrance, a half block up on the west side. "Better yet, what say we sup like proper folks?" Adding, "Sonny's busy helping out with the show anyway. And what I got to say to that man's been on a low boil since we left Hoxie, and it's best served on a full load." Clara not even sure why she was getting steamed again, knowing he had reason not to trust her. Telling herself she had her own reasons.

"Well, let's go sup, then." Mildred hooked her daughter's arm, the two of them stepping in the place with the air of visiting royalty.

The shopping bag meant the woman had money. Looked like a new hat. The waiter offered a bow, betting those were new shoes. Testing the French accent he'd been working on, hoping it would land him a spot as maître d' at some fine New York City eatery, get him out of Topeka as soon as the tips stacked high enough.

"Yeah, we'd like to eat," Clara said.

"*Oui.*"

"Yeah, us two." Clara wagged with her fingers, thinking again she ought to get her nails done.

"*Très bon.*"

Narrowing her eyes, she held up the two fingers for clarity.

"For Pete sake's, girl, the man's speaking foreign to you." Mildred said to the waiter, "Got to excuse her, she ain't Topekan."

Walking puckered, the way he guessed a Frenchman would, the waiter led them to a table by the kitchen, snapping his fingers for the busboy to get water glasses filled, drawing a chair for the older woman first, then the younger one.

Smoothing the black dress, Clara scraped her chair in, accepted a menu from him and flipped it open, saying, "So starved, I could eat a scabby donkey." Loving his bewildered look.

"Think we'll just stick to the menu." Mildred smiled at the waiter, holding back from kicking her under the table. "I'll just go with the chophouse chicken."

Taking his pencil and pad, the waiter jotted, kept any more French to himself — Clara going for the slow-cooked ribs — keeping his stretched smile, sure it would land him a decent tip.

. . . FORTY-FOUR

Lighting his last Black Hawk, Willis in his sitting room, looking at the Grant Wood painting over the mantle, his money stashed in the wall behind it. There was no clacking of Granddad's carriage clock, no heartbeat of the house, coming from down the hall, not since Whitey Adler's goons smashed it all to hell. He dared come back to the house with Adler out of the way, needing to make the call to Ringling's man.

Flirting with the call girl making the connection eased his nerves, liking her sultry voice. The girl saying he had the Spencer Tracy lines, wondering aloud if he had the looks to go with it.

"Keep talking, maybe you'll find out." Asking her name, then saying Dolores was a nice name on a girl. Willis tried to recall the girl's name in Hays, the one he took to supper. That one sure could eat but wouldn't do much more. Gave him a peck goodnight and jumped out of his car, ran up to her door, her mother looking out the front window.

Dolores giggled on the line now, Willis saying he could fix her up with free passes, come down and see the Happy Mustard show, Saturday night. His usual lines. The girl saying that sounded swell. Willis asking if that would be two passes.

Ringling's man came on the line. "That you, Taggart?"

"In the flesh."

Jack Spenser gave a sigh, saying, "Well, probably catch hell for it, but guess I can see my way . . . high as a thousand."

"Keep looking."

"Joke if you want, you're paying the call."

"Talked to my brother. He needs to hear more than a thousand." Willis lying, holding his breath.

Ringling's man let go a dramatic sigh, saying, "Fine, eleven hundred, but it's got to be transferred clear and unencumbered."

"Well now —"

"Not one cent more. You don't want it, I'll let Mr. Ringling know you're twisting his —"

"Man can twist anything he wants. I need time to —"

"You know, Taggart, you keep talking like you got more time than I do. Gave you twenty-four hours, now you got, what, about twenty-two left. Use it, don't use it, just don't waste any more of mine." Ringling's man hung up.

"Shit." Willis looked at the stone faces in the painting. Looked at the receiver still in his hand, saying, "Dolores, you still with us?" Waiting a moment, then hanging up.

•

The giraffe necks walked past his Airstream Clipper, carrying their belongings. Not a word of English, yet they had the sense to leave. Maybe it hurt to talk with their necks stretched out like that. Not a bad thing for a woman, Willis opined, stepping back into his trailer, understanding their fear of the White Knights.

At least he was done with Whitey Adler. Sonny Myers and Handy Phibbs didn't have the size, but they sure had the hard bark, or maybe it was just thick. Willis smiled, thinking how he crushed that old man's hand, Adler not coming back anytime soon. Uncapping the bottle, he splashed more whiskey in the jelly glass. Surrendering to it. Gulping it down and pouring more. Years of keeping the show alive through the thick and thin, scraping the bottom, dealing with his brother and that bitch wife, borrowing from the likes of Whitey Adler. He was done with it, thinking what he'd say to Ringling's man.

Mort tapped on the door, calling his name.

"Go away," Willis called, the whiskey claiming the feeling in his feet.

"We got a mob of hate coming, one with a bull horn, another on a horse. Just the deacon out by his pipes, and no cops."

Should have hired the strike breakers. Should have stayed at the house. Taking the Colt, Willis stuck it under his jacket and filled his glass.

•

The cooking fire burned down to embers from the late lunch, heat coming off the coals, a tendril of smoke puffing up. Mort, Hagar and the deacon sat around on folding chairs playing pinochle, a crate for a table. A break before the evening show, like they did between most shows. Mort asking if anybody wanted to bump their bet, when the haters were coming.

Walking between the trailers, Sonny checked for coffee in the pot. Pouring some in a tin, blowing on it. Watching the card game.

Mort asking if he wanted to sit in, Sonny shaking his head, sipping from the tin. Had things on his mind.

Mort saying that usually meant a woman.

"Matter of fact . . ." Sonny saying he had a wife.

"How long you been hitched?"

Sonny thinking, then saying, "Going on nine years."

"Was hitched myself a time," Mort said.

Hagar looked surprised, saying, "How am I just finding that out?"

"Sometimes hard to get a word in." Mort frowned at him.

"How long you hitched?" Sonny said.

"Long enough to learn what I know about women wouldn't fill a hat."

The others nodded, Sonny sipped the coffee.

"Was a fine gal too," Mort said. "Always figured we'd last forever. Went by Mary, Queen of Tots. The two of us working the Rubin & Cherry Shows in Florida. Worked alongside Percilla the Monkey Girl, before she took up with Emmitt the Alligator Man. The bunch of us warming up for Lady Olga. You know of her?"

Hagar did, saying, "The bearded wonder with the chin whiskers down to here, fine as cotton candy."

"That's right, wind always blowing it around. Anyhow, me and Mary got hitched in Gibsonton. And it went right for a time, then I don't know, it just come undone, the way things do. Still causes me regret." Looking at Sonny, saying, "You know, I got to come clean about something." Telling him about taking bets on the show's demise. "With only you and Handy standing in their way. And us wagering who comes the closest, just not right. Well, not everyone. Thelma and Minnie Plum wouldn't do it. Got more sense, I guess . . ." Mort glanced at the others, then to Sonny, saying, "Was me that got it started. So, you want to sock anybody, suppose I got it coming." He looked up, didn't see a fist coming.

"Mighta taken some of that bet myself." Tossing what was left in his tin at the fire, Sonny clapped Mort on the back, said he best get ready. Stepping from the square, he walked the show grounds, heading by the Airstream Clipper.

Willis, seeing him from the small window, came to the door, saying, "Ought to know, I sold the show, at least maybe I did."

Sonny stopped.

"Maybe not worth you two mixing it up with the parade of idiots," Willis said. Glancing to the front, "Got part of a bottle in there." Nodding inside. "Beats hell out of buttermilk."

"Maybe later." Sonny heard the commotion out front, kept walking. Some of the performers getting ready for the evening show stopped and were looking that way.

Thelma kneeled by her Indian, couple of tools on the ground.

"Thinking of riding that highway with no end?" he said, guessing she got wind Willis was selling the show.

"A straight line for some distant mountain, sure keeps me from getting heavy." Thelma looking to the front, a worried look.

The seesaw of Minnie Plum's nap time sounded through the trailer's window, catching some winks before more fortune telling. Sonny hearing the calliope start up.

Thelma glanced at him. "Feel like I got both sides of an argument going round my head. About going or staying." She took up a box wrench. "But likely, I'll be heading out first thing. How about you?"

"Going home, me and the missus gonna find our way. See if we can see things the same."

"Maybe meet someplace halfway."

"Clear you two never met."

Thelma smiled.

"Wheat, Thelma, that's pretty much what I know." He wished her well and he turned to go.

"Oh, I think you know plenty," she said.

Handy stepped from the supply trailer, scuffed boots in hand, hopping on one foot, getting one on at a time.

"You find hobnails?" Sonny said.

"It look like it?" Handy showed the wrecked leather, sat on the Zephyr's bumper and laced on his boots.

Thelma watching them walk to the front.

•

The time of the evening show had been scrawled on a board with a dip pen, the board leaning between the tractor wheel and harrow. A decent crowd gathered. Mort, wearing a bowtie, stood by the wooden gate. Deacon Leathers got behind the calliope, set to pipe "Turkey in the Straw."

Somebody in the crowd blasted a Klaxon horn. A man with size pressed his way to the front, lifting a leg over the gate. The guy next to him doing the same.

Expecting they were with the White Knights, Mort blocked the way, Greeny next to him on his stilts. "That foot comes down, promise you boys won't like it."

From the back of the crowd, a teen lit the wick of a Brocks firecracker, lobbing it. Making Mort jump, catching Greeny from falling. The crowd cheered, thinking it was part of the show. A candy corn box was tossed, then a drink cup, splashing Mort's pants.

"Maybe let them in," Handy told Mort, swiping something sticky from his shirt. Mort frowned and pulled back the gate, the clowns taking the nickel admission, coins jingling in their floppy pockets.

Sonny and Handy stood to the side, looking through the crowd. Sonny first to see the ragtag parade coming. Not the route the city approved. About two dozen men in robes and hoods, some with axe handles, some with bats.

Heads in the crowd turned, the singing of "Onward, Christian Soldiers" getting their attention.

The deacon stopped piping and took off.

"Hope he's getting back-up," Handy said, thinking of their guns stashed on the floor of the calliope, in easy reach. Willis not wanting them armed by the gate, scaring off the customers.

"Gimme the keys." Sonny held out his hand.

"We taking off?" Handy looked hopeful, then saying they were in the car.

"Got an idea." And Sonny hurried off.

Handy watched them come, the line of show-goers dispersing around him. The brotherhood marching up, the grand wizard on his horse, pumping his staff in the air, the kleagle next to him.

Hagar and Tigor came forward, stood by Handy. Tigor with his knives, Hagar with a length of pipe.

"Can't stop all of us," Hollis Capp called to them as the parade stopped before the gate. Handy recognizing the voice coming from under the hood.

"Gonna start with you — yeah, I know it's you, Capp," Handy told him. "See where it goes from there."

Tigor showed the brace of throwing knives, taking a blade and flexing it.

The klansmen gathered behind the grand wizard, axe handles and bats ready, waiting for him to call it.

Handy wished Sonny would hurry up, not sure what he was up to.

The explosion caught him off guard, knocked him right into Hagar. Feeling the rush of heat at his back. He turned into it. Thick smoke billowed up over the supply trailer.

. . . FORTY-FIVE

Clara watched as the couple of well-to-dos headed for the door, the waiter ready with his *merci* and *au revoir*, grateful for their tip. The busboy bumped through the swinging kitchen door, juggling a stack of empty plates. Clara and Mildred sipped coffee, Mildred reining in a belch, giving a light pat to her chest. The busboy backed through the doors, wheeling a dessert trolley.

"Hold up there," Mildred said, eyeing the sweets, guessing they'd help with her digestion, the wine with dinner putting her halfway between woozy and tipsy. Past caring about what the meal cost. "How about you plate a couple of these, hmm, and wrap up two, three of them little ones. You know, a doggy bag. Sure you seen them."

The busboy nodded, saying he'd be happy to.

Clara reminded her momma she was tapped, hoping Mildred had enough to cover the bill, her mother eating like it was her final meal.

Dabbing a napkin at her mouth, Mildred worked her tongue between her teeth, sucking and calling to the waiter, "You got any kind of toothpick . . ." Prodding with her tongue. Asking Clara, "And suppose they got them little mints?"

"Why you asking me?" Clara leaned back, tipping her chair on two legs, pushed the swinging door open and called inside, "Hey, you got any mints?"

"And toothpicks, make sure he don't forget," Mildred said, cursing the gaps between her damned teeth.

•

The toothpick snapped, and Mildred pincered the fragment between her fingernails, trying to get her tongue in there, dislodging the stubborn bit of chophouse chicken. Looking around for the waiter, thinking she could use more coffee. Her eyes swept past the front window. A newsboy stood outside, getting on his soap box at the corner, under the lamplight. Freckles and a sport cap too big for his head, showing under the yellow light. Lofting the evening edition, he called for folks to read all about it.

The rumble shook the restaurant.

"The hell was that?" Clara shoved from the table, thinking a duster was bearing down. Looking out the front. Not sure if Mildred had her car windows rolled up. It made her uneasy, had her moving for the door.

Her daughter acting strange again. Selecting a couple of bills from her bag, Mildred topped it with some change, as an anchor. Shoving up, she followed, her stomach feeling like sausage in a casing.

With the bag of pastries and the bill in hand, the waiter came through the swinging pass door, seeing the pair hurrying for the front. Second set of deadbeats this week. Cursing, forgetting his French. Maybe the food wasn't much, but his service was first rate and deserved a tip. Angling past an incoming couple, he told them to sit anywhere, he'd be right back. The offenders moved for the corner. Catching up easily, he put a hand on the older one's shoulder, turning her. "Good thing you're dames." Holding the bill in his fist and shaking it.

"Who the hell you talking to?" Mildred shrugged him off.

"You dames are duckin' the check."

"Money's on the table, nickel tip, too," Mildred said.

Backing up, he held out the bag of pastries, apologizing in French as he backpedaled. Saying they were on the house.

"Got a good mind —" Mildred snatched the bag.

Clara was walking past the newsboy, moving in the direction of the mental hospital, Happy Mustard's camp next to it in City Park, the smoke rising over the rooftops. That bad feeling was growing. Crossing the street, she practically ran for Mildred's Buick.

FORTY-SIX

Couldn't run in the shoes, Clara tugged them off, grasping them in her hands. Calling over her shoulder, "Come on, Momma." Looking over the building tops, past Bethany College, the top of the State House, the smoke hanging in the air. The Rock Island line chugged and blasted its whistle.

"Just ate, now you got me running." Mildred making an effort to keep up, going past the signs posted along the street, marking the parade route, declaring no parking.

"You heard it."

"Could be nothing."

"Why you got to head butt me? Wasn't nothing." Clara snapped her fingers. "Give me the key. Never get there with you driving."

"Oh, for Pete's sake." Reaching in her bag, Mildred dug for the key.

Snatching it from her, Clara hurried to the driver's side, got in the Buick, went about starting it up. Pulling out the choke, trying again, careful not to flood it.

"Acting strange since we left the farm." Mildred settling on the seat, shutting her door, saying, "What's wrong? I didn't gush enough about the dress? Well, you're pretty in

273

it, okay? There you go. High on the list of pretty, right up with Irenie."

"How about you hush now. Had my fill of that growing up." Clara turned, feeling the anger rise. "Hearing Irenie this and Lizzie that. One pretty, one smart."

"Oh, this again? I always treated you girls fair and square, fifty-fifty."

Clara put a tight grip on the wheel. The White Knights of the Great Plains showed far up the street, not in parade formation, just a ragtag bunch, the grand wizard out front on his horse, heading their way, looked more like they were in retreat. City folks lined on either side.

"That's right, fifty for Lizzie, fifty for Irenie. That don't slice up three ways, does it, Momma?" Clara tried again and got the car started.

"Guthrie was wild as a gypsy. Would've left you flat and broken-hearted. Irenie spared you that hurt, that's all. Did to him what he surely would've done to you. Gave him a taste of his own medicine."

"Gave him a taste alright, but it wasn't of no medicine." In spite of the detour sign, Clara drove up the street.

"What are you doing?"

"I coulda been a dancer."

"Blame me, blame the bunions." Mildred looked at the group of White Knights. No music, no floats, just a bunch of fools in oversized nightshirts, hating anybody defying their notion of the American way. "You best watch —"

"Always picked Lizzie's side anytime we squabbled . . ." Clara stomped her foot on the pedal, her eyes on those men, some the ones who burned her barn.

"Called you out when you were wrong, same as them." Mildred braced a hand against the dash. "Oh, my God, what are you —"

"Way you turned a blind eye on Irenie, with all the heck she got into." Pressing the pedal all the way down, giving it more gas. Fingers gripping the wheel. "That girl, sowing her wild oats as you called it. How about my oats, Momma?"

"Landsakes, if your daddy was here . . ." Mildred pointed up the street.

"Well, he ain't here."

"Turn, turn here . . . take Western." Starting to panic, Mildred looking out the back.

The White Knights stopped ahead in the street. Nobody singing "Onward, Christian Soldiers." And not a cop in sight.

"Never said a word when Lizzie poked her wedding day ahead of mine. Landed like a dung pile, and you never did a thing." Clara practically shouting.

"Stop!" Mildred feeling her gorge rise.

"Jinxed us right from the get-go, me and Sonny."

"How was I . . . there was the Sweeney reputation . . ."

The Buick flew, Clara shoving open her door, tossing the shopping bag in the street, her old feed-sack dress and shoes inside. "And how about Irenie stealing Guthrie while he was calling on me? You never said a word." Tears fell on the new dress.

"Oh, girl, you got yourself locked in a dream." Mildred putting her feet on the dash, arms around herself, bracing.

"Only place I was ever happy." Clara looking at the confused ranks, the one out front on the horse raising his arms for her to stop. "Me and Sonny was cursed since we got hitched. First the land goes barren, then me."

The kleagle jumped first, making a grab for the reins to the horse.

Klunk.

Clara parted them, her fender catching one of them. The car cut a swath down the middle. Men jumping out of the way. The ones behind her cursing and yelling, some on the ground.

"Done with living in that cracker box on that dried-out farm. Getting out of this Timbuktu-bit life." Clara was calm now, like it was a Sunday drive. White Knights jumping and falling in the street, one hurling a rock. "Get there while I still got a good head of steam. Me and that man gonna have a talk. Got no right to keep things from me."

Mildred ducked her head down, heard the rock hit the car, knowing her girl would have more than Sonny to talk to. The police and highway patrol would be coming for her.

Clara turned up Polk and began crying and singing some old song at the same time, the one about the circle being unbroken. About a better home awaiting. Looking out the windshield at the sky, the moon showing early in the afternoon sky. The Happy Mustard camp just ahead.

. . . FORTY-SEVEN

"I got a headache, comes in the form of you," Clara had it in mind to spit the words at him, wanted to shake Sonny and get him to tell where he hid the money. Tell him he had no right. She lived the hard years right along with him. It was her losing the churn, the stove and her sewing machine. And him acting like he didn't trust her. Sure she'd done some things, and he'd done some things too, but in the end, she was the one who stuck it out and stood by him.

She'd gone through every inch of the house, pried up the floorboards where the three-burner had stood, behind the pipes of the potbelly, the storage bin, looked down the well, walked out and toed through the rubble of the barn. Choking from that acrid smell. Poked around the backhouse. Pulled up the buried pickets where his mother's garden had been. Not a sign of the money anyplace.

A sign pointed to City Park, and there was the Happy Mustard show. A couple of police cars blocked the entrance. She'd be arrested for bowling through the damned parade. Telling herself it was worth it. She'd blame it on the brakes, or explain how being a woman, she couldn't get the pedals right, mixing gas and brakes with panic. Didn't matter, Sonny would have to use the bank money he hid, pay her bail.

Parking along the road, she got out and walked past the gate, the cops paying her no mind, Clara looking through the crowd for Sonny. There was no show going on. No clowns, no kids with balloons. The smell of something burning. A cop was questioning Willis Taggart over near the calliope.

Then Handy found her, coming to her with the long face, hugging her close. Saying the words.

Clara wasn't really hearing him.

Mildred bawled and tried to clutch Clara in her arms.

Clara ran to what was left of the mayor's Zephyr, past the door that hung from a single hinge, the glass all gone, the burned seat, the smell of burned rubber, the wreck worse than the Moon Roadster that burned in their barn. Then she was held back by a cop containing the scene, Clara kicking his shin. Saying she was Sonny Myers's wife, goddamn it. Crying more. Mildred came and took her from the officer, holding her daughter. Clara not believing it. The cop explaining they took him to Topeka State, pointing in the direction of the hospital.

Mildred saying, "That's the nuthouse."

"Was the closest place, ma'am." The cop said he was gone by the time they got Sonny on the stretcher, saying he was sorry for their loss.

Thelma and Minnie Plum led the crying women over to where they had their campfire inside the squared trailers, sat them on the camp chairs. Thelma offering a tin of buttermilk, saying Sonny was a good man.

Taking a sip, Clara gave it back, needing something stronger. Just wanting Sonny to hold her, tell her it would be alright. Wanted to hear him argue about her dancing dandy, paying that jigger Guthrie more heed than him. Talking about his roots and how he couldn't leave this godforsaken land. How the rain was coming. His high talk of picnics and days of feelings gone by. Trying to keep them together. Running Eugene Cobb off for giving her the twinkle eye.

"The twinkle eye, what's that even mean?" she said out loud, then she was taking a bottle from Handy, feeling the whiskey's burn.

Mildred drew her close again, and Clara slumped into her this time, not letting go of the bottle.

"Used to argue. I'd tell him how if my mouth wasn't so dry, I'd spit. And he'd say go ahead, the ground can use it."

Handy eased the bottle from her, took a drink, wiping the top of the bottle, passing it to Mildred.

Looking at her feet, Clara said, "Told him living with him was like living alone." Dragging a bare toe along the ground, no idea where she'd dropped the new shoes. "Sometimes felt that way."

Thelma and Minnie Plum were crying too, letting her talk.

"First, the land's dead, everything dry and blown off," Clara said, looking to the heavens. "Now you go and leave me." Tears rolled down both cheeks.

Mort led a pair of troopers from the highway patrol between the trailers and nodded over to Thelma. They had the kleagle between them, Hollis Capp in his white robe, with his hood off, the younger officer holding him by the Iron Claw restraint on his wrist. The older trooper had the look of experience, a corporal's insignia on his sleeve, knelt beside Clara and said his name was Marty Fisher. His partner was Dewey Cline, tall and by the book, had the look of a rookie and a good grip on their man. Fisher offered his condolences, then rose and looked to Thelma, pointed to Capp and asked if this was the man who assaulted her that night in the camp?

She looked at him, recognition coming to her, nodding her head. "Yeah, that's him. One who hit me."

"You got me wrong," Hollis Capp said, then to Marty Fisher, "You gonna believe this blue-ink freak woman over me?"

Dewey Cline yanked Capp's restraint, told him to watch his mouth.

"You know how these people feel toward the brotherhood," Capp argued. "They'll say anything."

Marty Fisher asked if she was sure.

Thelma looked at him, replayed that night and nodded. "No mistaking him."

Taken from her grief, Clara handed the bottle to Handy and got up, saying to Marty, "You say he killed Sonny?" Not waiting for an answer, she ran at him, kicking and punching and yelling.

Taking his time, Marty Fisher stepped over, nodded for his partner to step in, Dewey grabbing a hold of Hollis Capp, pulling him back, Hollis trying to shield himself from Clara's blows.

"Goddamn, I want her arrested. Ought to take her to that loony bin, just like her old man."

Mildred came from his blindside, first time in her life she threw a punch, landed it against the hater's ear with a smack, a blow that would have knocked Hollis on his ass if Trooper Cline wasn't holding him.

Holding his hat in his hands, Corporal Fisher said to Clara, "I sure am sorry about your husband, ma'am. Where are you staying while in Topeka?" Writing down Mildred's address over in Silver Lake. "That over in East Drucker?"

Then he asked Thelma to hang around until he came back for her statement. Telling them a patrol would be passing by during the night, they led their prisoner away.

Mildred turned to Handy. "You mind driving us out to Silver Lake?" Her mind on readying Clara's old room, thinking she'd stay a while. A coat of paint would freshen it up, a nice pink or sunny yellow. Remembering a bolt of cotton she'd been saving, had seashells on it, maybe enough for curtains. They could shove that old chifforobe down the hall. And she had an old stand-up mirror in the attic. Get Clara some of that oh-de-toilet she was talking about at supper. Help her comb the sand out of her hair.

Town Marshal Billy Joe Blake pulled up, spoke in a low voice with one of the troopers, then offered Clara his condolences, but saying he had some questions of his own.

"Fuck off, Blake. You got no sway outside of Hoxie," Clara said. "That enough answer for you?" Letting Mildred lead her off.

Turning to him, Mildred said, "Can't you see we got grieving going on?"

Handy passed Blake the near-empty bottle and followed the women. Told them to wait by their car, going to get the few belongings he and Sonny had at the trailer.

. . . FORTY-EIGHT

Thelma Hart walked behind them to her trailer, drinking from the tin of buttermilk, watched the Myers women walk from the camp, Handy going with them. The moon danced off the chrome, the Indian on its kickstand, tempting her to go right now. Climb on and ride the 66, take it west, find liberty on that ribbon of highway. Nothing holding her here. Didn't matter the highway patrol told her to stick around.

Going inside, she looked at her cot, knowing there would be little sleep tonight anyway. Minnie Plum's blanket ruffled. Guessing she'd end up by the fire, get into her cups with the rest of them. Mort, Tigor, Hagar and the deacon coming back around the flames, talking about what happened, saying words about Sonny, toasting him with something that wasn't buttermilk. Still angry about that stupid bet, she made up her mind and climbed into her jeans. Guessing she'd find Willis at his trailer, ask him to settle up. Making up her mind to get out of there.

.

Mildred was saying how much she hated driving at night, telling Handy to keep the old sedan to the center of the road, heading west on the 24. "Sure I feel a wheel wobble, you feel it?"

"Alignment might be off a bit. Could just be front tire needs air."

She nodded, saying East Drucker wasn't far off. Trying to put the horror of Sonny being in that blown-up car from her mind, she thought of the way the youngest of her Sweeney girls cleaved through that parade of bigots. Stirred her pride, but still no way she would ever let Clara behind the wheel again. Thinking she'd put Handy on the sofa for the night. Tomorrow she'd ask him to knock the fender in shape while she fixed breakfast.

Leaning against the passenger door, Clara was staring out at the passing landscape, still crying.

Handy was thinking he'd be the one to tell the mayor what happened to his Zephyr. And how Clara ended up with none of the bank money, nobody knowing where Sonny hid it. A tug of war going on in his mind about cutting her a piece of his.

Mildred told him again, keep to the center of the road. "Can see anything jumping from the ditches." Telling him about the deer Henry hit one time when they returned from Kansas City. Henry had done the driving all those years. Leaving her to twist on the seat and tend the girls lined across the back seat.

"Yes, ma'am," Handy said.

"You could bank on Henry's driving, and me, I made good sense of a map, even with all the jiggling and giggling going on in the back. Yeah, this old car sure lent good service to the Sweeneys. Still on the road." Eyeing the gauge, she told him to keep it at a steady forty-five. Put his hands on either side of the wheel the way Henry used to do it.

"Yes, ma'am."

Then Mildred turned to Clara. "Keep up the water-works, you gonna dry out."

"Gonna find it if it's the last thing I do."

"That highway patrol's sharp, even if your town marshal ain't. They'll put two and two together."

"Just got to keep looking and digging."

"Look to the Lord and dig for strength," Mildred said.

"*Phhtt*," Clara mouthed.

"What's that supposed to mean?"

"Means *phhtt*."

"Motherhood's one bad business," Mildred said to Handy. "You wipe ass the first year, then you take poo the rest of your days."

Headlights reflected in the rearview, Handy glanced, a vehicle closing fast and bearing down, then more lights behind it.

The DeSoto rolled up, wanting to pass. Had to be Hollis Capp or some of his people.

Handy held to the center, the DeSoto swung wide into the oncoming lane, somebody whoo hooing out the window, then barreling on. Truck lights bearing on them from behind.

The DeSoto slowed in front of them, Handy worked the wheel, swerving, trying not to get sandwiched. The car hopped the opposite shoulder. Bouncing. Screeching tires. Gravel striking the undercarriage. The .38 falling from under Handy's jacket.

Headlights of an onrushing Streamline tanker topped a crest, blinding them. The Buick rocked the gravel, humping a sand drift. Handy cranked the wheel hard, the car bolted the ditch, bottomed hard, their heads smacking the roof, windshield and dash. Grinding to a hard stop. The tanker's air horn cursed till it was out of sight. Son of a bitch didn't bother to stop.

"Oh Mary, mother of Jesus." Mildred put her shaking hands together in prayer. Dust rose around them, their remaining headlight cast a dim light over the dead ground.

A funk of gas and urine, Clara shoved open the passenger door and stumbled out, the car and trucks gone. Clara knowing who it was, payback for bowling through their parade. Didn't matter Sonny had just been killed. They had a hand in that too. A bomb, the trooper said.

Their lone headlight shone at a billboard across the open field, that colonel smiling with a drumstick as big as a bush in his hand, his other hand holding a plate of crispy chicken. Like, you nearly got killed, now have some chicken. The headlight dimmed and went out. A hissing from under the hood was the only sound.

Clara asking if Mildred was alright.

Mildred got out, took a few steps and retched.

Handy was looking at the guy on the billboard holding the plate of chicken. Reaching inside, he fumbled around on the floor, finding his .38, thinking the Knighthawks might come back. Didn't feel any broken bones, he was thinking again of making his way down to Uncle Ezra's in East Baton Rouge Parish. Make shit out of gator. His share of the bank money would be enough, even if he gave Clara some.

Clara looked at him. "You okay?"

"Yeah, you?"

She took the pistol from him, aimed it and fired it at the colonel. "I been better." She handed it back.

Mildred yelped, then cried.

"How about you, Momma, you okay?"

The woman couldn't speak, her head nodding and shaking.

"That was some driving." Clara said to Handy, going around and hugging her mother close.

Every inch of her felt raw, nerves jangling and heart thumping. Mildred pushed off and stepped over the ground, just wanted to be alone. The night chill told her she was wet below, her bladder no match for this kind of terror. Her son-in-law was dead, and her daughter had gone crazy, shooting off a pistol for no reason. Walking past some scrub, she lifted the Mother Hubbard and peeled down the knee-lengths, skipping out of them as best she could. She sailed the soaked garment off her shoe, it catching on a thistle. "Wish those vermin the fires of hell."

Handy stood looking at the car.

"You fix it or not?"

"Ain't a magician." Putting some back into it, he got the hood up with the grind of metal, both headlights out, the grillwork smashed, bumper and fender twisted. The moonlight barely let him see under the hood. Feeling for the plug wires and the distributor cap. One of the wires loose. Might be enough car left to roll them out of there and get them to the phone box at the Paradise Motel. Maybe if he got past the crazy aunt, Crawford Miller could help out.

"What's funny?" Clara said.

He shook his head, thinking of that Cricket woman and her trash poker. Yanking and tearing the hanging fender from the driver's side, keep it from puncturing the tire, careful not to cut himself. The metal groaned as he pulled. Looping some loose wire, he rigged a sling around the dead headlight, holding it in place.

Seeing Mildred was out of earshot, he wiped his hands on his pants, saying to Clara, "He give a hint what he did with it?"

Clara shook her head. "Just that he hid it. Guess I give him reason, not trusting me."

"Never mind that. Got to be there somewhere." He went and turned the key, and the engine coughed to life.

Helping Mildred onto the bench seat, Clara could smell that her mother had wet herself.

Rolling the wreck over ground like hardtack, Handy got the Buick up the stony ditch and got back on the 24. Close enough to East Drucker to drop the women off first.

Mildred was mumbling a prayer. "And forgive us our debts, except them bastards that trespassed on us. And lead us not into temptation, but deliver us from evil."

"Amen," Clara said, thinking about where Sonny hid the money.

•

"Think somebody's gonna beat you to it?" Handy said as they drove from the house, just the two of them heading west again on the 24.

"Not taking chances. They already burned my barn." Clara looked at him.

Handy nodded, knowing his station could go up in flames too. His share hidden behind the old toilet tank.

"What are you gonna tell Flint about his car?" Clara said.

"Don't matter. Already told him something was wrong." Handy waved a hand. "Just worse than I thought."

Both of them laughing.

Then he asked, "You find the money, you gonna stay?"

"Not living like that, a broke-down place with a bunch of dirt clods. Only thing grows comes when the living kills you and you push up daisies. Gonna take care of Sonny, get a nice spot next to his folks, then, I don't know, guess I'll go west."

"You find it, the money, best you leave it hid . . . a while, anyway." Handy looked at her, knowing she'd take it and run. Hardly blame her for it.

Then he was thinking of putting the Conoco up for sale, ask Nora O'Mara to leave with him. Take some of the money and buy a decent car, drive down to Uncle Ezra's. Learn to make boots and belts, sell it to the tourists. Maybe she'd see it as stitching hide beat working for some jerk who kept her on her feet on Sundays.

. . . FORTY-NINE

Woody Herman was blowing "At the Woodchopper's Ball." The channel drifted in and out, Cricket Miller getting an earful of Kansas static. Twisting the knob, she got another signal, the announcer declaring it was coming up on midnight and time to hit the hay, the station going off the air. Nothing after that but more static. Cricket shut it off.

Didn't need to be Sunday to address the wooden Jesus over the office door, Cricket Miller talking to Him, working late on the books like she often did when she couldn't find sleep, expecting the supper of chilies and beans didn't help. A nightbird called from the sugar maples out back. And if that cup of mint tea she had didn't settle things pretty quick, she'd be making a late trip to the backhouse by those trees. Then she got thinking a cinnamon bath might do her good, help her to sleep, though she'd likely wake everybody in the joint just by going about boiling the water. There was only one guest and her nephew, but these walls were like paper.

Jesus over the door had no opinion.

The Paradise sign cast blue against the wall, the thin curtain at the window not helping much. Somewhere on the highway, she heard an engine coming this way. She guessed from the east. Maybe more than one. Finally, she heard the whir of tires turning into the gravel lot, the protest of brakes and the engines cutting off.

The Ealesburg bread truck wasn't due for some time yet. Cricket raised her head enough to see the clock. The closed sign lit under the office's porch light. Under the light of the Paradise sign, she made out a car and a couple of trucks parked by the phone box. A big Confederate flag stretched across a spare tire on the back, a cross rigged to the bumper of another. Men stepped out and walked this way. Nobody making a call.

"Morons of the first degree." Knowing who they were, Cricket picked up the phone, having heard on the news about what happened in Topeka, somebody blowing up a car at the Happy Mustard show. One man killed. Wondering if Crawford was still awake.

The call girl was Jenny, Cricket asking her to connect her to the highway patrol. Asking her to do it quick. Waiting and looking up, asking Jesus if He knew where she left that poker.

A couple of the men stepped up on the porch, one rattling the knob, looking in and knocking. Cricket called they were closed. The man saying he heard there was a dust storm coming this way, they just needed a couple rooms, not like this place couldn't use the business. Then someone at the highway patrol picked up the other end of the line. Turning her back to the door, Cricket tended to the call.

"You fellas ought to come back when we're open," Crawford Miller said from the far end of the porch, doing up his shirt, knowing who these men were from the fight at Valentine's diner. "Worth it just to try a slice of my aunt's dirt cake."

"We look like we eat dirt?" Dale Telfer said. "What we need's some rooms."

"Dishes it up 'longside that new Instant Whip. Mmm-mm." Crawford walked along the plank porch running along the front. Taking his time.

"Just after some rooms."

"Said we're closed, the sign says so too, don't it?" Crawford kept it friendly. "Give you a tip though, word is there's one of them Hoovertown camps up the road, five or so miles I guess. Look for the Danville side road, then go right. Doubt they got pie, but mebbe you can spend the night."

"Yeah, a place like this." Telfer looked around, knowing who Crawford was now, not seeing any of his buddies from the diner. "Likely catch the pocky warts off some unsalted gal you no doubt got around. Making money on the side."

"Not sure how it is up the road, friend, but got nothing like that here," Crawford said, taking Telfer for their leader, the one Sonny hit not among them. "What else they got, I don't know, pocky warts, postcards, guess you got to ask." Stopping a foot from the man, he said, "And you don't like what I'm telling you, complain to the highway patrol. Call box's right there." Crawford nodded to the Paradise sign. "Cost you a nickel."

"That the way it is, huh?" Telfer said.

"Already called the highway patrol. Be here anytime now," Cricket said through the window, pulling back enough of the lace curtain, the trash poker in her hand.

"What's that?" Telfer said, grinning to the men. "You smell smoke, Stonewall?"

Talking was over, Crawford threw a solid jab and caught Telfer on the chin while his head was turned. Followed it with a good hook as the man stumbled.

Slipping an overhand right, Crawford threw the same jab, then sent a cross to the jaw. The man knowing a thing about counter-punching. The Knighthawks crowded in. Someone blindsided him, sending a ringing from one ear to the other. Shaking the cobwebs, Crawford pressed Telfer, throwing a right. Doing it like he'd seen Kid Chocolate do that time in Philly. Blocking and throwing a shot at the man's middle, a rocket with knuckles, knocking him back. Taking a punch to the kidneys. One of the Mulligans kicking at him. Crawford seeing double. Knowing he wouldn't last. Throwing an elbow and taking a punch. Not much left in his tank, Crawford staggered back and covered up. Going down as Aunt Cricket came bolting out the door, swinging her trash poker.

Lobbing a forearm into the crotch of the man grabbing at him from behind, Crawford pulled himself up on the doubled-over man, pulling the shirt up over the man's head. He saw a car pulling into the lot past the forest of legs. No headlights on. Hoping it was the state troopers.

•

Handy jumped out of the Buick, wading in and pulling a man off. Turning Dale Telfer around.

"Goddamn, it's the prairie nig—"

The punch cut Telfer's words, putting him down. Clouting somebody else, Handy grabbed a fistful of hair, twisting and punching.

Clara got the carbine from Sonny's belongings, the one he took from Capp's store, cocked it and fired into the DeSoto's back tire.

She held the rifle at the ready, the only sound was the hissing tire.

"You fuckers get blood or snot on my new dress, sure gonna tick me off."

Before the tire settled on its rim, they heard the far-off siren.

. . . FIFTY

The troopers sat in their black Plymouth, the radio tuned to WIBW, the station the highway patrol used for information. Marty Fisher was closing on his twenty years, on the brink of getting that gold watch. Saying it was colder tonight than it had been all week. Realizing the rookie had dozed off again, Dewey Cline's head tipping against the passenger-side window. He'd been talking about wetting a line out by Wiley, Marty saying yeah, he knew a spot. Dewey asking, "Any big ones?" Marty telling him about the back bays with the slop and pads, showed with his hands the size of the lunker he nailed on a jig. Dewey gave a whistle, saying they should go some time. Marty telling him, "You want a big one, you go in June." Marty looked out again now, thinking this night was never going to end.

A million stars above him, as many crickets sounding out past his window. Taking his cap, Marty turned it in the near dark, rubbing at an imagined smudge on the brim, thinking of that poor woman, losing her husband like that: blown up in a car. Thinking of his own wife at home in their bed. Gladys under the quilt. The woman always complaining of cold, but her body always putting out heat. Thinking of lying up against her now. God, these graveyard shifts had no end. His partner not known for his sparkling exchange, Dewey going on tonight about a bomb getting stuck under that Hitler fella's chair, and how the feds let Al Capone out of jail. Dewey feeling they ought to give that crook the rope. Then he had a good recipe for perch.

His arms folded across his chest, Dewey's head bobbed, then snapped up, woke himself with a snort. "What's that, Marty?"

"You nodded off." Reaching to the floor, Marty grabbed the Picnic Jug, gave it a wiggle, hearing sloshing inside. Uncapping the Thermos, he took the final swig of cold and bitter coffee.

"Any more of that?" Dewey asked.

"Drained her, sorry." Marty picked grounds from his tongue.

After a while, Dewey said, "Read about that bank job in Hoxie, you hear about it?"

"What about it?"

"Article compared it to the ones Bennie and Stella done."

"That so?" Marty thinking, here we go.

"Locked the banker in his vault. Got clean away with no shots fired. Paper talked how Stella got dubbed Sure Shot Stella after she shot out some pursuing patrol car's tires."

"Except they got caught."

"Yeah, G-men shot Bennie eating a hamburger at some stand in St. Louis. You imagine that, *hmm hmm*, taking a nice bite of meat and pickle, and *pow*. Nabbed her next day, over in Kansas City. Doing a ten-stretch as we speak."

"Why we speaking about it?"

"Just thinking, in a way, they're our people, from Kansas, I mean."

"Not my people." Marty tipped up the empty Picnic Jug, forgetting it was empty. Didn't want more coffee anyway, just something to do.

A broadcast came through the hiss of static on the radio, the announcer reporting a duster blowing up from Oklahoma, likely to pass through Wiley.

"Just our luck," Marty said. Thinking they might have to dash over to Topeka, or just wait it out, put up with the blowing sand. Looking out at the night sky, no sign of the duster yet.

"Fellas robbed that bank live long enough, gonna have something to blow on about in their old age."

"Make their mommas proud."

"'Course they got us out here, ready to take 'em down and lock 'em up."

"Right now, I just want to figure how I'm gonna end with no sand in my crack holes." Marty leaned and looked at the night sky.

The radio announcer's voice cut over the airwaves, a rush of static following, "Got ... *sss* ... urgent ... *sss* ... car ... *sss* ..."

"He say Car One?" Dewey leaned an ear to the set.

"Situation ... *sss* ... Paradise ... *sss* ... shots fired ... *sss* ..."

"Shots, oh my God," Dewey felt his stomach flip, thinking it was the bank robbers.

A spate of static, then the call cut out, and the radio set went dead. Dewey rapped the side with his knuckles. Switched it on and off, getting nothing.

"Probably the duster," Marty said, fumbling with the ignition key. "Damn time for a storm." Cranking the engine to life, he got the car turned around on the two-lane, rubber squealing. "Closest motel's the Paradise."

Getting the howler and flashing lights, Dewey put his hand on his service revolver.

Marty glanced at him. "Remember that thing I told you? About breathing easy, down to your finger, the one on the trigger, 'case you got to draw on somebody. Don't look them in the eyes, you look here." Marty pointed at his throat.

"See what their hands are doing." Dewey wiped at his brow.

"Right." Marty looked at him, saying, "You think old Creepy Karpis coulda busted loose?"

Dewey forced a smile, saying, "You ever do it, draw on a man?"

"Right now, best we just get there, huh? And remember what I said, about breathing to your finger."

"Sure I will."

The tarmac and the gravel shoulder blurred past, the blue-and-red lights strobed over the dry fields, the howler blaring. The sand storm looming somewhere ahead.

"So, Wiley you said, the big ones come in June, uh?" Dewey said, licking his lips, his mouth feeling dry.

Reaching the rolling Picnic Jug off the floor, Marty tossed it into the back seat, saying, "Yuh, June."

FIFTY-ONE

Stubbing the cigar butt in the overfilled ashtray, Willis called, "Hold on." Opening the drawer with the pistol, he went to the trailer door, listened and pushed it back. "Something wrong?"

"I'm quitting," Thelma said.

Opening the door wider, he nodded to the chair, sat behind his desk and shut the drawer. "Figured you'd stick around, pay your respects."

"Stop in Hoxie on my way through." She looked at him. "Was hoping to get paid the rest, what you owe me."

He topped his glass, slid it to her. "I sold to Ringling."

"The rest of them know?" She slid it back.

"In time." He shrugged and looked at her, hopeful. "Why not wait till morning, leave then?"

"Got it in mind to make Wichita tonight."

He picked up the glass. "Leave me an address, I'll send it to you."

"Rather have it now, no offense."

Willis frowned and went to the lockbox bolted to the floor in the corner, unlocked it and took out some banded cash and handed it to her. "Where you gonna end up?"

"Someplace I never been."

Standing at the door, he watched her fasten her packs and kick the Indian to life. The roar of the engine faded over the Melan Arch bridge. Standing on the stoop, he looked up at the night. Not sure why they never slept together. Willis blaming the tattoos.

Thinking about her, he wasn't aware of headlights swinging in out front. Didn't look until Lips was practically on him, Willis backing a step.

"Move, and I bust your arm."

Willis stopped.

"The hell happened?" Lips looked at the wrecked car. The most Lips ever said to him. Willis saying somebody planted a bomb, told him the cops had been in and out all night.

"Not working for Whitey no more."

"That right?"

"Gone solo now."

"But you're still asking after his money."

"You're a smart guy, Taggart." Lips grinned. "'Fore I do ask, you should know, one answer gets you a busted arm, other answer gets you two, your choice."

"Always nice to have a choice."

Lips pushed him inside the Airstream. Willis going behind the desk, moving his hand in the drawer.

Quick for his size, Lips slammed the drawer on the hand.

Willis yelped, clutching his wrist.

Reaching in the drawer, Lips took the .38, emptying the cylinder and tossing it in the corner. "How much you got?"

"None here." Willis looked at his watch, said he just sold the show to Ringling. "Sending a man by with the money, be here tomorrow."

"Asked how much you got right now. And you say nothing again, I'm gonna give your hand another slam. Up to you."

Not looking in the direction of the lockbox, Willis reached the bottle with his left, needing to ease the pain. Not wanting to look at his broken fingers.

Lips stopped his hand, grabbed the wrist and unstrapped Willis's watch, putting it on his own wrist. Then he took the bottle and drank, saying, "Now, the question . . ."

Willis heard footsteps on the steps, then a tapping on the door.

FIFTY-TWO

"Busted a knuckle, but got to admit, it felt good doing it." Skimming his tongue across his teeth, Handy was glad none were missing. The flashing red-and-blue lights shone off everything, the highway patrol pulling in stopped the fight. He had a hold of Dale Telfer, the fight gone out of the man. The rest of the Knighthawks wheeled out of there, one truck riding on a flat, both trucks heading toward the duster.

The passenger door of the police car opened and Dewey Cline got out, his pistol in hand, watching the trucks roll away.

Shutting off the engine, Marty Fisher climbed out and told him, "Put that away."

Cricket helped Crawford inside, said she had some ice. Looked like he could use stitching up, a piece of meat hanging from his lip, his nose bloody and bent.

"Wailed the tar out of them no-hopers, Marty. Called me an old biddy, and they got schooled." Cricket looked back at Clara standing with the rifle. "And that girl, got pure piss and vinegar flowing in them veins. God bless her. Sent them sons of bitches riding on their rims, right into that hell. Duster's gonna hit 'em like the fist of God." Cricket saying she was putting on a pot, telling them to get the cars around back, park in the lean-to, saying there was a tarp they could use against the sands.

Marty stepping over to Clara, held out a hand for the rifle and asked her what happened. Needing the other hand to keep the wind from blowing off his cap.

"It was them killed my husband." Letting go of the carbine, she pointed a finger at Dale Telfer, then nodded up the highway. "Rest are getting away."

Looking the way fleeing trucks had gone, Marty turned the other way as a motorcycle pulled into the lot. Thelma Hart getting off and coming over, recognizing Clara and Handy.

"Our sergeant'll be out to the camp in the morning," Marty explained to Clara, "sift around the Zephyr for physical evidence." Feeling the winds pick up, he guessed if there was any, there may not be by tomorrow, but didn't say it.

Thelma pointed at Telfer. "Your buddy's the one hit me." Stepping closer, looking at him, nodding her head. Explaining how she caught Hollis Capp lurking at the camp, getting out of the Zephyr and cold-cocking her when she asked what he was doing there. Sure he had accomplices in on blowing up the car.

Denying it, Telfer tried to shrink away, Handy renewing his grip. Dewey stepping up and taking over.

"One of the ones drove up to my house, making threats," Clara said, pointing at him. "Just ahead of my barn getting burned down."

Marty gave Telfer that cop look, Dewey reaching for his cuffs.

FIFTY-THREE

The door of the Airstream Clipper was pulled back, and Mort stood at the bottom of the steps, looking up at Lips. "Want a word with Willis."

"He's busy," Lips said.

"Want to know if he sold the place." Mort sounding indignant.

"Best get lost, little man."

"Not till I get my back wages," Mort said, folding his arms, putting a foot up on the step.

"Not the best time, Mort," Willis called out.

"How am I gonna make ends meet?" Mort said, holding his ground as Lips reached out for him. "You lay a hand on me, you gonna be sorry."

Lips smiled, saying, "Let's see how far I can pitch a midget." Started making the grab.

The iron hand came from the side and clamped his wrist, stopping him. Lips tried but couldn't break the hold, letting go of Mort. Mort taking a step back. Hagar yanked Lips down the steps, spun him and shoved him against the trailer wall, getting a two-handed grip. Had Lips up on his toes. Mort stepped in and felt for the pistol under Lips's jacket.

Willis stepped to the door. "One minute you're slamming my fingers in that drawer, now this, huh?" Showing Hagar his broken hand.

"Hurts, huh?" Hagar said.

"Fuck do you think?"

"Think Mort ought to give you the pistol." Hagar forced Lips's hand flat up against the trailer, the man unable to pull away.

Mort took out the shells, let them fall in the dirt and handed it to Willis barrel first.

Getting his meaning, Willis reached with his good hand, hefted it by the barrel, used it like a hammer and smashed the hand, then again.

Lips groaned, cried out the second time. Hagar still pressing the hand flat against the Airstream.

"We square now, asshole?" Willis raised the barrel to strike again.

"Yeah, yeah, square, square." Lips locked his eyes through the pain.

"Just to be sure," Willis said, nodding to Hagar.

Hagar got his meaning and jerked up the other hand, shoving it against the trailer.

Willis slammed with the pistol.

Grinding his jaws tight, Lips locked his eyes and moaned.

Willis unstrapped his watch from the man's wrist, taking it back.

Hagar let go, and Lips tried clutching his hands together, not saying anything, just walking from the camp, past the Packard, with no way to drive it.

Willis clapped Hagar on the shoulder, saying, "Got an idea about a new kind of show."

Hagar just looked at him.

"Men in tights wrestling, no holds barred."

"Count me out." Hagar shook his head. "Go broke working for you."

"What if I got the money?"

Hagar shook his head.

"Hear him out," Mort said, looking at Willis. "Go on."

"Growling, hitting and tossing. Fists and sweat, kind of like boxing, only more of a show."

"You mean in a roped-off ring?" Mort said, seeing the possibilities.

"Right. With you doing the announcing," Willis said to Mort. "Hagar takes all comers, maybe at the end, you can give the crowd some kumbaya, play your guitar."

Hagar twisted his mouth, thinking about it now. "Wrestling, then singing."

"Maybe we start with the singing and build it up. An opponent laughs at you and your guitar, see?" Willis tucked the pistol in his belt, going inside his trailer, wondering if he had another bottle. "Yeah, see, that's how the fight starts."

"Never liked being laughed at," Hagar said, following him. "You see."

Mort telling Hagar it was just an act, but, yeah, he could see it, getting on board with the idea. Asking Willis about that money they were talking about.

. . . FIFTY-FOUR

Looking out at the drifts of sand that last duster had blown in, this one not as bad as the one the week before when he went and burned down that barn. The Iron Claw restraint was on one wrist. Sitting in back of the squad car, Hollis Capp couldn't see the sense in it. He could reach over the seat and clout the dopey young cop on the passenger seat, but instead he used the squared edge of the cuff to scratch.

"Who's this judge I got to see?"

"Uncle Willy."

He wasn't worried about the arrest, no evidence and a tattooed witness. Maybe the White Knights weren't what they had been a decade ago, but they retained some top-drawer legal help.

"So you're telling me this judge is your uncle?"

"Just what everybody calls him, on account he's been around a long time," Dewey said, then to Marty, "Now, there's a fella can fish."

"Got that right," Marty said. "Had old Willy up on the Menoken this summer. Got himself a big one."

"That the eight-pounder on the courthouse wall, one he nailed on the red-and-white?"

"That's it, but think he got it on a Paw Paw plug."

"Been meaning to put a couple in my box," Dewey said. "They work, huh?"

"I'm falsely accused, and you two go on about fishing." Smiling, Hollis guessed he'd be free by noon.

"Well, according to Dale Telfer you ain't exactly that. From what he told us . . . well, was up to me, I'd pull over and beat you silly right here." Marty turned and looked at him. "Beating on women, blowing up a man in his car." Marty shook his head.

"Uncle Willy's gonna throw away the key," Dewey said.

"Had nothing to do with that car," Hollis said. "Had a permit to parade. You want to arrest somebody, ought to be that crazy woman tried to mow us down."

"Except you got no witnesses," Dewey said, then to Marty, "How about this weekend, you and me, we go wet a line?"

"Got a spot in mind?"

"Up by the Shawnee. Might do alright, never know."

"'Course, you want a lunker for the wall . . ." Marty looked at him.

"Got to wait till June," Dewey said.

"Yuh, June."

. . . FIFTY-FIVE

Kicking the toe of her shoe at the ashes. Everything black, the smell of it stinging her nose. Handy had driven her back nearly a week ago, and she'd been over every inch of the place. Walking through the wrecked barn again, Clara stepped over the scorched beam. If she didn't find the money soon, she'd end up living at her momma's. Her bedroom of pink and calico, her mother leaving it just like it had been. God help her. The button eyes of her dolls looking down from the shelf. Recalling the names she'd given them. Photos of her sisters on the dresser, their jurists' eyes and their told-you-so smiles.

Dreams of dancing the Palais Royale had kept her from going crazy. Guthrie in his tux and tails. Handsome and young and full of promise.

Then she was thinking of Sonny again. The man worked his fingers raw, never hit her, treated her okay. Wasn't his fault the dusters blew away any chance they ever had. Nothing going the man's way till he robbed that bank. She felt bad living with him, but it was worse without him. She started to cry again. Would have collapsed to the ground if everything around her wasn't charred black. She kicked at the blackened handle of a maul, the wood snapping from the blade. Looking up at the sky, not aware of the circling buzzards. "Damn you, Sonny. Where in hell is it?"

Stepping out of the ruin, she took the blackened shovel and went behind the house and up the slope. Back to thinking of herself hugging the pillow, in the bedroom of her childhood, the embroidered words Home Sweet Home in needlepoint. Remembered how she used to sit and stare out that window. That old oak dropping its last leaves around this time, along the street where the kids of the kids she'd known were playing hopscotch or skipping rope. Walking up the slope, she started humming that old *Gold Diggers* tune. She could see getting another sewing machine and making dolls for kids. While away her days and turn spinster old, living with her momma.

"Clara?"

She jumped and turned around.

Handy Phibbs came walking from a beat-up red Dodge. Hadn't heard him drive up. She leaned on the handle and waited for him, giving him a curious look.

"Didn't talk much last time I saw you," he said.

"Yeah, funerals are like that."

"Come by, see if you need a hand."

"You mean with no man around?"

"Not like that."

"You mean help me find where he hid it?"

"More like that, yeah." Handy recalled what Sonny told him that day at the Conoco, how she just ran off without a word. How he didn't trust her. Still, Handy felt bad for her. And if they couldn't find it, he'd give her some of his.

"Been over every inch of soot, checked the house, the old garden, the goddamn backhouse, the shed. Two, three times.

Was just going to where he planted them trees. Maybe I missed some."

"How about where we buried the mule?"

"Yuh, checked there."

"Got another shovel?"

She said she didn't, and they started up the hill, hearing a truck roll up the county road.

"You bring a gun?" she asked, thinking it could be the Nighthawks, back for more, finally recognizing the rangers bringing more trees. The driver pulled up, his arm hanging out his window, calling to her and asking where she wanted the trees dropped.

"Don't want 'em at all," she said. "Never did."

The driver looked confused, calling, "Sonny around?"

"He's gone."

The driver looked at her a while, finally driving off.

She looked at Handy. "Let's go dig up some trees."

... FIFTY-SIX

Evening settled on the Sheridan County courthouse. Eugene Cobb's mortar sat near the twelve-pounder. Eugene Cobb's last day. His Cobb-busters, ramrods and pails were stacked next to his trailer in the lot out the back. Eugene had shot up an uncooperative sky and got his money from a reluctant mayor. Townsfolk were calling him a flim-flammer. The graybeards at Grainger's declared he ought to be fined for the smell of sulfur he left hanging in the air. Betting he was going to see headlines like "A hoax on Hoxie," "The ground dry, city coffers drier." Last thing Mayor Flint said to him, he had a good mind to get the town marshal, Billy Joe Blake, to run him from town, tarred and feathered. Turning in, Eugene curled in his bedroll, thinking of Clara Myers. Knowing his career as a rain man was over.

•

The lights at Grainger's Mercantile dimmed. Emmett Grainger flipped the closed sign for the evening. The only lights on the block came from a few doors up: Hollis Capp's

Square Deal 'n Wheel. The only place in town that seemed to prosper.

Silhouettes moved around behind the lamp light, the sound of high spirits coming from inside, the meeting of the White Knights of the Great Plains. Hollis Capp had been released due to a lack of evidence. Grand Wizard Braxton Early held up his hands, delivering his words, keeping it casual tonight, nobody in garb. Welcoming a couple of new members. Early called the Topeka parade a pure success, the next one set for Cheyenne.

Jesse Mulligan said something about how they delivered a message to the Happy Mustard freaks. Getting a hear-hear from his brother Levon.

Coming from his slump of worrying about the assault charges against him, facing six months of hard time, Dale Telfer said, "It's a damn shame we still got the Conoco up the street, run by that prairie nigger, that Handy Phibbs nothing but trouble."

One of the new ones said something should be done.

"Only place this side of Hays to get ethyl," Stonewall Bradley said.

"That make it right?" Braxton Early said. "This town needs a fair-dealing place. A place a man can go."

"Goddamn right," Hollis Capp said, happy to be released, but looking at Dale Telfer, worried he could rat him out, soften his own sentence.

"So, what's to be done?" Early was saying, "We gonna stand by and let a nice place get turned to Niggerville?"

"No!"

"Bad enough we got the Catholics."

"Ought to send them a message too."

"Damn right." Early pointing at the man who said it.

"That Conoco and its fuel tanks right in the ground, woo hoo. With old Handy Phibbs sleeping in the room right out back. One good match and no more problem."

Heads bobbed in agreement.

Levon Mulligan rolled an empty bottle across the floor. Alcohol and brotherhood filling the room.

Grand Wizard Braxton Early smiled, raising his hands again, the way he liked to do. Then something caught his eye out the front window.

Someone moved on the courthouse lawn. A figure with its head covered cradled something, at first Early guessed it was a woman with an infant. Maybe another bastard child left on the courthouse steps.

It was a woman's voice calling, "Hey, you sons of bitches. You asked what can be done about it. Well, here's something." The figure stopped by the rain man's mortar, held out what Early thought was an infant, and dropped it down the mortar's maw. Why would anyone do that to a child? The way it looked to Braxton Early in that final moment.

Some of the men turned, looking in the direction he was facing. In time to see the mortar shell dropped down the barrel.

Dale Telfer dove for the floor. Hollis Capp tried for the door, got his hand on the knob as the blast ripped the night. Pieces of the storefront boards blasted into the sky, dust rising up, glass shattering, the roof beam crumbling and smoke rising.

. . . FIFTY-SEVEN

"I couldn't shine your shoes, Sonny . . . never could."
Looking up at the looping buzzard, Clara squinted away
tears. Scraping a handful of earth, letting it sift it through
her fingers. Regret turned to tears, then to loneliness. Heavy
with that cemetery guilt. Feeling Orin's gray eyes on her,
guessing how the old man had seen her, had always seen her
that way. Never missed much.

Looking at his headstone, saying, "Means you were right,
old man . . . about me, anyway." Scraping her nails along for
another scoop of earth.

"A man's got to hang onto the rope and stick by his con-
victions." She remembered him saying it, words Sonny stuck
by. Trickling the earth on Sonny's plot. "You just weren't a
man wanting things. That was me. I was blind for the want
of things. Now I'd settle for it to be the way it was." Tipping
her head up, unaware of the angry sky, saying, "Just shut
up, Clara. Even a fool knows time don't tick backwards."
Wanting to say the Lord's Prayer or something, if only she
remembered all the words.

A raindrop tapped her on the forehead. At first, she
didn't open her eyes, felt a few more, cool and wet on her

313

skin. Hadn't seen the dark amassing across the land. First time the sky had filled with clouds not made of sand in near a decade. More drops touched her, her cheeks, her forehead, her hair matting. She held out her hands, letting the shirt get heavy with the wet. The earth around the headstones pocked with tiny puffs. Dust rising like the ground was reveling.

Keeping her head tipped, she blinked the drops from her eyes, the sky letting go. And a deluge poured down. Clara loved the sound of it, the scent of the earth waking. Rain roused the clay and soil and bedrock. Coming back to life. She danced around the stones, not thinking of Guthrie and the Palais Royale. Putting a hand on the top of his cross, Handy saying he'd take care of getting Sonny a proper stone. Looking at Orin's cross, she said she'd make good on that too, get him that stone Sonny promised, if only she found the money Sonny hid.

The hardpan was getting soaked, rivulets forming. The air turning cool, the patter whispering its promise. Saying goodbye. Stepping in a puddle, a rill running like a vein through the cracked earth. Going to the red Dodge Handy let her have, telling her it would get her to that new beginning. That and the five hundred he pressed in her hand. Clara feeling the years of drought coming to an end. Just like Sonny said it would.

She drove back to the place, set to pack up her belongings. The rain coming heavier as she drove. Could barely see past the swishing wipers. Stopping in the yard, she hurried barefoot over the slippery ground. Couldn't remember the last time the earth felt like that. Hopping up the steps, she missed her footing, breaking through that busted step. Falling headlong up the steps. Thinking she twisted her ankle.

"Goddamn it, Sonny." Feeling the pain as she pulled her foot free of the splintered boards. Looking at her chafed and bleeding ankle. Then she saw something under the broken board. Snapping it away, she forgot about her ankle, saw the first of the bank sacks lined underneath.

ACKNOWLEDGEMENTS

Gratitude and appreciation to publisher Jack David for his ongoing support. And a big thank you to everyone at ECW Press for their commitment to making every book the best it can be. I've said it before, and I'll say it again, Emily Schultz is the best, a talented author and my favourite editor. I get wonderful comments on the great cover designs, so thank you to Michel Vrana for this one, and a nod to Peter Norman for his amazing copy-editing talents. I am so fortunate to be working with these people.

And here's to the many writers who have inspired me along the way with their stories, and to those who have been generous and supportive of me so that I can share mine.

I also give thanks to the readers for their continued support which encourages me to do what I do.

And to Andie and Xander. My two rocks. Thank you isn't enough.

At ECW Press, we want you to enjoy this book in whatever format you like, whenever you like. Leave your print book at home and take the eBook to go! Purchase the print edition and receive the eBook free. Just send an email to ebook@ecwpress.com and include:

Get the eBook free!*
*proof of purchase required

• the book title
• the name of the store where you purchased it
• your receipt number
• your preference of file type: PDF or ePub

A real person will respond to your email with your eBook attached. And thanks for supporting an independently owned Canadian publisher with your purchase!